RETURN TO EDEN

Sirius Loss Discoveries

Ad Majorem Dei Gloriam

Tim Edwards

WESTBOW
P R E S S®
A DIVISION OF THOMAS NELSON
& ZONDERVAN

WestBow Press books may be ordered through booksellers or by contacting:

WestBow Press
A Division of Thomas Nelson & Zondervan
1663 Liberty Drive
Bloomington, IN 47403
www.westbowpress.com
1 (866) 928-1240

ISBN: 978-1-5127-4149-0 (sc)
ISBN: 978-1-5127-4151-3 (hc)
ISBN: 978-1-5127-4150-6 (e)

Library of Congress Control Number: 2016907558

Print information available on the last page.

WestBow Press rev. date: 5/17/2016

For my loving parents, Phil and Margaret Edwards and my loving in-laws, Ben and Frieda Edinger.

PREFACE

For those who have not read <u>Sirius Loss</u>, the following story picks up where that one ended. It is an exposition of the personal lives of an ordinary family who experience the most dramatic celestial event in human memory, the envelopment of Earth and our entire solar system by an enormous Dyson sphere of alien origin. The mother of this family is Dr. Jennifer Bass, an astronomer at the University of Texas' McDonald Observatory in Fort Davis, Texas. She makes a series of extraordinary discoveries beginning with the disappearance of a nearby star, Sirius. Then Dr. Bass finds evidence that Sirius was swallowed up by a black hole that is headed toward Earth. She leads a team of elite scientists who work to gather information while the government works secretly to prepare the world for the proximal passage of the black hole in several years. During their work, she discovers the Sphere at some distance as it speeds toward Earth, with an arrival time of only forty days. Uncertainty, concern, and curiosity dominate humanity as attention turns to the gigantic object that is fast approaching. The suspense mounts until the day when the Earth is taken inside, along with the Sun and all the planets. The detection of numerous civilizations on the interior surface of the hollow sphere suggests that this is a rescue mission. The book ends with plans underway for a mission from Earth to the surface or rim of the Sphere to make first contact. Jennifer and her husband, David Lopez, are selected to lead this mission. Between the books, they move to Houston to begin training at the Johnson Space Center.

CHAPTER 1

Mission Aborted

A bright August-afternoon sun baked the balcony of David and Jennifer's condo on the top floor of the Endeavor Tower at Clear Lake. A warm, muggy breeze blew steadily inland from the Gulf of Mexico. David and Jennifer were taking a rare Saturday off from their training at the Johnson Space Center in Houston, where they had undergone intensive astronaut training during the last two years. Frustration was as sticky as the climate as they restlessly reclined in chaise lounges.

"It's all wrong, David," Jennifer said in frustration that had become all too familiar lately. "I am beginning to wonder why we ever said yes to all of this."

"Well, we have certainly done our part," David mused. "There have been those endless training exercises that have made us fitter than Arctic wolves. Then we have read and assimilated thousands of pages of speculative writings on what we might encounter out there. You and I have also become pretty good pilots in many different kinds of air- and spacecraft."

"I'm sick and tired of all the wrangling about who will go with us on the voyage. Every celebrity, politician, and journalist wants a seat on the trip. And there is no consensus among the various national space agencies about the design or capacity of the ship. Maybe they're going to give us a bunch of helium balloons, smartphones, and a bag of granola bars, then send us on our merry way in these lounge chairs," she said with a hint of despair.

"That would probably eliminate most of the volunteers who are lobbying to get a ride. Did you hear that one of the princes from Saudi Arabia has offered to pay for the entire trip if he can take his harem? He also said he wanted us to pilot the vessel," David responded.

"Oh, how I miss everything—the way things were before we left Fort Davis and moved here to Houston. I miss the quiet solitude, the wonderful neighbors, our church friends, my colleagues at the observatory, the cooler, drier weather, and most of all, looking at the stars," Jennifer said sadly. She reached over and fondly touched the Meade Max twenty-inch ACF telescope they had moved from home.

"It all happened so fast at the beginning, when we were enveloped into the Dyson Sphere," she continued after a pause. "But now, two years later, we don't even know where we are in the cosmos anymore. And whoever is running this sphere hasn't even attempted any contact. The only stargazing left to us is either the sun or the 120 white dwarfs that all read identical in spectrographic signature and mass, all in a uniform, symmetrical grid hovering a couple of million miles above the interior of the Rim. All of our astronomical instruments have become tools of cartographers and geographers, and they have just scratched the surface. I still don't understand the radio and TV silence from the rim after the first couple of weeks. Why are we still inside? Where are we going? Will this voyage ever take off?"

Changing the subject, David asked, "Do you remember where Allison was going today?" Their precocious, energetic daughter had grown remarkably in the two years since leaving Fort Davis. She had struggled to adjust to attending a school that had more kids than the entire population of their home county, and the culture shock of moving into a wealthy, fast-lane suburban enclave had taken its toll. Allison was now a couple of weeks away from starting ninth grade. She was frequently on the minds of her parents, who worried how all the changes impacted Allison's life.

"She left early this morning with some friends to go shopping," Jennifer replied with a searching look of recall. "She said they would be back by midafternoon."

"Ever since last spring, she began to settle in and stopped begging us to move back home," David said, reflecting. "Who is she out shopping with? Who is the driver?"

"I don't know," Jennifer said, growing concerned. "It's two thirty already. Maybe I should call her. But that would only annoy and embarrass her. Let's give it another half hour."

Even in the clammy breeze, they grew silent and dozed off in the shade of the overhanging roof.

Suddenly, their rest was rudely disturbed by the sound of excited adolescent, female voices fueled by frozen caffeinated drinks.

The elevator door opened to reveal Allison with four other girls. Allison's guests stepped out with looks of awe at the top-floor condo now occupied by the Lopez-Bass family. They went silent as they surveyed the interior and then scurried to look out of the windows at the wide vistas. One took snapshots with her smartphone.

David and Jennifer rose and entered the room to welcome the guests.

Allison spoke with excitement. "Hey, Mom and Dad! These are some of my friends. I think you know Julianna and Marleigh." She pointed to two of her classmates, who had become recent friends. The other two were strangers to David and Jennifer and clearly older. "This is Carleigh, Marleigh's older sister. She's a junior." The taller girl nodded and smiled. "And this is Jacqueline. She's the head cheerleader and a senior." She looked older and more sophisticated than a seventeen-year-old and exuded an air of confident self-assurance.

Allison stepped back, uncomfortable with taking the lead for the group. Immediately, Jacqueline stepped up and said, "You can call me Jackie. It is so good to meet you, Mr. and Mrs. B. You look even better in person than on TV. I must have your autographs and pics!" Jackie grabbed some paper and a pen from the counter and handed them to Jennifer. She then took another sweeping look around the room and said, "I really like your place. My parents almost bought this a couple of years before you moved here, but it didn't have enough room to make us comfortable." She then turned to look at the other girls and, focusing on Allison, said, "I can't wait for all the great parties we can have here."

Jennifer was already on her guard with this older, affected girl but struggled to keep an open mind. She shot a glance at Allison, who was faking a smile and nodding to cover anxiety over the thought of hosting a party. David wished the girls would soon become bored and leave.

Jackie, having completed her quick scan of the condo, moved on with her agenda. "Let's get into our swimwear and go down to the pool. Those guys better still be there. Come on, girls; let's use Allison's room to change. Mrs. B, get some towels out for us. We forgot to bring our own from home."

The clutch of girls hustled off to Allison's room to do as Jackie suggested. David stepped down the hall to get the needed towels. Still stunned by the encounter, Jennifer decided Jackie was dangerous to her daughter. It was a good thing Jackie was too young for the mission to the Rim. Otherwise, she would have shown up and quickly made a place for herself before anybody could have stopped her.

Within minutes, the girls, dressed for the kill, headed to the elevator before Jennifer had the chance to stop Allison to question her about the brand-new two-piece bathing suit she must have purchased with the encouragement of the other girls. David was shocked into silence to see so much of his daughter, who was wearing so little of a pink, two-piece bikini that would have fit a seven-year-old. Jennifer noticed Allison's clumsy overapplication of makeup.

"I don't like that Jackie or care much for the others," Jennifer snarled after the elevator departed. "What is their agenda with Allison? Why are they using her?"

"Let's not be too hasty, dear," David interjected. "Remember how we worried about Allison's adjustment our first year here? Allison's school is full of kids from affluent and sophisticated families. Shouldn't we be glad she has finally been accepted?"

"I don't see acceptance in that group. They are a bunch of groupies for Jackie. I don't know anything about those girls or their parents. I miss the simplicity of Fort Davis," said Jennifer, sighing. "What's next? Are we losing our girl, David?"

Not wanting to face that question, David looked at her with sympathy.

Just then, Jennifer's smartphone rang. "Hello?" Jennifer listened intently.

David noticed her face growing pale. Whatever it was, it was bad news. He worried it might be something about her mother in Midland or their married son and daughter-in-law in Austin.

"Thanks for the call, Chantal," said Jennifer. She disconnected and laid down her phone. Chantal Jackson was their immediate supervisor at NASA and a dear friend. "Let's check the computer for the president's radio address. Chantal said he's made some major changes that are detailed in his speech."

They raced to their home office to check the usa.gov website for the text of President Barton's address. Jennifer and David had met him briefly for a speech he had made at the Johnson Space Center about a year ago, but they had not become as close as they were to his predecessor, President Freeman. Bill Barton was never a big fan of space exploration and had made no progress on resolving the complex issues of the international mission to the Rim. Now they would get to see where he was leading the mission.

Jennifer was able to access the video clip of President Barton's address. As it played, their concern grew.

The president said, "The time has come for us to advance in a constructive direction on this most historic moment in human history, when a handful of humans will make a nine-month journey to make first contact with the people on the interior Rim of the Dyson Sphere. While it would be wonderful if everyone who wanted to join could make the trip, limited funds and resources have made it necessary to select only a handful of our brightest and best. Only six people can be fitted in the vessel now under development at our Goddard Space facility outside Washington. Since geology, astrophysics, and other hard sciences are no longer the central purpose of this unprecedented mission, specialists must have diplomatic, commercial, and leadership skills. Given the international nature of the mission, only two of the astronauts will be Americans. The others will come from Russia, China, Saudi Arabia, and Japan. The Americans will be George Sharkos and his close friend, the CNN anchor, Millicent Grant. Well known to most of us, their high intelligence and business experience will serve us well as they make the sacrifice on a journey of unprecedented time and distance. As a cost-saving measure, all other NASA facilities will gradually be closed within two years. We are all grateful for their immense contributions to science down through the decades."

Jennifer cut off the rest of the recorded speech and turned with a blank look to David. "What now?" she ventured. "It's not surprising this president would send his closest friends and greatest contributors on the mission. Too bad he didn't go himself. I just wish he would have told us directly. After all we have been through; it would have been a decent thing to do."

"I'm sorry, Jennifer," David replied. "It's not really surprising we would be bumped off the most desired flight of all time."

"What now, David?" Jennifer asked again. "What are we to do? Should we move back to Fort Davis? I can't do astronomy anymore. Should I retool and try cartography? After all, the interior surface of this Dyson Sphere is fourteen billion times the size of the entire surface area of Earth. We have mapped only a tiny fraction and still have no clue where to go. Any mission could miss civilization by millions of miles. In a way, I'm more relieved than disappointed. Maybe now we can focus more on Allison before she grows up. In a few short years, she'll be gone and off to college."

"How about a vacation before Allison returns to school?" David asked. "We haven't had any time off together since we stayed at Rockport over two years ago."

"Speaking of Allison, let's go down and rescue her from those girls who are trying to remake our daughter into someone we won't even know. It's time for their pool party to come to an end. We can tell them you and I had planned a family dinner out tonight to the Aquarium. Allison loves that place. There we can break the news that her parents will soon be unemployed."

Both Jennifer and David made the thirty-story journey down to the ground floor and out to the pool where the girls had three college-aged young men cornered in the pool for horseplay and silly conversation. Allison tried to look annoyed when her parents brought it to a sudden halt with the announcement of dinner plans. She was inwardly grateful for the break.

Within half an hour, the four other girls were dispatched for destinations unknown, while David, Jennifer, and Allison headed out on NASA Road One on their way to the Aquarium, a seafood restaurant on the waterfront at the Boardwalk in Kemah. They were all silent, lost in their thoughts. Allison was engrossed in texting her friends about their adventures with the boys in the pool.

At the restaurant, Jennifer insisted that Allison stop texting. She sat and sulked, watching the fish swim by in the massive tank near their table. Jennifer was drawn to watching a large sailboat passing in the channel outside the outer deck of the restaurant.

The order was placed, and David decided it was time to break the ice.

"Allison, how did it go for you and your friends today?" David cautiously asked. "This was the first time I had met the two older girls. What do you think of them?"

"I don't appreciate your breaking up my pool party or prying into my personal life," Allison said sullenly, rolling her eyes.

The tone of the reply brought Jennifer back into focus on the conversation. "Since when do you address your father in that tone, young lady?" Jennifer retorted. She remembered her own mother saying something like that many years before.

"Mom, these girls are the most popular girls in the entire high school, and they have included me. Now you ruined everything," Allison returned.

"If they are truly friends, this interruption would be no problem for them," Jennifer replied. "What kind of friends would they be if they dropped you just because you had to end the party to do something with us? Do you feel that the older girls are really interested in you? What kind of things do you have in common? Did they engage you in conversation where they showed interest in you?"

"Mom!" Allison was beginning to flush red, her anger rising. "I don't want to talk about it anymore. I just want to live my own life."

"Allison," David interjected, hoping to steer the conversation in a different direction. "Your mom and I got word from Washington while you and your friends were in the pool. The president has decided to make big changes in the mission. We have been taken off the journey to the Rim and our jobs will come to an end soon."

This news was even more unwelcome to Allison, who felt that her own social future was about to collapse around her. She searched her parents' faces to read how they were taking the news.

"We wanted you to hear it from us first," Jennifer said. "Your dad and I are still in shock but also somewhat relieved. We have been worried about our long hours of training that have taken us away from you."

Just then, the waiter brought their salads. They returned thanks and began to eat.

"That is so not fair! Are we going to move back to Fort Davis?" Allison asked huffily. "Can I stay with my friends here if you go back? What about your jobs? What are we going to do?" She was a little unnerved by her parents' calm.

"We thought we would take a three-week vacation, just the three of us," David said. "Your mom and I have really missed you, and this would be a great way to get reacquainted with our wonderful, amazing daughter. It's been almost three years since we have taken a trip somewhere. Where would you like to go?"

Allison was in no mood to leave and travel anywhere, especially with her parents. She simply shook her head and picked away at her salad.

"Well," offered Jennifer. "Let's sleep on it and talk about some options tomorrow. Our passports are current, and our vacation time and savings are ample. Since we won't be traveling into space, let's see some of our own world."

With that, the rest of the meal continued in peace as dusk settled in. When they left the Aquarium, the last blaze of color from the sunset was giving way to the steady and symmetrical pinpoints of white light glowing from the white dwarfs that illuminated the Rim at its great distance.

Unseen by anyone on Earth, a glowing, silvery sphere about two meters in diameter left a hovering space station several hundred miles above the Rim. It began its long journey to Earth. Soon it was traveling at almost 5 percent of the speed of light. The arrival at Earth would be a little over a week. Everything would soon be ready.

CHAPTER 2

Meeting the Past

Several days later, a BMW raced over the winding, narrow roads of the Spanish Pyrenees. Jennifer was driving. Allison was riding shotgun, holding her left hand out the open moonroof to test the feel of rushing wind but trying not to show enjoyment. David was navigating with maps and a GPS system from the backseat.

"Are you sure we're going the right way?" Jennifer asked David.

"I'm having trouble matching the map with the GPS. It's in Spanish. Maybe Allison can figure this out," David said.

"Don't get me involved. Once we left Barcelona, I lost my signal, and the map app won't work." Allison said, trying to ignore her parents' worries. "This whole goose chase wasn't my idea."

"Going to Padre Island with your friends didn't work for us," Jennifer replied.

"Mom and I wanted to get a taste of how our ancestors lived centuries ago. Most of my people were Basque, and half of hers were Icelandic, so it made sense to come to Spain and then Iceland."

"I don't care where they came from. I'm worried about my future when I start high school next month," Allison said with a hint of self-pity. "You two are out of work. I'm out of the country, away from my social life. And none of us has a clue where we will be in a month. We might even have to go back to Fort Davis." She sighed.

"It is strange we are doing this trip facing unemployment," David said, pondering. "Normally, we'd be furiously mailing out resumes to colleges looking for science professorships. I'm still on the faculty at Sul Ross with an extended unpaid leave of absence. Maybe we needed to travel after two years of preparation to journey into our future on the Rim and then losing our seats. Going back to the past intrigued us. Maybe it can help us forget the pain of being put off the voyage."

"I could go back to the observatory, but working with cartographers mapping the Rim has no appeal," Jennifer added thoughtfully. "The best part is that we now have time to reconnect with you, Allison. I had the fear we were beginning to lose you."

Allison chose not to respond. She was engrossed in playing a game on her iPhone. Getting closer to her parents was the last thing she wanted to do.

"I think you need to turn left up ahead," David directed as he checked his GPS against the map.

"The last time you sounded like that, we were lost for hours," muttered Allison. "What are we looking for anyway?"

"We're due to stay at an etcholak, a shepherd's cottage, for a couple of nights," Jennifer offered, choosing not to answer the bigger implication in the question. "It's the time of year when Basque shepherds stay in these mountains, grazing their flocks. The hiking and biking will be great."

"Oh, great. Are we going to join the herds and shear the sheep? Will we keep watch over the flocks by night?" Allison grumbled, rolling her eyes.

David and Jennifer exchanged looks through the rearview mirror.

"It's a bed and breakfast with running water and indoor plumbing," David offered.

"How long will we have to put up with this?" Allison replied, pouting.

"Probably four days, including the polombière," David said.

"The what?" asked Allison, turning to look at her dad in the backseat.

"It's a special event for the Basque shepherds where they set nets along the ridges to trap migrating wood pigeons," David explained.

"I hope we don't have to eat any of them," Allison sneered.

"It's considered a great delicacy and will be a featured dish at the upcoming feast," David said.

"I knew I should have packed my own food," Allison replied, turning back to face the front and slumping in her seat.

They continued on in silence through the rocky, rolling terrain. The treeless mountains accompanied their path to the northwest. The winding, twisting road kept Jennifer's hands tight to the wheel. David was beginning to feel like he was back in a simulator at NASA during a training session with a surprise disaster. As they rounded a sharp curve, Jennifer slammed the brakes, and the car screeched to a stop inches from a flock of wooly Latxa sheep crossing the road, being managed by a couple of Basque sheepdogs. The dogs were staying close to the black-faced sheep, barking and even nipping at any strays. Two older shepherds followed at an unconcerned pace, without even looking at the car.

"Are all these people this crazy?" Allison asked with irritation after messing up on her game.

"It's their way of life, dear," David ventured.

"Well, I wish they would live their lives somewhere else." Allison frowned.

Looking again at the maps, David squinted ahead at a rough, rocky road that dropped off, almost to the next hairpin turn. "I think if the travel agent's map can be trusted, the next turnoff will take us to our etcholak. I can't tell whether it says one mile or ten when we leave the highway," David said.

"Let's give it a try," said Jennifer.

One of the dogs had finished chasing the last of the flock across the road. Jennifer drove down a steep lateral angle over to a sharp drop-off. It looked like the rocky trail had run off into the sky. Jennifer took it too fast. Everyone gasped as the car careened downward at an angle similar to that of a dive bomber.

"I didn't think cars could hold the road at this angle." David's voice quivered.

"How are we going to ever get out of here?" Allison demanded. "I thought vacations were supposed to be fun."

Jennifer, stressed from white-knuckle driving, slowed the car and turned to her surly daughter. "We are doing our best. If you don't like it, then you are welcome to get out and walk to the cottage or...back to the airport!" Jennifer gave Allison a maternal look that warned her of crossing a kind of mental line. "Your dad and I are sick and tired of your attitude. If you can't enjoy yourself, then sit there and sulk. If you can't say anything good, then just shut up." Jennifer raised an eyebrow while lowering the other with intensity. She surprised herself by using the phrase "shut up" but hoped it might help.

Allison looked Jennifer right in the eye, trying not to show surprise at her mom's outburst. She slouched down in her seat again but remained silent. Before long, the rocky trail came over the shoulder of a descending ridgeline. It entered a secluded grove of oak trees in a small, sloping valley, huddled around a cluster of stone buildings. They looked as if they had grown up from the bedrock in ancient times. Jennifer slowed the car to a crawl and looked hopefully in the rearview mirror at David. He returned a smile of relief. They had arrived.

David and Jennifer slowly emerged from the car, stiff from the long ride. Allison made no attempt to get out, as if they would turn around and drive back to Barcelona. A short, full-bodied woman came out of the main building and walked over to greet them. She was dressed in a heavy woolen skirt with a similar dark woolen shawl over a white blouse. Her hair, tied neatly into a bun at the back of her head, was a dazzling mixture of black and silver. Her severe expression gave way to a blazing smile.

"Hello! Welcome to Ibarretxe, our home. It is Basque for 'house in the valley.' I am Josefina Alegria," she said in accented but clear English. "You must be exhausted after such a long drive. I will show you to your etcholak." Josefina began to march across the compound. Allison, fearful of being left behind, quickly got out of the car and joined her parents. "There are four here. Yours is the largest and the only one we rent out. Shepherds use the other ones."

Halfway across the tree-covered nest of buildings, three men rounded a corner and stopped, looking down at the ground. Josefina walked up to them and turned around to face Jennifer, David, and Allison. She placed her hand on the shoulder of a burly but worn-looking man, "This is my husband, Gorka." He nodded and lowered his gaze. Then Josefina pointed to the old man next to him, saying, "This is our chief shepherd, José Mari Legorburu." This thin, tall man, aged beyond time, looked as if he had been carved from the weathered, gray rock ubiquitous to the Pyrenees. He gave an intense, expressionless stare from dark eyes set above an unruly white mustache and almost hid beneath great white eyebrows. His bushy mane of white hair reminded Jennifer of Einstein. Jennifer immediately recognized them as the two shepherds they had nearly hit back up the road.

Then Josefina pointed to a slender, whiskerless young man standing tall but a half step behind the other two. His dark hair and olive complexion reminded David of his son, Justin. "This is our grandson, Ixidro Trincado. He spends his summers here, helping us old ones. Ixidro will be attending the University in Pamplona in two years." He timidly looked up and nodded to David and Jennifer but let a smile show when he saw Allison. Ixidro then blushed and looked at his feet once again, only to steal another quick glimpse at Allison, followed by another smile.

This was not missed by Allison, who found herself blushing. She couldn't take her eyes off Ixidro.

Josefina broke the spell when she said, "They will take you out tomorrow to the polombière at dawn. It's about ten kilometers to the site. You have arrived at the peak time. We should have plenty of pigeon for dinner tomorrow. But enough of that for now. Up here is your etcholak."

The low, dark granite building before them seemed to be partly swallowed by the mountainside. The stone walls were spotted with lichen and moss. A warm light beckoned from the window. As they entered the front door, what had seemed like a cave was transformed into a warm and cozy nest, modest in size but decorated with colorful Basque folk art and furnished with time-worn, handmade furniture, including two bountiful feather beds covered with Basque quilts. In the corner sat an aged, smoke-stained fireplace with a low fire burning in a generous hearth. The chill of the cool, damp mountain air fled as they looked at the fire and the cluster of comfortable chairs facing it, just waiting for occupants.

"Gorka will bring your supper in about an hour. The bathroom is in the next building over. Be sure to knock before entering. You will be sharing it with José and Ixidro. There is also a basin with a pitcher on the dresser for you to wash. Please make yourselves at home and let me know if you need anything. The men come and go, but I am around here all the time. The fields and mountains are their world; the home is mine."

Josefina left. David and Allison returned to the car to fetch the luggage. Jennifer gave a closer inspection of the handcrafted textiles on the walls and beds. Soon David and Allison returned.

Allison looked carefully around the room. "There's no electrical outlet! How am I supposed to charge my iPhone? How do they make those lamps work?"

Fighting a smile, Jennifer replied, "Back home, those are called hurricane lamps. They are fueled by kerosene. A century ago, every home in Fort Davis was lit with them."

"And we have to share a bathroom with a couple of stinky shepherds," Allison remarked, though she was still intrigued with Ixidro and couldn't wait to have a chance to talk with him and to gaze into his fascinating face. "How come they are bringing supper to us in here?"

"Basques are very shy and private people," David replied. "They don't often eat with people who are not part of their family. Meals are treasured times for families to be together and to enjoy food and talk. They would assume we are the same way."

"Did you hear what Josefina mentioned about the polombière?" Jennifer remarked worriedly. "We are leaving at dawn and hiking ten kilometers up into the mountains. That's about six miles at four thousand feet of elevation."

"Just be glad we're not running with the bulls at Pamplona," David joked.

"We had better bathe right after supper and go to bed early," Jennifer said. "I'm still jet-lagged with my time all mixed up. It will be hard to go to sleep and even harder to rise in a time zone that is seven hours ahead."

They began to unpack when Gorka entered with a cast-iron pot full of lamb stew and set it on the table. He added a generously long loaf of homemade bread similar to French bread. Gorka then set three places at the table with plates and flatware from an adjacent cabinet. He finished quickly, muttered something in Basque, and left. They sat down, gave thanks, ladled out the stew, broke the bread, and ate with surprising hunger. No leftovers were to be found. Soon they prepared for bed and sat quietly by the fire.

"Mom, I'm sorry about being so awful today," Allison said with contrition. "Everything is so different here, and I'm afraid about what will happen to us when we go back."

Jennifer reached across from her chair and took Allison's hand in hers. "I understand how you feel. If I let myself think about it, the uncertainty scares the willies out of me. But then

I remember that only two years ago, we all faced something far more terrifying than just losing our jobs or moving. Remember how the Lord brought us through to a better day?"

Allison looked into her mother's eyes. "Life sure is complicated right now. I wish I knew more about what the future holds for me."

Listening thoughtfully, David chimed in. "If we knew more about the future, it would lose all of the joy of surprise. The Lord loves to surprise us with wonderful things. I can still remember the overwhelming joy I felt when the doctor handed you to me right after you were born. Ever since then, you have been giving us many wonderful surprises."

Jennifer looked at her daughter wistfully. "I know you get tired of hearing me say this, but only thirty years ago, I was much like you are now. How often I am reminded of those experiences every time you struggle with something. You will make it, and you will like how you will turn out when that future becomes today. In the meantime, don't miss out on the joys of your age today."

They smiled knowingly at each other and enjoyed the warm comfort of the fire for a while longer.

"I hate to be the bearer of bad news, but it's time we all get to bed. Dawn is coming quicker than we want," Jennifer said.

They rose, held hands, each one praying in turn, hugged, and then turned in. Soon they were nestled in the hug of their feather beds, falling into a deep and gentle sleep.

CHAPTER 3

Songs in the Mountains

Just before daybreak, a rooster crowing nearby stirred everyone into wakefulness. David crawled out, lit a lamp, and put more wood on the fire. Soon they were all dressed. David sported a beret and a chamarra, a traditional Basque woolen cape. He had purchased them the day before at a shop. After a breakfast heavy with bread, eggs, and roast mutton, they met Gorka, José, and Ixodro. Without a word, Gorka presented each with a worn makhila, a shepherd's staff carved from gnarled dark wood that smelled of cedar. They headed up a steep path accompanied by the sheep and dogs on the way to mountain pastures. Lingering darkness kept everyone watchful for footing on the ascending path. The dogs, sheep, and shepherds moved quickly upward, driven by old memories of a familiar way. In the cool early-morning air, David stumbled and caught himself with his makhila. Jennifer and Allison tiptoed around sheep droppings. The shepherds never slackened their pace. After about an hour of endless fast walking with sharp turns and steep climbs, they reached the pasture for the day. David and Jennifer were grateful for their rigorous astronaut training, but Allison was beginning to wear down. Gorka came over to them.

"Now we go to the polombière. José remains with the sheep and dogs," Gorka said. "Two hours and we get there." He pointed to a cluster of jagged peaks rising before them. There was a lower break in middle that formed a high pass into France.

Though relieved to leave intimidating, old José behind, Allison was dreading the rest of the climb. She longed for the cramped quarters and smooth power of their rental car. Just as she became aware of the aches in her feet and legs, Ixidro walked over to join her on the path. He shyly lowered his head, watching the path and building up the courage to talk. Allison was beginning to feel much better.

"Did you rest well last night?" Ixidro asked slowly in a soft voice with a hint of accent. He glanced at Allison briefly, smiled, and returned his gaze to the path ahead.

Allison chanced a look at him. "Yes, thank you. I have never slept in a feather bed before. It was like, well, the best sleep I have ever had." She squeezed her mind like a sponge to think of something to further the budding conversation. "What's it like to live here all the time?"

Ixidro looked at her directly with his searching, deep-brown eyes, "It is a good life. I do not live here all the time. During the school year, I live with my parents in Pamplona. In summer, I come here to help my grandparents with their farm." He looked away again, fearful he had talked too much.

"Is your home in Pamplona like this?" Allison asked, feeling easier.

"No, we have an apartment. It is much more like what you must have in America. Tell me about life in America," he said.

"Oh, I go to school, see my friends, and do my studies," Allison replied, not sure how much detail to share.

"What do your parents do? Do they work in a factory?" Ixidro queried.

"No, they are scientists. Dad studies and teaches biology. Mom studies the stars. They were training to become astronauts but just found out they lost their jobs," Allison said.

"Oh, I am so sorry to hear that. What will they do now? Maybe that Bass woman—you know, Jennifer, the one who found the giant sphere that came to Earth two years ago?—maybe she can help your parents," Ixidro offered.

Allison looked directly at him with a big grin. "Jennifer Bass, the woman ahead of us, is my mother."

Ixidro blushed. "I am sorry. I hope I did not offend," he said apologetically.

"No problem. Mom and Dad found out last week that they were not going to be on the voyage to the Rim, so they decided to take a vacation and look for other work when they get home," Allison replied.

"How wonderful to have such famous parents," Ixidro exclaimed. "It is so sad that they will not get to meet the ones who brought that sphere here to save us from that black hole."

"I think they are taking it okay. Mom never sought out all the fame and attention she received when she discovered everything. It might be nice to return to the way life used to be for a change," Allison said.

"Where was that?" Ixidro asked.

"We lived in a small town called Fort Davis in the mountains of west Texas. There are about a thousand people there," Allison said.

"Do you have a farm and sheep? We live well with our flocks. This way of life goes back tens of thousands of years for my people," Ixidro said with a sense of pride.

"No, we lived in a home in the town where Mom and Dad were doing science even before that," Allison replied.

Those in the lead came to a stop before a spring of water that bled out from the side of cliff. Gorka cupped his hands and began to drink from the icy water. Without any instructions, the others followed his example. Ixidro went to his grandfather and began to talk in Euskara, the Basque language, while looking at Jennifer. She and David filled up on water and sat on a rock shelf.

Jennifer looked at David and smiled. "Notice how much happier Allison is today?"

"I haven't heard a single complaint. Maybe it's the fresh air, feather beds, and hearty food," David joked.

"Allison was fascinated yesterday when she first saw Ixidro. He was also keenly interested. Do you realize she left her beloved iPhone back in the cottage when we left?" Jennifer noted.

"She didn't need high tech to get in touch with the one who's most important to her now." David smiled.

Gorka stomped up to Jennifer, followed by Ixidro. "So you are the Bass woman who changed the sky?" Gorka looked accusingly with a raised eyebrow.

Jennifer was blindsided. "Mr., I mean Señor Alegria, I am Jennifer Bass, but I didn't change the sky. I only saw it all coming and told everyone so that our leaders might be able to respond," Jennifer offered.

"Forever, my people here in Euskal Herria have shaped our lives by the stars, sun, and moon in the sky. Our stories begin and end there. For two years, there have only been these faint white lights that look like city lights. Bring back our stars. When will you do this?" he demanded.

"Señor Alegria, I wish I could bring them back. I miss them too. My life was given to watching them with a great telescope, and now I am out of work," Jennifer said, trying to appease him. She gave a quizzical look and shrugged her shoulders.

Gorka narrowed his eyes and gave a hint of a grin. "Then maybe you can raise sheep too," he mused.

Ixidro went over to sit close to Allison. They were doing more gazing into each other's faces than talking. Gorka shocked him into action, saying, "Ixidro, go ahead. Check the nets and find our decoys. Quickly! It must be ready for our guests."

The young man stood up and immediately trotted onward at a quickened pace, soon going out of sight around an upward bend in the trail. Allison already missed him.

After another half hour, they made it up to the broad, grassy area of the polombière. Black, handmade, fine mesh nets were strung like cobwebs at various high points across the expanse. They were tied to short, weathered trees, rocks, and occasional posts. Ixidro had already collected and dispatched a dozen pigeons he had found in the nets. There were other Basque men checking nets and removing their catches.

Gorka barked at Ixidro, "Give me a decoy. Too many birds are flying above the nets." He took a decoy and climbed atop a rock near the middle of the grassy field. Soon Gorka was swinging a beautifully carved falcon decoy at the end of a long cord in oscillating circles above his head. Incoming pigeon flocks panicked and dove for cover in lower reaches, many getting tangled in the netting. Allison was worried by the capture of so many beautiful wild things. David began to look around for insects, though he had no way to collect any he found. Jennifer wandered for a while and sat down on the grass, looking wistfully up at the cloudless sky. Gorka was annoyed that his guests were not helping in the gathering of pigeons.

It seemed like time slowed down in this timeless place. After awhile, Allison found Ixidro and began to help him, but she still shuddered for each one that was removed from the net, only to have its neck broken. By midday, the men across the pass began to gather around a big fire to talk and clean some of the birds for roasting on skewers set above the fire. Over two dozen had come together, and talking began to change to singing Basque folk songs. At the start of the singing, David came near and began to move in rhythm. The Basque men ignored him and continued with their songs. The plaintive spirit of one song caught everyone's heart:

Urtzo churis, urtzo churia
Errani zaddak othoiegina
Nundat buruz houndonen...

Return to Eden

White dove, white dove,
tell me if you please,
where were you traveling,
your route so straight, your heart at ease?

From my country
I departed with the thought of seeing Spain.
I flew as far as the Pyrenees—
there lost my pleasure
and found pain.

Gorka lifted one of the skewers, pinched the roasted bird, and motioned for everyone to come close and take a skewer. A barrel of fresh cider was opened, and ceramic mugs were passed around for everyone to help themselves. A man produced several loaves of bread and laid them on a rocky outcrop. Soon everyone was enjoying a simple feast under the dazzling midday sun.

Ixidro came over to where Allison sat and joined her. They ate without talking but occasionally exchanged glances. Soon the singing resumed. As quickly as the feast had come together, it was cleared away, and the men made ready to return to their homes with the bulk of harvested pigeons. Ixidro rose first, took Allison's hand to assist her, and then, while looking into her eyes, kissed the back of her hand. Allison felt her pulse double and hoped Ixidro wouldn't notice her sweaty palm. She smiled and longed for more, but he turned and left to carry a large bundle of pigeons. Allison felt as if she could float back to the cottage. David and Jennifer noticed her budding romance with concern.

CHAPTER 4

Romance on Horseback

Shortly after breakfast together in their etcholak, Jennifer, David, and Allison went outside to leave for another hike. Ixidro came around a corner, leading two domesticated pottokak, a breed of small, sturdy horses indigenous to the Pyrenees. He looked at David and asked, "Would it be okay, sir, if I were to take your daughter for a ride?"

David looked at Jennifer, searching for some way to say decline, but with no answer forthcoming. Allison, flushed with excitement, gave him the look of a starving child. He caved in. "Well, sure. I guess it's okay. Allison has ridden horses only two or three times."

"I've ridden plenty," Allison blustered with false confidence. "No problem. I love all animals, especially horses. I'll help you get saddles on them, and we can go right away."

"We don't use saddles," Ixidro replied.

"Oh," Allison hesitated. "Great! Let's leave now."

Though the horses were of small stature, Allison wasn't sure how to mount up. Ixidro leaned over, offering his hands for her left foot so she could throw her right leg over the pottokak's back, which she did with a happy smile for Ixidro.

Jennifer leaned over to David and said, "I'm just not sure about this. Allison has never had a romantic relationship before.

This is all new to her, and we've only known this boy for a couple of days. He's two years older."

David put his arm over Jennifer's shoulder and comforted her. "What could go wrong out here? Besides, he's from a traditional culture where there are strict rules about courtship. Did you notice he asked me and not Allison?" Jennifer nodded with misgiving.

Ixidro threw a leg over his pottokak, looking almost comical as his long legs almost touched the ground while seated on his stout but short mount. He took up the simple rope reins and led his horse down to a trail. Allison grabbed her reins and shook them, having no effect. Ixidro, without looking back, said a simple command in Basque, and her horse began following at a trot. Allison gave a quick backward glance and wave to her parents as she rode off in pursuit. David and Jennifer looked searchingly at one another and then headed out on their morning hike, complete with their makhilas from the previous day. Their pace was much slower as they descended a trail leading to some grassy meadows in the lower reaches of the mountains.

At the same time, Allison and Ixidro rode on silently for a long time, their horses following a winding trail that surprised her with grand vistas at nearly every turn. Though she longed for the sound of his voice, Allison was content to simply be the object of his attention. It was even better that the two of them could be alone without interference. She was so glad her parents had decided to make this trip. Allison mulled over how her friends back home would react when she texted them her news and pictures of her newfound love in such an exotic place. Perhaps even Jackie would be impressed.

Allison was growing sore when, while passing through a shady glade, Ixidro stopped suddenly and dismounted. He came to Allison and helped her dismount.

Not sure of what would come next, she offered, "Do you want me to tie my horse to one of these trees?"·

"No, we let them graze. They will come when I call," he said with a look that hinted at something beyond horses.

Ixidro took Allison's hand and led her off the trail and down to a secluded bushy area nestled up against the slope. There was a small stream of water trickling down in one corner. Ixidro cupped his hands and took a drink, then offered up his hands to Allison. She gratefully drank, looking affectionately into his eyes. He then led her to a benchlike shelf of rock where they sat down.

Ixidro drew close and wrapped his arm around her shoulders. Allison felt a chill run through her body as she looked reverently up into his eyes.

"I have never seen eyes like yours," he said softly. "They are so enchanting."

Allison smiled as her pulse quickened.

"Your hair—it is so unusual. May I touch it?" Ixidro asked as he reached out to handle her long, straight auburn hair. "I have never seen a girl with such bewitching hair."

Allison nodded and labored to breathe. He then caressed her cheek with a slow tenderness, sending a shiver through her. Then, without any words, he kissed her full on the lips. Allison melted. Ixidro held her closer and extended the kiss. Allison felt a thirst she had never known before. After a few moments, she felt his tongue enter her mouth. Allison's eyes popped open in surprise and then she held him tighter.

The sound of hooves and feet drew near. Suddenly, Gorka walked into their hideaway and stopped in front of the couple. They stopped to look up at him.

"So you are at it again?" Gorka growled in a tone that warned of an approaching storm.

"Grandpapa, I am sorry I didn't tell you where I was going," Ixidro offered, trying to deflect what was coming.

"This is not our way! There is no honor in what you do. You have learned too many foreign ways in that school in Pamplona,"

Gorka yelled. "You did this same thing last week with that girl from Germany, and the week before—"

"But, Grandpapa, I love Allison," Ixidro said in desperation. He then looked at Allison, who was still partly in his embrace. She was stunned into shock. "Allison, you are different," he tried.

At that moment, Gorka reached out and took him by his ear as a prelude to an old-fashioned Basque slap down. As Ixidro was pulled upward, Allison came to herself and boiled over in a rage, smacking him hard enough on his cheek that it echoed off the rocky hillside. She quickly rose and left to walk back while wiping away hot tears.

"Allison, wait. I can explain," Ixidro offered weakly.

"You will explain it all to me," Gorka demanded, turning him around to face judgment.

David and Jennifer, having returned from their morning hike, were enjoying a lunch of bread and lamb stew in their etcholak when Allison stomped in with a tear-stained face. She was sweaty from her rapid hike back. When she looked to her surprised parents, she burst into another round of sobs and buried herself in her bed.

Jennifer turned to David with a knowing look, raising an eyebrow. She rose and went to her daughter, sitting on the side of the bed and placing a comforting hand on her back. "I'm sorry, Allison," she said softly.

"He's awful, just so awful," Allison muttered. "How could he play with me, after having done the same thing several times with other girls only weeks ago?"

"It's so painful when someone we want to love hurts us," Jennifer said.

Allison sat up and cuddled against her mom. "The worst part of it is that I went along with what he was doing," Allison steamed.

David and Jennifer looked at each other with looks of concern.

"What was he doing?" David ventured.

"He took me off to this secret place where he put moves on me, hugging and kissing me. His grandfather, that Gorka man, walked in on us right after that French kiss and began to shout at Ixidro. He then said he had done this same thing with other girls before me! I feel like some kind of band instrument. He was just playing with me!" Allison said in disgust.

David and Jennifer shared an unspoken look of relief.

"Some boys are like that. They get into a pattern of manipulating girls to see what they can get them to do," David said. "I'm afraid he's already becoming a predator. You are lucky Gorka walked in on you. Allison, Ixidro was trying to seduce you."

"If they're all like that, I'm through. Who can I trust?" Allison said peevishly.

Jennifer gently rubbed her back. "There are some good ones you can trust, like Justin and your dad, and many others as well. You have to be careful," Jennifer said. "If a boy really cares about you, he won't rush the physical aspect. He would be content to simply spend time listening and talking with you. Another good measure is the strength of his faith. Go into a relationship with your eyes wide open. Also ask God to guard your heart."

Allison looked up to her mom. "I just want to go home. How can I face him after what he did to me?"

"Well, we leave tomorrow to go to the coast and a short stay at Gueterria, where there is a wonderful beach," David said. "This afternoon, we will head down to the village of Orbaizeta for a festival they call San Fermín. This time of year, our people celebrate this all over the region with song, dance, and parties."

"It's a good thing we missed the running of the bulls in Pamplona," Jennifer chuckled. "No telling what your dad would have done in the face of a frantic bull. Allison, let me get you something to eat before we go. You may want to clean up after your walk back."

Soon they were in the car and on their way down the winding mountain roads on their way to a nearby village of Orbaizeta for the festival of San Fermín, an annual festival celebrated across Euskal Herria, the Basque homeland. Jennifer, David, and Allison walked along all the main streets, taking in the atmosphere of the small mountain town. There were several fascinating shops with handmade woolen garments and Basque craft items. They ate dinner at a local cafe and then went out to the plaza to take in the festival. People gathered. Some sang, others talked, and some danced. There were a couple of clusters at tables playing *el mus*, a Basque card game. The singing subsided when two men in Basque traditional dress stepped forward and faced each other. These *bertsolari* began to sing in counterpoint against one another. The crowd grew and cheered as they battled back and forth in song.

The music wore on as the day gave way to evening. Sunset burned into the western clouds in yellows, moving through orange to red and magenta. A shrill tone was heard as a *tchirula*, a flute, announced the beginning of dancing. The player emerged from the side of the crowd, playing his tchirula in one hand and beating an *atabal*, a small drum, in the other, sounding a tune as old as the mountains themselves. The crowd continued to dance. David and Jennifer rose from their seats to try to follow. As they began to master the steps, the music finished, and the men moved back, with some sitting down, leaving the women alone to dance the *Makil* using the shepherd's staffs. David and Jennifer rejoined Allison at their small table off to the side of the plaza. The women moved rapidly in ancient patterns that Basque women had danced for millennia.

As the women finished, they retired from the dancing area to be replaced by men, all in costume, moving with practiced dignity and motion. As the music began, they started the *Zamalzain*, the oldest of all Basque dances. In the music and dance, the ancient contest between good and evil was reenacted between two groups dancing around a wine glass set in the middle of a flimsy table.

At first, the good group danced with fury around and over the glass, missing it by millimeters, much to the gasping and cheering delight of the crowd. Then a group representing evil followed a similar pattern and tempo. Near the end of their time, the cuff of the trouser of one of the men touched the glass enough that it began to wobble and then fell, crashing into shards on the stone pavement. The crowd cheered deliriously since this was considered a good omen.

"Tell me again why we came here instead of Paris or Venice," Allison said wearily.

"Allison, our ancestors were Basque. Several hundred years ago, our people lived around here," David said.

"No wonder they left for the new world," Allison replied, "with nothing to do but watch sheep, live in cold stone huts, and prey on young women."

"The traditional ways are deep and gave a sense of order. Ixidro has been confused by the ways of the modern world, much like many boys back home," David said. "Traditional Basque customs for courtship are very strict. Physical contact was restricted until after marriage. Women are regarded with a high status equal to that of their men. If Ixidro lived by that code, he never would have touched you like he did."

Jennifer jumped in. "Tomorrow, we will get a change of scenery. Your dad has planned this part of the trip. We will be staying on the coast at a small fishing village with a wonderful beach."

"It's the place where several of our ancestors lived and worked on the sea," David said. "I'll even introduce you to the most famous one. He was one of the greatest explorers of all times."

Allison perked up at the thought of a beach. Then she gasped as she recognized Ixidro in the dancing crowd. "He's here," she whispered, "and he's got two girls with him, holding them like he did me!" Allison felt a mix of anger and jealousy swell up. "What if he sees me? What will I do?" Allison panicked.

"He's too busy with those girls to even notice you," Jennifer reassured her. "He's already beginning to work on them. Watch and learn."

"Someone should tattoo a warning label on his forehead," Allison fumed.

"If Ixidro cannot grow out of this pattern, he will never be able to sustain any lasting relationship," David said. "His future could be very unhappy. You, on the other hand, will have a terrific life and will someday meet that wonderful young man that God has for you. Your mother and I have been praying for your future husband since you were born, just like we did for your brother, Justin. Look at what a great wife he got."

"I wish I could know him now so there wouldn't be any more pain and hurt," Allison lamented. "I would call him or text him, and we could start making a life together."

"The time is not right yet, Allison," Jennifer reminded her. "Besides, all the surprise would be gone. If you knew and contacted him, telling him you were going to marry him, it would terrify the young man. It's better to let it happen in God's time. Both of you have a lot of growing up and living to enjoy first."

"Tomorrow will come early, and we mustn't keep our famous explorer waiting," David said as he rose and started for the car.

"Count me in, Dad," Allison replied with relief.

CHAPTER 5

Meeting the Voyager

After a quick breakfast the next morning, Jennifer, Allison, and David loaded up their car and began the three-hour drive to the Spanish coast. The cloudless sky welcomed the dominion of the rising sun with a dew-filled landscape as fresh as the first day.

Temperatures rose as they approached the coast. The land came to an abrupt end at the low cliffs and slopes that held the ancient fishing village of Getaria. They parked in a lot off the plaza and soon found the little inn that would be their home for the next couple of days. It was a welcome change after the bracing air and rigorous pace of the mountains. The steady sea breezes coming in off the Bay of Biscay pumped optimism into the family. After a light lunch at a cafe overlooking the sea, the family took off on foot to explore their new surroundings.

At the city hall, they came to a large statue of a man in ancient costume, looking out to the sea with a fierce gaze. Jennifer came closer and tried to make sense of the Spanish on the plaque at the statue's base.

"Is this the Elcano guy you have been talking about, David?" she asked. "He lived from 1475 to 1526, and there's something about sailing for three years."

"Yes indeed, that's Captain Juan Sebastián de Elcano, to be exact," David replied with a stance of pride. "Not only did he sail for three years, he sailed in 1519 with Ferdinand Magellan and two hundred sixty-five men in five ships to circle the world."

"Wow!" exclaimed Allison. "That must have been hard with the level of technology back then. Wasn't Magellan the guy who first sailed around the world?"

"He made it only halfway and was killed in the Philippines," David said. "Elcano was the only officer to return with a single ship, the *Victoria*, and seventeen other survivors in 1522. He was Basque, born and raised in this village. Elcano was from a long line of daring Basque sailors who had braved the waters of the Atlantic. It is said that the Basque were the first Europeans to find the Grand Banks off Canada in search of fish during the Middle Ages. This was centuries before Columbus ever sailed westward. Most of his crews were Basque sailors because they didn't fear the sea."

"Talk about brave explorers," Jennifer exclaimed. "They found their way without GPS, charts, or accurate instruments. No one else had circumnavigated the world until they did. I wonder why the world gives so much credit to Magellan and so little to Elcano?"

"Maybe it's because Elcano led a failed mutiny against Magellan as they neared the southern end of South America," David ventured. "Elcano and many of the crew were losing their nerve. Remember that no European had ever sailed the Pacific before them. They knew nothing of what lay beyond."

"What happened to Elcano after his mutiny failed?" Allison asked curiously.

"Magellan slapped him in iron shackles and sentenced him to hard labor for five months, which was much of the Pacific crossing," David said. "In those days, most mutineers were executed, so Elcano was lucky."

"After such a hard journey, did he ever go to sea again?" Allison wondered.

"Yes, after four years here, he couldn't resist the chance to return to the South Pacific on another voyage. Elcano was like the rest of our people; the sea called, and he answered. He died there in 1526, probably from malnutrition or disease," David said.

"Dad, you seem to have a special interest in this man," Allison said.

"Years ago, my mother did our family history and was able to trace us directly to this man," David said as he flourished his arm upward to point at their ancestor.

"Wow! Dad, I never would have guessed you had that in you, what with your keen interest in animals and bugs," Allison said, chuckling.

"Well, Juan Sebastián hungered to explore lands beyond the sea. I hunger to explore very small worlds where amazing little creatures make good lives for themselves," David replied. They turned to look out to sea—the warm, gentle breeze blowing on their faces.

"It makes the cancellation of your place on the Rim mission especially hard to take," Allison said. "That is *so* not fair! Elcano probably would have taken a ship and gone anyway."

"Who knows," Jennifer ventured. "We may still get to go. As it is, we still have much to learn here on Earth, especially as you get to explore with us. I was not happy about leaving you behind when your dad and I were preparing to take off for a multiyear voyage to who knows where to find who knows what. I felt like we were going to lose you. That's too high a price to pay for any voyage."

Allison hugged her mom and said, "I wasn't very happy about having you two gone for three or four years of my life. Besides, who could I turn to for help with dating, college, and careers? Thank you for the great ways you have loved and guided me. I love you guys."

Jennifer beamed, grateful for a rare affirmation and show of affection from a fourteen-year-old. Out of habit, she leaned over to kiss Allison's head. She was surprised that she had to step up to kiss her forehead. Allison had continued to grow. The three then return to their inn to change for an afternoon at the beach.

Half an hour later, they found an unoccupied space on the limited beach east of the peninsula that served as a breakwater against the vigorous waves of the Bay of Biscay. David and Jennifer were relieved to see that their daughter was wearing a more modest one-piece swim suit in lieu of the scanty two-piece bikini she had displayed two weeks earlier. Jennifer stretched out to sun herself on a towel after having lathered up with full-strength sunscreen. Allison set herself down on the sand a few feet below Jennifer and near the incoming waves. She set to work building an elaborate castle complete with moats and levees. David walked down the waterline for a while, looking for small mollusks and crustaceans. He soon joined Allison in her work on the wet sand.

"Dad, do you realize we're building mounds in the sand just like ants?" Allison asked.

"We do a lot of things like the ants," David replied. "It's basic to intelligent life to do things similarly."

"Do you believe the people or creatures living on the Rim will build communities and civilizations like we do?" Allison wondered, looking up to David.

"Maybe. Then they also might surprise us with using materials in different ways and living in patterns new to us," David said. "We won't know until we get out there."

"It's taken over two years, and all that has been done is a lot of talk." Allison frowned. "And now they are shutting down NASA's manned program. It's like we're taking several steps backward."

"Your mother and I, as well as many other people, are very frustrated by the lack of progress from our leaders around the world," David said, agreeing. "It doesn't look like any viable mission will get underway for years. Maybe our friends out there will have to make the first move, like they did with the coming of the Sphere."

Allison picked up a small pinch of wet sand, spread it across her palm, and then picked up an even smaller cluster of grains on her wet index finger and held it up to the sunlight. "These little grains look almost like miniature gems. They are really beautiful. There must be trillions upon trillions of them right here under us," Allison said in wonder.

"Think of the fact that at one time, every last one of them was connected to much larger pieces of quartz before being crushed into so many small fragments," David said. "It's an amazing world God has made."

She took her treasure over to her mom. "Look at the amazing little gems I found," she said playfully.

Jennifer sat up and looked carefully at Allison's grains of sand. "Just think, Allison, no two of these are exactly alike," Jennifer said, adding to Allison's wonder.

"Mom, you've told me many times how there are more stars than all the grains of sand on Earth," Allison said, looking her in the eye. "That boggles my mind. Do you miss the stars?"

"Of course I do," Jennifer said. "We still have our own sun and the one hundred twenty white dwarfs that hover above the Rim, but those dwarfs are all identical in size, temperature, and content, which suggest they were manufactured somehow. Once you've studied one, you studied them all. It's pretty boring, except for the mystery of how they manage to periodically occult the light from each of them to give the Rim night after day."

"Do you think we will ever see the stars again?" Allison wondered. "And will they be in the same places?"

Jennifer looked at Allison seriously, "I believe someday we will, but I have no clue whether we will see them in the same ancient constellation patterns. It depends on how far the Sphere has moved everything."

"What are you going to do now that you won't be going to the Rim and there are no stars to study?" Allison said, worried.

"I don't know, dear," Jennifer said with a warm look of reassurance. "It's odd, but I have a peace about it all, except for this strange urge that Dad and I had to travel over here to voyage back to our roots. We had never considered a trip like this before, but it's like we're on another kind of mission to find something else, and we don't even know what it is." She looked Allison in the eye and smiled. "The best part is that we all get to be together for this adventure. Who knows what we'll find next when we head out in two days for Iceland."

"Mom, you said we knew of living relatives we have there now," Allison began. "Who are they and how do they fit in our family?"

"Remember our family story, how my dad was a young soldier in World War II and stationed in Iceland?" Jennifer started. "It was there in Reykjavik, the capital, where he met my mom. They dated, fell in love, and married. After a lot of paper work, he moved her back to America and, after the war, they moved to Texas where I was born."

"Have you ever been there to see our relatives?" Allison asked.

"Your grandmother and grandfather did, going back once before I was born," Jennifer replied. "My mom was an only child. So when her parents, your great-grandparents, became frail in old age, we moved them to live with us in Midland. They died before you were born. They would have loved knowing you. Someday, you will meet them. There are some third cousins still in Iceland on a farm in the rural eastern side of the island. Before we left on the trip, I called them, and they insisted we come to stay with them. I have never met them in person, but we often wrote and e-mailed over the years. The farm where we'll stay is in a gorgeous valley. There are some horses to ride, miles of hiking in wild terrain, and a small, wild river we can kaya, with water so clear and fresh that we can drink it whenever we want. I know you'll love it there."

Allison returned for a while to sand-castle construction with her dad, but the waters of the incoming tide soon made their work impossible. She looked up at him with disgust. "It's no use. Maybe we should have used concrete. Within a few hours, there will be no trace of all this work."

"It's another reminder of how temporary everything in life is," David said. "Someday, even the pyramids in Egypt will finally disappear into the sands of the Sahara. But even now, you are building something far more important than any sand castle or even a pyramid."

Allison looked at him with a half-raised eyebrow, knowing this was another one of his fatherly teaching moments. "All right, I give up." She grinned. "What am I building now?"

"You are building the foundations of your future life," David said with a warm smile. "Your mom and I are the primary members of a larger team of people who are helping you design and build yourself into the woman God wants you to become. He's the architect, and you and the rest of the people in your life are the carpenters, painters, electricians, and so forth. You have learned so much and have come so far. Sometimes I wish you could look back and see what you were like even a few years ago. As your father, I am blessed to see how far you have come."

"And how far do I have to go?" Allison said in self-condemnation. "I still feel like such an idiot after that time with Ixidro."

"No one gets everything right the first time. We all make lots of mistakes. But the important thing is that we learn and grow from those mistakes. Be patient with yourself. You're only fourteen, and your whole life is before you. Enjoy it now and love who you are becoming. Always keep an eye open for where the Lord is leading you and an ear tuned to what he is saying. Who and what you are is eternal, made in his likeness. With your faith and life in him, you will outlast the sands, the pyramids, and even the stars," David said.

Later, in early evening, after cleaning up after the beach, they all enjoyed dinner together. Then they took a walk to the end of the peninsula to a park, where they found a bench to watch the sunset and the constant movement of the waves. Occasional fish would jump from the water, trying to escape predators. Gulls skimmed the waters to pick up small bits of food or a small fish. As the sky burned slowly into deep, warm colors in the west, beyond the coastline, the same white stars came out to accent the sky in their uniform, symmetrical grid pattern, still beckoning the people of Earth.

CHAPTER 6

Land of Fire and Ice

Two days later, after clearing Icelandic customs at the Keflavik International Airport, David, Jennifer, and Allison found the rental-car desk. They made their way to the door leading to the lot, where their car was waiting in the early-morning light. As soon as they stepped outside, an insistent north wind began to push them so much that they had to tack upwind. Allison was glad for a heavy suitcase for ballast to keep her earthbound. They found the assigned car, loaded it, got in, and couldn't get it started. David went for help, returning shortly with an attendant in a cart with jumper cables. As they labored to start the car, a honking sound came from the trunk. Jennifer jumped out in alarm and grabbed the keys from David to access her suitcase. She frantically opened it on the parking-lot asphalt while David and the attendant ran to catch garments that started to blow away in the wind. Jennifer continued digging for the strange noise, which turned out to be the special phone she had used years before when serving as a Cabinet member. She frantically grabbed the honking device.

"Hello!" she gasped. "Yes, this is Jennifer Bass. Who is this?" To hear better, she climbed back into the car and closed the passenger door, leaving David outside to return the suitcase to the trunk.

"I still can't make out what you are saying," Jennifer said, almost shouting into to the phone. "Please call me back on my iPhone." She gave the number, and her phone began to ring. Jennifer drew her iPhone out of her purse and activated the call, which indicated a video stream. To her delight, the face of Dr. Otto Prather from the McDonald Observatory was there, with several other colleagues in the background.

"What a surprise to get a call from you," Jennifer beamed. "How's everyone back home?"

"We had trouble tracking you down," Dr. Prather said. "After the announcement of the closure of the Johnson Space Center in Houston, we couldn't find anyone still on duty who could tell us where you had gone. Even your condo complex couldn't help. Finally, I remembered these special phones the government had issued a few years ago when they set up the base here. By the way, where in the world are you?"

"We've been to Spain, and now we're on to Iceland, where we have just arrived," Jennifer replied. "Since NASA was closing down, David and I decided to take a long overdue vacation. We have missed you so much."

"We have missed all of you too," Dr. Prather said.

Jennifer knew something was up and looked over at David with a raised eyebrow.

Dr. Prather continued. "Since you and David left for Houston over two years ago, things have gotten a lot quieter here. The government left all of the scientific instruments and connections. Since we couldn't look at stars anymore, we have been doing a lot of mapping and scanning of the Rim's interior. In all this time, we've charted less than five percent of the entire surface. The call is about something much greater than all of that."

Dr. Prather paused to catch his breath. "About half an hour ago, we picked up an object with the Spitzer and then confirmed it with Hubble. It is small, only about two meters in diameter. It has no coma, so we ruled out a comet. The surface is highly reflective, almost luminous, suggesting it is artificial, possibly metallic, and it is coming our way at high velocity. This thing is hard to get readings on, but our best guess is that it will arrive here within a day."

"Have you called anyone else?" Jennifer asked.

"We felt you should be the first to know, even before we call President What's-His-Name." Dr. Prather smirked. "Currently, we've been shut down as a government base, so there's no protocol for where to go with this news. Dr. Jackson has retired, so we lost a valuable connection there. Maybe you can tell us whom to contact."

"Wow! What a discovery. You guys are great. Thanks for calling to tell me," Jennifer blurted out. "I don't know anyone in the current administration. Maybe you could contact our governor and go from there. I don't know."

"I feel bad to have disturbed your vacation," Dr. Prather said, "but it is great to see you and David, and is that Allison too?"

"Yes, indeed," Jennifer said. "For now, I think I should continue with my itinerary. That small sphere will hold something wondrous when it gets here. Please keep me posted."

"Will do. Dr. Ellis, Rachel, Lucy, and the others all send their best. Come home soon," Dr. Prather concluded. "Good-bye and Godspeed."

"Good-bye," Jennifer concluded. She looked at David. "It's been too long. When we get back, let's go home for a while." Allison rolled her eyes, worried about losing her new friends in Houston.

"What should we do?" David asked. "Should we go back inside and rebook for Houston? It's only seven in the morning local time, and we could be back by early evening, Houston time."

"No, we haven't come this far to miss seeing my cousin and my family's farm," Jennifer said with certainty. "There's nothing to be done about it for now. Let's go. It's an all-day drive to Egilsstadir."

In the last minutes of fading evening light, they approached a remote stone farmhouse situated in a long, narrow valley with widely dispersed trees across rocky meadows. It seemed to erupt out of the hillside, with the moss growing on every slate shingle on the roof. The house was aglow with warm, lit windows that beckoned the weary travelers.

"Well, after all that ice, rocky scree, and endless wasteland, I thought we'd never get here," Allison said wearily. "That circle road seemed to go on forever."

"There's no place like it anywhere else on Earth," David responded. "It's some of the newest land on Earth, and one of the last to have human habitation."

"Are you sure there are any humans here?" Allison retorted.

Ignoring Allison and turning to Jennifer, David said, "So now we meet your cousin you have written to all your life in person. What is her name again?"

"Sigríður Magnúsardóttir, Sigi for short," Jennifer said. "And her husband is Jóhann Þólhallsson. Wow, this is the house where my mother was born, as were seven generations before her!"

"What a mouthful of a name," David commented.

As they pulled to a stop, a trim couple in their fifties walked out the front door to welcome them. The tall, white-haired woman came to their car immediately.

"Oh, Jennifer, it is so good to finally meet you!" Sigi said as she embraced Jennifer. "These must be David and Allison. Welcome! How wonderful to see you. This is Jóhann. You must be exhausted. Please come in. I have fixed a dinner of Þorramatur. We can get your luggage later."

Just then, a boom sounded from the east, followed by a faint roar high above. They all looked upward to see a bright cone of light that was followed very closely by a tiny luminous sphere.

"Is that a meteorite?" Sigi ventured.

"No, it's moving too slowly, and there appears to be an object behind the main fireball," Jennifer said, squinting upward, wishing for binoculars. "We haven't had any meteorites at all since Earth was enveloped over two years ago. This is not behaving like any regular meteorite."

"Will it land here in Iceland?" Jóhann asked.

"No, it's too high," Jennifer replied. "My guess is that it will land somewhere in North America."

"Well, there is nothing to be done about it," Sigi said. "Dinner is waiting."

After a sumptuous dinner of smoked leg of lamb, boiled salmon, rye bread, and black pudding, Jóhann helped David with luggage and showed him to a tidy room with modern furniture and sparse decor. They rejoined Sigi and Jennifer for coffee in chairs of Scandinavian austerity that circled a blazing fireplace. Allison excused herself to take a long soak in a tub of hot water.

"Jennifer, it has been wonderful getting to know you and your family. We hope you can stay for a while," Sigi said.

"The pleasure has been all ours," Jennifer replied. "It has been wonderful to see this old home after hearing my mother and grandmother's stories and seeing the old photos. Nine generations of our people have made this home. You and Jóhann have done such a fine job of keeping it up. Tomorrow, we look forward to exploring the farm too."

"Jóhann and I are not farming anymore," Sigi said with a note of sadness. "There's no way we could sustain ourselves raising sheep. A dairy company leases the land to graze their herd, and they built a milking barn down near the highway. Jóhann works for the Icelandic Postal Service, and I have recently retired from teaching school in Egilsstadir."

"Are you happy here?" Jennifer asked.

"We do not know anything else," Sigi said, "but we have no children and since we are also only children, there is no direct relative to take the place after we die. I guess everything comes to an end. Sometimes I wish I had come to America with

Grandmother Arna when she left to join Helga, your mother, twenty years ago."

"You both would be most welcome to come our way," David said.

"Our roots are deep here," Jóhann said. "It would be so hard to pack up and leave the only place we have ever known forever."

"Jennifer, we have known each other so well through our years of letters," Sigi said, changing her tone. "There is one thing I cannot understand about you. With all your scientific training and accomplishments, I was shocked to hear you talk about God and faith when you were on TV when you made the discoveries. Surely as a scientist, and an astronomer at that, you would have shed all those primitive notions long ago. How can you be a good scientist and still believe in a God?"

Surprised at her question, Jennifer was slow in her answer. "My faith and my science have never been in conflict. When I look up at the stars, I also feel I am looking up to the one who made them. My science deals with the 'how' and 'what' questions, while my faith addresses the 'who' and 'why' questions."

"But surely you must know that there can be no God with all the great discoveries of science. All we know today has shed light in all the dark places where people used to see God," Sigi said with growing intensity.

Jennifer again paused before thoughtfully responding, silently praying for wisdom to answer in love. "Sigi, the more I learn from science, the more questions arise, humbling me with how great our reality is and how great the Creator must be. For me, God is not a god of darkness or superstition, but the God of truth and light. Science is just another tool we have to learn more about how his creation works."

"Like much of Europe, we have downplayed religion for years in our schools. We believe it is important to rid children of the shackles of religion that have been so destructive in our history," Sigi said.

"That's sad. I am grieved to hear that," Jennifer said, a growing fire within. "My read of history is that the evil done by people in the name of any religion, or even the lack of religion as in communism, has an equally bad record. As I see it, the fault does not lie with the religion, but with the people in power who abuse it. I especially fear societies where religion becomes the enemy. All absolutes are removed except the absolutes of the government as well as those in control of it and the media. Nazi Germany was a prime example of such a utopian atheist state. I don't want to live in that kind of world."

"You intrigue me, Jennifer," Sigi said, with newfound respect. "I want to visit with you about this again."

Jennifer sensed it was time to let it go. "Sigi, thank you and Jóhann so much for everything. I think David and I will excuse ourselves to prepare for bed. We look forward to breakfast with you at six a.m. tomorrow."

With summer mornings beginning at four in such northerly latitudes, the sun was well up in the sky by the six a.m. breakfast time. Jennifer and David made their way down to the kitchen, followed by a sleepy Allison. Sigi and Jóhann had prepared a smorgasbord along the kitchen counter, laden with pancakes, skyr, cheese, dark rye bread, pickled fish, smoked salmon, and roasted lamb kidneys. A roasted sheep's head was the edible centerpiece. Everyone was encouraged to fill their plates, but Allison exhibited deliberate caution, avoiding all the dishes she couldn't understand. She welcomed the strong Icelandic coffee when she joined everyone else at the table.

"How did you sleep, Allison?" Sigi asked.

"I'm not sure that I'm not still asleep," Allison said faintly as she sipped her hot coffee. Everyone else smiled.

Jennifer noticed how grown-up her daughter looked, with a large cup of coffee in her hand. Allison had already passed her in height.

"Last night you said you wanted to kayak the river through the valley down to Seyðisfjörður at the head of the fjord," Sigi said. "Jóhann will have to go to work in an hour, but I will be here all day. Please excuse me from that water sport. Perhaps later in the day, you will want to ride some of our horses up into the highlands."

"Thank you. That would be wonderful," said David.

"Jennifer, if you do not mind, I want to return to the discussion we had last night," Sigi said softly. "Your talk about your faith has caused me to think about things I have not thought of in years. Is everyone in your family a believer like you?"

"Yes, we are," David said. Allison nodded.

"Do you believe because you are afraid of something, maybe of death?" Sigi asked.

"We have no fear of God in our faith," Jennifer said with a warm smile. "We are very happy and blessed in our lives and home. We are rich in love for each other and our Lord. For us, there's peace and joy, a contentment that is like solid ground under our feet."

Sigi continued. "The God I remember being taught about in childhood was terribly mean, always watching us for mistakes and then ready to punish us with illness or misfortune. He was to be feared."

Jennifer looked at Sigi intently. "I am sorry you grew up with that kind of belief. No wonder you wanted to abandon a god like that. The God that David, our children, and I have come to know, love, and trust is nothing like that. We know him best through his son, Jesus Christ. We feel his presence with us often, especially when we pray or read Scripture. He has been especially close in times of happiness, like when our children were born, and in bad times, like when my brother was killed in that car accident."

"I remember how hard it was for all of you, especially your mother, Aunt Helga," Sigi recalled. "Why would your God let that happen since you love and trust him?"

Jennifer slowly shook her head, then looked to Sigi. "I don't have the answer for that, Sigi. Tómas was so young. It was horrible. But through all the tears, shock, and grief, I knew that the Lord was there, and he was hurting too. I also believe that I will see Tómas again when my time in this universe is done."

Sigi knitted her brow in doubt. "Again, how can you as a scientist, and you, David, also a scientist, believe in those tales of an afterlife? I have seen people die. Then we bury them in the ground, and that is it."

Jennifer continued eye contact with a slight smile of reassurance. "Sigi, there is so much more to reality than what we can detect with our senses. God is so wonderful. He loves us and made us like him in our souls. That part of us will last forever, beyond this life and into life beyond time, space, and dimension with him and those we love, free from all of the suffering, limitations, and mortality we experience here."

Sigi raised an eyebrow. "So what is the purpose of life here and now?"

Jennifer continued, saying, "It is to do all we can to love one another, love the Lord, and to live following his example and teachings, trusting him by faith for life here and life to come."

Tears came to Sigi's eyes. "I would give anything if I could have a faith like yours. I'm not good enough."

Jennifer placed her hand on Sigi's hand. "I know that you can. You have opened the door to your heart. Jesus loves you even more than we do, and he wants to relate to you and become part of your life. If you come to him openly and honestly, he will forgive anything in your past and open a whole new future for you. Let's pray about it right now."

"I want to believe too," said Jóhann, with tears streaming down his face.

David put his arm around Jóhann's shoulders. They all joined hands around the table and bowed for prayer.

After a deep sigh, Jennifer began softly. "Dear Lord Jesus, thank you for answering our prayers for Sigi and Jóhann. We love them, and we know you love them even more. Please make yourself known in their hearts right now. Take away their doubts, sin, fears, and guilt and fill their hearts with the light of your Spirit. Heal their souls and lead them to love and follow you the rest of their days. In your holy name we pray. Amen."

"God sent you to us," Sigi said in a choked voice. "This is the most wonderful thing that has ever happened to us."

They got up from the table and gave hugs all around. Even Allison had tears on her smiling face.

"I will give you my Bible," said Jennifer. "It's in English. I hope that is not a problem for you." Sigi and Jóhann both shook their heads. "I also urge you to prayerfully seek a community of believers who can share the journey of faith with you."

Sigi brightened. "I know just the person—a fellow teacher in my school often talked about her faith. I used to think she was a fanatic. She kept saying she was praying for me. I will call her as soon as you three head out to kayak. This will come as a real surprise to her."

"I want you to feel free to call us anytime," Jennifer said. "I'm never too busy for matters of faith. You both have made us so happy."

Moving fast in bitterly cold glacial meltwater, David, Jennifer, and Allison guided their kayaks into a slower section of the river. Their bodies felt conflicted with the exertion of vigorous paddling to avoid rocks and steep parts of the rapids. They were chilled by the persistent cold wind and spray from the icy water.

"Tell me again why we didn't take the horses instead of these kayaks?" Allison said with a hint of disgust.

"This is a great way to get close to this fierce land of ice and fire," Jennifer said. "Just think, Allison, your ancestors lived with this land and water for over a thousand years."

"No wonder Grandmother got out," Allison retorted.

"You know better than that," Jennifer reminded her. "She fell in love with Grandpa during the American occupation in World War II."

"I want to remind you both that my Basque ancestors probably sailed near here centuries ago and kept on going," David said with a grin.

"Put me down for that boat," Allison grinned in reply. "Where do we finish and what do we do with these rental kayaks?"

"We will meet the rental people and our ride back at Seyðisfjörður, where this river drains into the fjord," Jennifer said. "I'd guess we're almost there. No more than a mile or two to go."

The whirr of distant chopper blades drew their attention and silence.

"Someone must be lost," David said.

The chopper drew closer, passed overhead, and then circled back, dropping quickly to land on a sandbar a few hundred meters away. Jennifer, David, and Allison were so stunned that they stopped paddling. An American Air Force officer got out of the chopper with a bullhorn and came in their direction.

"Dr. Jennifer Bass?" he shouted into the horn.

Jennifer nodded and waved.

"All three of you are to come with us immediately," he shouted again.

CHAPTER 7

From All the Corners of the Earth

(Previous day, City of Rahat, southern Israel)

Dr. Fatima al-Tarabin unlocked the door and wearily trudged into her fourth-floor apartment, turning on the lights and dropping her bag on the table. She took off her *tarha*, the black shawl worn even by urban Bedouin women. In exhaustion, she fell onto the couch. It had been a grueling morning at the hospital in Rahat, testing her thirty-five-year-old strength to its limits. Fatima had been called in at midnight after a terrorist bomb detonated prematurely in a makeshift weapons lab in another apartment only blocks away. Dozens of her fellow Bedouins were injured and maimed. She had operated nonstop, trying to save as many as she could. Fatima began to cry as she recalled the little girl she had tried so hard to save. Her last words were cries for a mother who was already dead.

A shadowy figure darted out from her bedroom. Fatima looked up and began to scream until she realized it was Mahmoud, her younger brother. He was gaunt, unshaven, and anxious.

"Mahmoud!" she exclaimed. "What are you doing here? How did you get in? I haven't seen you since you quit school almost a year ago."

"Fatima, my elder sister," Mahmoud began with a hoarse voice. "I am here on an urgent mission. I have been sent by the imam who leads Tawhid wa Jihad with a message for you."

"So you quit school and deserted our family to join a terrorist group?" Fatima said with scorn, readying to give a scolding. "Let's see, Tawhid wa Jihad means 'unity and holy war.' It was you and your friends who were responsible for that bomb blast that killed and wounded two dozen of our own people this morning. How many have you killed since you joined up?"

"The bombs went off by accident," Mahmoud said with rising anger. "It was written. We call them martyrs."

"Nothing was written," Fatima countered. "Someone got careless, lit a cigarette, and killed fifteen women and children, who are innocent victims of hatred. Their blood is on your hands."

Mahmoud quickly glanced at his hands. "It is all the fault of these infidel Israelis and Americans who have taken our land and imprisoned our people in these apartments. Someday we will be free thanks to Tawhid wa Jihad."

Fatima looked gravely in his face. "No, someday all of you will be dead, along with thousands of innocent victims. Mahmoud, my beloved baby brother, give this up and come back to us," she pleaded.

Mahmoud darkened. "You have brought dishonor to our people, our family, and our father! You are a collaborator. You are responsible for our parents' death. You are the one who must change."

"Our father died of cardio myopathy fifteen years ago and mother died six months ago with cancer! Where were you when she needed you?" Fatima argued. "The Israelis educated me. They sent me to Ben Gurion University. I have become a doctor. I am no collaborator. What do I have to change?"

"Every life you save prolongs their occupation and, worse, encourages others, especially our women, to abandon our ways," Mahmoud said.

"You talk of honor and our ways," Fatima replied. "We Bedouin were people of peace to all who came our way. Now you have gone and brought hatred and death. You take life! I work to save and give life!"

"As the head of our family, I come here to give you a chance to save your life, to join up with us," Mahmoud said. "Your place as a surgeon in the hospital, respected by the enemy, would be valuable to us. You could even help us with creating biological weapons."

"I will do no such thing, and if our father were here, he would beat you," Fatima said in disgust.

"The imam said that if you refuse to join us," Mahmoud said in a lowered and threatening voice, "he will issue a fatwa against you. Every one of us will be bound by honor to kill you on sight."

Though short and stocky, Fatima rose from the couch in rage and grabbed her taller, lanky brother by the collar. "Get out. Get out! And don't come back until you have gotten over your hatred!" She shoved him out the door and slammed it, double-checking the lock. Her encounter with her brother and his threat unnerved her. In agitation, Fatima busied herself in the kitchen, trying to fix some coffee and a snack. Nothing seemed to help.

In a moment of impulse, she packed up a few essentials into a large carpeted bag, including her medical bag. Fatima knew what she must do. Since she was off for several days, she would travel to al Tawani on the northeastern edge of the Negev desert. There she would be safe as she spent time with her uncle, Abdullah bin Hassan. He and his family spent the summer months grazing their small herd of sheep and goats in the desert. Uncle Abdullah was a decorated veteran of the IDF (Israeli Defense Force) and a hero among Bedouin and Israelis alike. Fatima began to put on her tarha but replaced it with her mother's dark blue *abaya*, the traditional long coat. Somehow she felt safe inside that traditional garment.

No one noticed when Fatima left her apartment, headed to the bus stop dressed head to toe in the abaya. By the time she reached the stop, Fatima was blending into the crowd. Soon she was on her way to Be'er Sheva to catch a connecting bus up to al Tawani. There she would walk a couple of kilometers into the hills to a nameless *wadi*, where her mother's brother had camped and grazed his flocks like his ancestors for countless generations before.

The sun was descending in the west when she arrived at Abdullah bin Hassan's *goum*, a small cluster of tents. She knew from childhood where to find her family. Several male cousins and her uncle Abdullah embraced and welcomed her. Fatima entered the *bait ashshar* and went into the mahram, the section reserved for women. Fatima drew off the hood of her abaya, a sign she was home with family. Immediately she was warmly welcomed and hugged by her aunt, female cousins, and the wives of male cousins. Preparations were well underway for the evening meal. Fatima pitched in to help and joined in small talk, as if she had always lived there.

In honor of Fatima's arrival, the meal was elevated to a *mansaf*, a feast with roast lamb on rice, garnished with pine nuts and drenched in yogurt mixed with butter. Side dishes included *feteer*, handmade bread as well as cheese and dates. *Gahwa*, the traditional strong, bitter coffee seasoned with coriander, was the beverage of choice. With respect to Bedouin ways, Fatima assisted her female kin in serving the male family members in the *es-shigg*. Then she retreated to the mahram through the *saha*, a woolen curtain partitioning the bait ashshar. She was revived by the wonderful feast. Afterward, Fatima helped with the cleanup, a traditional role learned from summer visits to her mother's side of the family.

After sundown, her uncle sent for her to join him outside by a campfire. The clear desert sky was full of the grid of pure white pinpoints of light, all in a grand symmetrical pattern across the heavens. As Fatima sat down next to him, she knew he was concerned. Her keen sense of medical diagnostics came from this branch of her family.

"Daughter of my beloved sister," Abdullah began with an air of gentle authority. "What brings you to us so suddenly?"

"I have had a very hard day," Fatima began. "I operated on seven people, including children, who were injured in the terrorist blast last night in Rahat. Two of the children did not make it."

Never in a hurry to converse, her aged uncle always knew which way to go with the conversation. He looked at her, and Fatima lowered her gaze out of deference. With a look of concern, he said, "I know you are troubled in your heart."

As tears began to run down her face, Fatima said, "It's not the loss of patients that disturbed me so much. I have lost people before, but Mahmoud broke into my apartment. I hadn't seen him in a year."

Abdullah looked at her with concern. "That boy quit school and disappeared. What did he want?"

Fatima looked up into the eyes of her uncle. "Mahmoud said I have brought shame on our family by becoming a doctor and that our parents would be ashamed of me because I have not followed the Bedouin ways for women."

He looked into her face and smiled. "Daughter of my beloved sister, you have never dishonored us. My friends in the government tell me of your medical achievements. They say you are one of the finest surgeons in Israel. Mahmoud is jealous of your accomplishments and still angry you rejected the arranged marriage he had planned for you with an old man two years ago. As the winds move even the great *uruqin*, so, too, must the Bedouin change. Your ways are new ways, but they are good ways."

"It is worse than that," she said. "He has joined Tawhid wa Jihad and tried to recruit me, even threatening me with a fatwa of death if I refused."

"In the old days out here, we would have taken care of that group and their imam with a well-placed dagger in the ribs,"

Abdullah said and then spat on the ground. "Your brother is mad with hatred. You are safe with us."

She leaned against him, and he held her close for a time of silence. A cousin began to softly play a *rebabe*. Soon everyone joined in, singing an ancient Bedouin folk song that told of the timeless stars that watched over them.

As their song wound down, a brilliant streak raced across the sky from east to west, accompanied by a low sonic boom. Everyone looked up to follow its path.

"*Subhaan il-Khaaliq*! (The Creator be praised.) That is the first falling star since we were gobbled up by that sphere two years ago. I wonder what it portends?" Abdullah said, wondering. Then, looking at his weary niece, he said, "Dear one, you have had a bad day. Go to bed now and get a real Bedouin sleep. Tomorrow will be good. *Inshallah*." (May God will it.)

The next morning, Fatima rose refreshed from a carefree desert slumber. It was after dawn and after a quick breakfast of feteer and goat's cheese, she and the younger women of the family left with a portion of the flocks to graze in hilly terrain to the northeast. Fatima loved the sting of the warm desert air, which awoke so many happy memories from childhood. She could remember every dune, hill, wadi, and tree. Even though she only spent summer breaks from school here, this felt like real home. At times, Fatima wished she could go back a few centuries and join her ancestors in these vast, arid lands.

As the heat of the day increased in late afternoon, Fatima and all the shepherds returned to the goam with their flocks. They noticed a land cruiser approaching across the dry wadi. It stopped about a hundred meters shy of the tents, and two men got out and approached on foot. The driver remained inside. Fatima and Thenwa watched from the corner of the bait ashshar as her uncle came out to meet them.

Thenwa squinted to try to identify their guests. "That looks like Ismail Tanaf, the cabinet minister," she said. "But who is that with him?"

Fatima's eyes grew wide with surprise. "I think the other man is Benny Goldberg, the prime minister! What would he be doing out here?"

They decided to enter the bait ashshar and try to eavesdrop on the mahram section. Abdullah met the two men only a couple of meters from the front of the bait ashshar. Tanaf approached in the lead. He was wearing traditional Bedouin attire—a white kibr that covered him like a cloak and a red and white smagg. Prime Minister Goldberg was wearing khaki trousers and a pale-green polo shirt.

"*As-salaamu 'aleikum!*" (Peace be with you.) said Tanaf as he held his right hand high and then lifted some sand into the wind.

"*Wa-'aleikumu s-salaam!*" (And to you, peace.) said Abdullah bin Hassan in return. He bowed and dropped his hand to the ground. Then he touched his heart and his head before clasping Tanaf's right hand, and each placed their left hands on each other's shoulders before embracing. Bin Hassan repeated the ritual for Prime Minister Goldberg.

"*As-salaamu 'aleikum and Daayme.*" (May your house be prosperous.) said Goldberg.

"Inshallah," replied Abdullah. "*Ahlan wa-sahlan.* (Our house is as open to you as the plain.) Come, let us share some coffee."

As the men entered the male only es-shigg section of the tent, Abdullah's wife and two daughters immediately served a plate of dates and ornate pots of coffee for each man.

"What brings you to my humble abode?" Abdullah asked as he poured his coffee into a delicate cup. "You have honored us with your arrival."

"We need your help to locate your niece, Dr. Fatima al-Tarabin," said Prime Minister Goldberg.

"Is she in trouble?" Abdullah wondered aloud.

"No," said Tanaf. "Everyone knows she is the finest physician in all of Israel and still so young."

Abdullah smiled with pride. "Tell me, why would the prime minister himself come all the way here to find my niece, the great doctor?"

"Her country, and even the world, needs her urgently," said Goldberg. "We looked for her at Rahat, finding her apartment vacant, and the hospital said she was off of work for several days. Tanaf knew you through your time together in the IDF. He suggested we speak with you.

"Our family is honored by your compliments, but there are many other fine doctors in Israel," Abdullah replied.

"It has to do with that meteor that came across the sky last night. I have come to bring her back to Jerusalem, where she must catch a flight for Houston," Goldberg said.

"So that meteor was a good omen," Abdullah said.

Overhearing the conversation, Fatima couldn't help herself. She pulled aside the saha and walked in on the three men. She realized her mistake. "I am sorry, Uncle. Please forgive me."

"Gentlemen, may I have the pleasure of introducing my sister's daughter, the famous physician, Dr. Fatima al-Tarabin," Abdullah said with bravado. "Please speak, my dear, what are your wishes?"

"Uncle, with your permission, I would like to go with them and fly to America to see what is needed of me. When they talked about it, I knew in my heart that I must go," Fatima said with excitement. "I can get my bag and join you immediately."

"Inshallah," said Abdullah with resignation.

"The gahwa was excellent. Thank you for your kind hospitality," said Goldberg, rising to leave.

"As-salaamu 'aleikum," said Tanaf as he also rose to depart.

Fatima said her farewells to all her cousins, finishing with her uncle. "*Allaah yitawwil 'umrkum*, Uncle," (May God lengthen your life.) she said as she hugged him.

"*Gowak*," (Strength may Allah give thee.) he replied, trying to be brave and stern.

(South Central Pacific Ocean between New Zealand and Hawaii)

The canoe armada had been under sail for a day after leaving Kiribati on the final leg of their voyage from New Zealand to Hawaii. Near noontime, the sun shone over the vast, easy waters of the central Pacific. Apiranoa Ngata, a thirty-something ethnopsychology professor from the University of Auckland, stood on a small platform at the rear of the canoe. His stocky stature and muscular build spoke of his Maori ancestry. He proudly wore *moko*, the traditional tattoos across his bare chest and arms. Having missed the first epic voyage of the traditional Polynesian canoe armada of a dozen *waka* from Hawaii to New Zealand, he worked diligently to be able to crew on the return trip. Two weeks earlier, they had set sail from Te Reringawairau, at the far northwest end of the North Island of New Zealand at Cape Reinga. This is where the Maori believe souls depart after death from the lone Pohutukawa tree to enter the afterlife. They left at sunset to mark the time of departure for those headed to Hawaiki, the final destination and original homeland. Navigation was done by wayfinding, the ancient Polynesian method of using currents, birds, wave sequence and shapes, and star patterns. The latter had changed considerably after envelopment in the Sphere, much to their dismay.

Apiranoa hailed from the Nfati Porou clan of Te Ika-a-Maui, the North Island. His people traced their origins across this vast expanse of ocean nearly a thousand years earlier as they set out from Hawaiki, the homeland of the Iwa or Maori people. After years of studying other cultures, it was inspiring to him to return to the ways and life of his own people. The other waka were in view from behind as Apiranoa's vessel took the lead. He was taking his turn at the helm and looked forward to a break to do some fishing.

Suddenly a large black object began to emerge from the water forty meters to the starboard side, matching the speed of the waka.

Spotting it first, Apiranoa clapped to get the attention of his crew mates and then pointed. Maori consider it taboo to shout so near to the sea. Three others joined him at his post at the helm and stared in wonder.

"Is it a whale about to breech?" Apiranoa asked as the black mass kept rising.

Before they could say anything, everyone realized it was the sail of a submarine surfacing from the depths. Soon the sail towered above their canoe as the long, black, curved body of the upper hull rose to a level of the canoe's deck. The upper vertical tail plane emerged, indicating the rear of the vessel. Atop the sail rose several poles, housing periscopes and communication antenna. At the forward end of the sail, an American flag rose, followed by the appearance of several naval officers. One of them held a megaphone and faced Apiranoa and his companions.

"Ahoy. I'm Captain William Remsing of the USS Texas. Our mission is to find Dr. Apiranoa Ngata. Is he aboard your vessel?" asked the officer.

Apiranoa and his shipmates were stunned by the request after the surprise appearance of the submarine. At the captain's question, Apiranoa's friends backed away from him as if he were a criminal.

Apiranoa stuttered his reply. "Yes, Sir. I am Dr. Ngata. What do you want from me?"

"Our orders are to take you to rendezvous with the aircraft carrier USS Nimitz and from there, you are to be taken directly to Houston, Texas," said Captain Remsing.

Bewildered by the request, Apiranoa asked, "Why? What have I done? Why would anyone want me to go to Houston?"

"I don't know any details. My orders came from the highest levels in Washington," the captain said. "Please pack your belongings and come with us. Commander Bayless is coming over in a launch to pick you up."

By this time, several other canoes had drawn near, and crew members gaped at the massive submarine in their midst. Some began to take pictures. They were surprised to see a sailor taking pictures of them as well.

Soon a couple of sailors deployed an inflatable raft. Commander Bayless got in and paddled up to the canoe. Apiranoa, now wearing a T-shirt, climbed down and aboard the raft with a modest duffel bag.

Immediately, the Maori crew members on the gathered canoes began a *haka* with ritualized posture and dance as they chanted, "*Ka ora! Ka ora!*" (It is life. It is life.)

Their haka ended with a loud cheer from everyone, including the American sailors.

As the raft headed back to the submarine, Apiranoa said, "*Haere raa.*" (Go well.)

His Maori crewmates responded, "*Haere raa, Paikea!*" (The legendary Maori whale rider who was the ancestor of them all.)

Soon Apiranoa and the sailors disappeared down the deck hatch. Captain Remsing, on the bridge at the top of the sail, saluted the armada and returned to his ship. As quickly as it had appeared, the submarine sank beneath the waves.

(On a narrow, dusty highway in southwest Botswana, Southern Africa)

It was a beautiful but cool winter day as N!amce Xamseb approached Ghanzi, his hometown. The sixty-something widower was showing gray in his peppercorn hair. The Basarwa, or San Bushmen, his people, would now consider him an elder. He had been gone for many years, living in Botswana's capital city of Gaborone, where he taught and studied cultural anthropology. N!ance, or Petrus as friends called him, had left his heart in this ancestral homeland of the bush-covered Kalahari Desert. During the winter break from his teaching duties, Petrus was determined to spend quality time with his grandchildren, who currently lived with their maternal grandparents. His son and daughter-in-law, school teachers in Ghanzi, had been killed in a car accident only a month before. No one in the family or the community had recovered from the tragedy. Tears would run down Petrus's high cheekbones whenever he thought of them. He worried about how the grandchildren were handling this most tragic of losses. It was now time to do for Toma, a slender boy of ten, and Kushe, an irrepressible girl of eight, what Petrus had done for their father twenty-five years earlier. He would take them out for a week in the bush to introduce them to the ways of their ancestors. Maybe together, they could find peace in the solitude of the vast, arid expanse.

When Petrus drove up to the metal-roofed concrete home where they lived, Toma and Kushe came running out to greet him with hugs and kisses. They were packed for their expedition into the bush. Their mother's parents came and spoke quietly and nodded a greeting to Petrus. He was struck again at how unassuming his people were. They invited him inside for some tea, while Toma and Kushe loaded their duffel bags into Petrus's pickup. Not caring for tea, they climbed into the cab, eager to get underway. After a brief visit with limited conversation, Petrus returned to his truck and off they went for an adventure back in time and space.

For what seemed like hours, they drove the dusty road deep into the Kalahari Game Reserve to the area where Petrus had spent his childhood. His people had wandered and hunted over the trackless bush for tens of thousands of years—since the beginning of the world, according to their legends. All of that had changed forever in a couple of brief generations. Petrus himself had been sent off to a missionary boarding school in Ghanzi, where he had excelled, winning scholarships for further education that eventually brought him back to Botswana and the University in Gaborone. There he had worked for decades to preserve and to share the culture and traditions of his people since they were losing their land and ways. Nearly every San lived in settlements and cities. Governments in their region had practiced years of forced relocation to remove the ones who persisted in living the old ways deep in the bush. Tourist dollars and the mining of vast mineral wealth were too much for national leaders to resist for the needs of a remote minority of people. Petrus knew this might be his last chance to connect his grandchildren to their people and their ancient past.

Toma and Kushe had been quiet, lost in thought and occasional naps, until a bump in the road awakened them. Petrus slowed the truck down and made a left turn into a dry creek bed, departing from the road and civilization. There were no signs or markings apparent. Petrus knew this land like his own mind.

"Are we there yet, Großvater?" asked Toma, reflecting the colonial influence on the speech of his land.

"No, we still have several kilometers to go before we get to the place where I want to camp," Petrus said, glad one of them finally spoke.

Not to be outdone, Kushe asked, "How do you know where to go?"

"When I was your age, I lived here. One of our family's *werfs* is our destination," Petrus replied, looking carefully at her.

"What's a werf?" Kushe asked, looking up at him with bright eyes.

Petrus looked at her, raised an eyebrow like a knowing elder, and gave a hint of a grin. "It's a place where our people would set up our *skerms*, like a small village, but temporary. I know your next question. Skerms are the grass-and-stick shelters our women would make for us, like a tent or a lean-to."

Toma looked concerned. "How did you ever stay alive out here? We're a long way from any store."

"We made and found everything we needed here. There was never a need for things from any store," Petrus said with a grin.

"There's nothing here but these short, worn-out trees, rocks, dry grass, and sand," Kushe said.

"During our week here, I will show you how we lived then," Petrus responded. "We hunted our food, gathered our vegetables, and dug for our water. This was our classroom, our playground, our town, our store, our home, and our world. Our people lived here for tens of thousands of years. It could be this is where people first learned to hunt animals for food. For most of human history, this is how everyone lived."

Kushe was wide eyed in disbelief. "You poor man. I am sorry you had to live your childhood like this. It is very good you now live in the capital city and teach at the university."

Petrus chuckled. "It was a very good life. I was very happy, as was everyone we knew out here. Maybe you can get a feel for what it was like for me and our people before we began to move to settlements and towns."

Toma gave a serious look at Petrus. "Will we or have you come back to this to live here for good?"

"No, we cannot come back and live here permanently, but we need to come here to remember and to understand who we are and where we came from. Too many have forgotten everything our people learned over one hundred thousand years. Even our songs and language are about to be lost," Petrus lamented. "I did this same thing for your father about twenty-five years ago. He never forgot."

Both Toma and Kushe grew silent for a time. They rocked along slowly, dodging rocks, stumps, and sand traps as they ventured ever farther from civilization. Toma was sure he could not find his way back to the dirt road they had left.

"Großvater," Kushe said with intensity. "If Daddy had moved here with us, would he and Mom still be alive?"

Petrus drew a slow, deep breath and answered her with gravity. "Kushe, terrible things like accidents happened here in the bush just like they do in town. Death came too often for old and young alike. My little sister died of a fever when she was only three years old. We were too far from the hospital and the folk medicine our people knew couldn't save her. Everyone in our family cried. We loved her so much. I still miss her almost sixty years later."

Toma knitted his brow. "Why do people die, especially younger people?"

Petrus stopped the truck and drew another deep breath. "I wish I knew the answer to that. It's one of the worst things about life in this world. My heart is still breaking for the death of your parents and for your loss. Often, I want to cry and hold each of you tight in my arms. I promise I will do everything I can to walk with you through this time."

"Was God angry with Mom and Dad?" Kushe asked.

"No. Nor do I believe God caused the accident," Petrus replied.

"Why didn't he prevent their deaths?" Toma asked.

"I don't know. I wish with all my heart he had done so. They had so much to live for and much to share with you as they loved you into adulthood," Petrus said. "God didn't prevent the death of his own son, Jesus. God used that to work the most wonderful blessing for all of us. Maybe God can work something good for us out of all this bad stuff."

"What are we to do now?" Toma asked with a hint of anger.

"Every chance I have, I want to work with you both as we try to figure it all out," Petrus responded. Tears began to fall from his high cheeks. Kushe wiped away some of her tears. She kissed her fingertips and then touched Petrus's face. They drove the rest of the way in silence.

Resonate

"This is the place," Petrus said as he stopped and turned off the truck, which was just shy of a small hillock that rose above the surrounding terrain. "Let's get out and make camp."

Toma and Kushe were slow in emerging. They squinted, looking around for any hint of human habitation. Seeing nothing but endless bush, they reluctantly took their duffel bags out of the bed of the truck. Petrus handed each of them some gear to carry as well.

"This is it?" Toma said with a hint of sarcasm.

"Yes," replied Petrus. "This is the same place our family came back to every dry season, year after year. It is the closest thing we had to a permanent home."

"There are no buildings. I don't even see any boards or stones. Where's the bathroom? I need to go," Kushe said urgently.

Petrus handed her a roll of biodegradable toilet paper and a small shovel. "Find a thick bush over there, dig a hole, and take care of your need. When you are done, fill it in with dirt."

Kushe looked exasperated, but seeing no alternative, left in a state of irritation.

Petrus looked at Toma, who was chuckling to himself, and said, "This will be different from anything you have ever known, but you can adapt, just as our people adapted to the modern ways now familiar to you."

Soon all three were busy setting up camp, complete with a sizeable nylon tent, water jugs, sleeping bags, a cooking stove, a camping table, bag chairs, a kerosene lantern, and food packed in a stout metal ice chest.

"Understand that this is nothing like the werf our people would have lived in," Petrus said. "We had no tents, sleeping bags, lanterns, packaged food, or the like. Our shelters were made of sticks and grasses by the women. We called them skerms. But we usually slept out in the open, under the stars, around the campfire. A skerm gave us shade in the afternoon heat. Our food was the meat the men brought from hunting wild animals for days as well as the roots and plants our women could gather. The water had to be drawn by strawlike grass stems from sandy low spots. It may have been up to a meter below the surface. One would suck up as much as possible into his mouth and then empty it out into a hollow ostrich egg for storage."

"Yuck, how nasty," Kushe said with revulsion.

"Life out here was hard, but it was good," Petrus said. "It may not have been sanitary by modern standards, but it helped us survive for millennia. Nothing was wasted."

"Where was your school?" Toma asked curiously.

"Everywhere around us," Petrus replied. "The animals, plants, our elders, and land were our teachers."

"Wasn't it terribly boring without TV and computers?" asked Kushe.

"There was so much to do. The stars, the rain, the moon, and sun were our TV. Our people even talked to them. Legends say they were once humans as we are now," Petrus said. "Go and gather a lot of sticks, and I will show you how to 'roll a fire.'"

Within half an hour, the kids had gathered enough wood to last through the night. With evening coming on, Petrus lit the cooking stove and began to heat some lentil stew. He gathered a small clutch of smaller sticks together, along with two carefully selected fire sticks, one of which he proceeded to roll between his hands. Kushe and Toma watched intently. Within ten minutes, he had started the fire, adding larger pieces as it grew.

"Großvater, wouldn't it be easier to start a fire with matches?" Kushe queried.

"Certainly, but we had no matches, so we used what God provided here," Petrus said. He prepared three long sticks to use as skewers and stabbed them into strips of raw meat from the ice chest. "Here, roast these over the fire. Be careful not to dip them into the fire, but hold them close enough to cook well."

Judging the lentil stew to be ready, Petrus removed three crude clay bowls and spoons made of animal bones from one of the packs. He served them the stew. "Let's give thanks to God," he said, as he sat down to join them around the fire. "O wondrous God who has made all that is around us and called it 'good,' we thank you for this food and water and this time and place together. Please keep Toma and Kushe's parents close to you and heal our broken hearts. In Jesus's name we ask. Amen."

After their meal, Petrus led the kids a short way across the hillock from their camp to the very top, where there was a clear view of the entire land around them as well as the heavens above. Since it was winter in those southern latitudes, the sun had set early, and the sky was full of stars. There were the planets and the symmetrically placed white-dwarf stars hovering above the interior Rim of the Sphere. Petrus began to sing one of their people's night songs to his grandchildren:

"Sirius!
Sirius!
Winks like
Canopus!
Canopus
winks like
Sirius!
Canopus
winks like
Sirius!
Sirius
winks like
Canopus!

"This was sung by our people in good times like this—in gratitude for an abundance of food," Petrus said. "We would watch the stars and planets and sing to them. The elders would tell us stories about them. They believed that all of them had been people in the beginning but had become very powerful and could help or hurt us. Children would be asked to bring a burning ember, called a fire stick, to an elder, who would point it up toward Sirius and Canopus in the belief this could make their light warm and friendly to us."

"Where are those stars now?" Kushe wondered.

"I don't know that anyone knows now that we are inside this great Sphere," Petrus said.

"Remember that Sirius was lost or devoured by that black hole," Toma reminded them. "And that happened before the Sphere swallowed up our solar system."

"What would our people have believed about this Sphere that came and took us away?" Kushe asked.

"It's hard to say," Petrus began. I think they would be very scared with the inability to see the stars they had known since the beginning. We still have the moon, the planets, and the sun. Our people called Jupiter 'dawn's heart' because of its brightness and faithfulness as it traveled the heavens. They believed that the moon was hollow, like the Sphere, and that it came to carry the dead away."

"What do you think will happen to our world now that we are inside the Sphere?" Toma asked.

"No one knows for sure yet," Petrus replied. "There's been talk that a mission will head to the inside surface of the Sphere to make contact with people or creatures out there."

"It would be so much fun to go there," Kushe said. "Just think of all we could see and learn."

"I'm not so sure they would be friendly," Toma said with skepticism.

"Well, it looks like they did come to rescue our world from the black hole," Petrus added. "Besides, if those people were advanced enough to build something so huge that it could hold all our planets and the sun, they must understand so much more than we do. If they didn't care, why did they come here to save us?"

"Tell us the stories about the moon," Kushe said. The early first quarter moon had risen above the horizon, waxing a bright crescent.

Petrus said, "The legends say the moon was once a human but changed form to go across the sky. He or she, would travel far in a month but would die at the time of the new moon, when the dark side of the moon is toward Earth. Then he would come back to life again as he became a crescent, half, gibbous, and full moon. We had to be careful not to look at the moon when hunting, even though its light helped us find game in the dark. It was thought this would bring bad luck and no food. There's a song we would sing to the young moon as he came back from the dead:

> "Young moon!
> Hail, young moon!
> Hail, hail,
> young moon!
Young moon, speak to me!
> Hail, hail,
> young moon!
Tell me of something.
> Hail, hail!
> When the sun rises,
> you must speak to me,
> that I may eat something.
You must speak to me about a little thing,
> that I may eat.
> Hail, hail,
> young moon!

They sat looking up at the skies for a long time, listening to the sounds of the animals out in the bush. Petrus identified the animal cries they heard. Finally, he added more wood to the fire to keep it going most of the night and settled Toma and Kushe into bed in the tent. He remained under the stars for a long time.

As the earliest rays of the dawn ignited the eastern sky, Petrus sat at the same place as the night before. He heard cries from the tent and ran back to find that Kushe had awakened after a bad dream. He picked her up and carried her back to the place where he had been sitting to welcome the sun.

Kushe rubbed her eyes and looked up to her grandfather. "Großvater, I keep having this awful dream."

"Tell me, child," said Petrus as he held her closer.

She said, "It's a dream I have a lot. I am in the car with Mom and Dad, and we are driving down the road real fast. Dad can't stop the car. Mom cries out that we are all going to die."

Petrus kissed her head, and they looked at each other. "I know just what to do about that, little one," he said as he rose and led her by the hand back to the smoldering campfire. "Pick up a rock and look at it while you think of your bad dream."

Kushe deliberately selected a fist-sized rock and scanned it careful.

"Now cast it into the fire," he said.

Kushe tossed the rock into the middle of the fire. A shower of sparks shot upward.

"That is what our people used to do for bad dreams," said Petrus. "It works for me every time. You should never have that dream again."

They turned to see Toma had joined them, so Petrus decided to prepare breakfast.

After cleaning up, the three of them headed out to explore the bush, stopping on the far side of the hillock, where they found a colony of meerkats. The animals were gathered near the entrance of their borough, facing the morning sun to warm themselves. At first, Toma and Kushe tried to get close to the meerkats by chasing them. No matter how hard they tried, the kids couldn't get near the creatures that skittered down various bolt-holes.

Laughing, Petrus said, "You will only wear yourselves out doing that. Come here and join me near the entrance to their manor. Lie down and be still. Speak softly and don't make any quick gestures. Let them come to you. Don't stick your fingers out to them or you might get bitten. If you listen carefully, they might even have something to say to you."

After ten minutes or so, the meerkats came out one by one. Gradually, some came closer to Petrus and his grandkids. He was humming some old San tune when one of the bolder ones came up to him and began to look him over. Before long, others followed, and a dozen or so had come and climbed up on Petrus, Toma, and Kushe. She fought back an excited giggle. The meerkats kept making a variety of squeaking sounds as they explored their new human friends. Toma was lost in wonder at one standing on its hind legs, looking him straight in the face only inches away, as Toma reclined on the sand.

As quickly as they had come, the meerkats heard the call of their dominant female and set out to forage for their breakfast of scorpions and insects. Hunger won out over friendship.

"So you think it is boring to live out here?" said Petrus with a big grin.

"Did you hunt and eat them when you were a kid?" Toma asked.

"Never," said Petrus. "Our people once believed meerkats were some of our most ancient ancestors. It was unthinkable to kill and eat them. We were always friends, though sometimes they would steal food from our sherms. Come, there is much more to see and learn out here."

After a full day of exploration, where Petrus continued to tell them about the animals and trees of the bush, they returned to camp. They sat down under a tarp canopy to enjoy some cold water. A man in a *kaross*, the traditional animal-skin garment, emerged silently from the bushes below them. He slowly approached with his eyes cast down toward the ground. He was soon joined by others—men, women, and children—who followed his lead, eight in all. They looked like ancestors who stepped out from the ancient past.

"Hello, I am Kwe Xamseb, and these are members of my family," he said with his eyes still downcast.

Petrus jumped up and ran down to the man, "Kwe, do you not know me? I am N!amce Xamseb, your father's brother's son. It has been years. What a joy to see you! Please, come and join us. Let your women make skerms at our werf, just like we did so many years ago."

"N!amce, you left us long ago for the cities in lands far away. I have not thought of you in years. Now you are here at one of our oldest werfs with these children," Kwe said with a warm smile.

"These are my grandchildren, Toma and Kushe," Petrus said. "Their parents, my children, were killed in a terrible car wreck a month ago. We have come here to remember our ways."

Kwe and his family members slowly shook their heads and made soft sounds of dismay. "May God comfort you all," he said. They came in and sat on the ground under the tarp canopy. Petrus told Toma and Kushe to provide water and snack bars for the guests.

Petrus raised an eyebrow and said, "How is it you are still here in the Kalahari when the government has ordered all our people relocated out of the bush?"

Kwe smiled wryly. "We made sure they couldn't find us when they searched for us. Still, it is harder than ever living here like our people always have. The drought has been bad for the last several years. Maybe you made the right decision to leave for the cities."

"I may have left in body, but my heart is always here," Petrus said. "I now work at Botswana University, where I study and teach the ways of our people and others around the world who have lived like we do. It is so important we don't forget our ways and past. Modern people of today need what we know."

They talked and reminisced for hours. By evening, the fire was rekindled, and the women and girls busied themselves fixing Bushmen rice, a term for a mix of native vegetables gathered that day, and skewered game meat from a *gemsbok* the men had killed earlier in the morning. Petrus also shared from his stock. Kwe's youngsters were amazed by the ice in the ice chest. They quickly taught Toma and Kushe several of the children's games played from time immemorial. After the informal shared meal, Kwe and Petrus entertained everyone with songs and stories. One of Kwe's sons played music on a *goura*, a five-stringed thumb piano made from the wood of a music tree.

Just as Petrus was finishing a traditional song about the hare and the moon, the sound of helicopter blades began to be audible from the southeast. Soon three large Botswana Defense Force helicopters were hovering overhead. One of them landed in a clearing about a dozen meters near the werf, and several uniformed men emerged and walked up toward the camp.

The lead figure, in civilian clothes, Petrus recognized as Botswana's prime minister. One of the uniformed men was General Sesana of the Botswana Defense Force. Petrus and his family were all stunned by this visit.

"Good evening," said the prime minister. "Please forgive our sudden intrusion. I am looking for Dr. Petrus Xamseb and his grandchildren, Toma and Kushe Xamseb. I need to talk to them."

Petrus almost fainted in shock but managed to walk unsteadily toward the prime minister, worried about what this visit might mean. "I am Dr. Xamseb, and my grandchildren are here with me, along with more of my family. Why have you come here looking for us?"

General Sesana said, "It is urgent that all three of you come with us at once. We will fly you back to Gaborone in this helicopter. Your family can take care of your camping gear and vehicle."

Still perplexed, Petrus asked, "What have we done?"

"Nothing wrong, but you three have been invited to make a great journey," said the prime minister. "You are needed in Houston, Texas by tomorrow."

"How did you find us?" Petrus asked.

"It wasn't easy," General Sasana said. "Satellites helped us locate campfires out here, and we have checked several before we found you. My soldiers have collected your papers, clothing, and personal things."

Petrus turned to Toma and Kushe, who were wide eyed with bewilderment and shaking with fear. "It will be okay, little ones. We are together, and God goes with us." He then came to Kwe and the rest of the family. "We shall see each other again soon, my father's brother's son. Use my truck and camping gear if you wish. May God go with you and yours and give you good hunting."

Within a couple of minutes, Petrus, Toma, and Kushe were lifting off in the helicopter to return to the capital city. Their travels were just beginning.

CHAPTER 8

Houston, We Are Coming In

(Outside a hangar at Keflavik International Airport, Iceland)

The helicopter landed, and Jennifer, David, and Allison were led off to an office in the corner of the hanger. Several American air force men carried their luggage, which was gathered from their cousin's home. As they entered the door, their eyes adjusted to the dark surroundings as a uniformed officer walked up to them.

"Jennifer, David, and Allison! How great to see you!" said the exuberant voice. "I am pleased to be working with you again."

As their eyes came into focus, they recognized the familiar face of General William Morris, the military chief of their base at Fort Davis two years earlier. They had never seen him so animated or expressive. Confused and boiling with questions, they simply stared in silence.

General Morris sensed their shock and took the lead. "I will explain more after we get on board the X-53. But first, put on these flight suits. We were able to retrieve yours from the Johnson Space Center, Jennifer, but I'm afraid Allison will have to make do with this generic female suit. Be sure to test their pressurization before we board. Jennifer, you will need to help Allison with hers. We will also check your communications systems before we launch."

In a few moments, he led them from the office and into the hangar, where they saw a large, stub-winged craft with a shovel-shaped snout. It had mottled colors with patterns that were constantly changing.

"It's a beauty, our new X-53 space-plane," the general said. "You are among the first to fly in her. She's our first fully functional SSTO vehicle, complete with gravitic drive, scramjet engines, and cloaking technology. With the capability of Mach 10, we will get to Houston in about thirty minutes."

"General." Jennifer was beginning to recover herself. "What is an SSTO vehicle?"

"It means single stage to orbit. We are about to go into space to take you home quickly. Let's get on board, and I will tell you more," said Morris as he led the way into the low cabin. It was only about five feet in height, Spartan in decor, much like a spaceship. There were six fighter-plane-type seats in two rows of three, with a narrow aisle on the left side. A pilot and copilot occupied the seats in the cockpit, open to the cabin directly in front of them.

Quickly, everyone was harnessed into place, with life support systems activated. David and another officer were seated in the back row. Allison occupied the window seat on the front row next to her mom, with General Morris on the side aisle. The plane was towed out of the hangar, the engines started, and the clearance given for takeoff. They felt the power of the engines kick in as they were pressed hard against their seats. Video feed was displayed on a couple of small screens in the front upper corners of the cabin, giving them outside views to the front and rear. The plane left the runway in a short distance and climbed upward to a near vertical angle, accelerating at 3.5 Gs. The earth fell away rapidly, and the scattered clouds were soon passed.

Jennifer looked over at General Morris and noticed he had four stars now, indicative of greater responsibilities. "What is going on here, General Morris?" she asked.

"I am now the commander of DARPA, the Defense Advanced Research Projects Agency. That's how I got this, the most secret of all our nation's black projects. It was necessary to find you and return you to Houston ASAP. As far as security concerns go, you never saw this space-plane, you never flew on it, and you never talked about it."

"But why the urgency?" Jennifer asked curiously.

The general continued, saying, "The meteor you may have seen last night was some kind of messenger from the Rim. It landed at the National Security Agency's CNCI Data Center at Camp Williams in Utah. Our new supercomputer has just become operational. The messenger was some kind of glowing sphere about two meters in diameter. It flew through a solid wall with no damage to itself or the wall and hovered above the control room, where it accessed the computer. Within seconds, it had bypassed all security protocols and downloaded a massive file that nearly filled the one yottabyte memory. Then the sphere left, returning to orbit, taking up position a thousand meters ahead of the International Space Station, matching its orbit."

"What does that have to do with us?" David asked.

"The downloaded information is a double gift of sorts," General Morris said. "There is a supermassive atlas of the Rim, containing enough geographical information to keep our people busy for years. But even more importantly is an invitation listing eighteen people, six of whom are children, to be guests and transported to the Rim in one of their vessels. These people are to meet their vessel at the International Space Station in a little over forty days."

"Why all the bother to get us?" Jennifer asked.

"All three of you are on the list, with you, Jennifer, listed as the leader," Morris replied.

Allison's mouth dropped, and she looked at her mom with wide eyes. David shot a glance at Jennifer at the same moment. She could only respond with a satisfied smile.

"Now you have to go with us, kid," Jennifer said with her heart full of joy. "Just think of all the schoolwork you will miss while taking another wild trip with your parents. This will make Iceland and Spain look pretty lame."

They noticed the acceleration of the space-plane had slowed, and the sky had turned black, with the atmosphere falling beneath them. They became silent as the plane reached the top of its parabolic arc, giving them feelings of weightlessness. Then, like a high roller coaster, the plane began its belly-first descent toward Houston and home. Hot plasmatic gases appeared outside as the ablative underside built up heat from atmospheric friction, beginning the slow-down process prior to landing. The sky soon returned to blue, and the earth grew ever closer. There was an inescapable feeling of uncontrolled free fall. Suddenly, the craft took a long, wide turn to the right with its belly exposed. This was followed by another hard turn to the left. Several more turns were made, and the velocity meter at the front of the cabin indicated they had dropped below Mach speed. The Houston skyline drew closer. The plane continued its descent in an approach to Ellington Air Force Base near the Johnson Space Center.

"Look, Mom, I can see our condo tower and JSC," Allison exclaimed.

As soon as they landed, the plane was towed into a hangar, and the doors closed. Massive fans were brought up to cool the still blazing underside of the plane. After several minutes, it was safe to disembark. Outside the plane, everyone stopped for final words and for gathering their gear.

General Morris looked at Jennifer with a serious intensity. "I'm sorry, but you won't have time to go home right now. We must get you to Building One immediately to meet with NASA Director Sanderson. He will brief you further on the details. I will need to return with the X-53 to pick up some more of the astronauts. They are scattered all over the world. Here's my card,

Jennifer. If there is anything else I or anyone else in the DOD can do to assist you in your mission, call anytime."

He then shook their hands and surprised them with a salute. David, Jennifer, and Allison were then led out to a waiting Suburban to whisk them to the Space Center.

On the top floor of Building One at the Johnson Space Center, Jennifer, David, and Allison were ushered into Dr. Franklin Sanderson's office. The slender, gray-haired man rose at once from his desk to greet them.

"Jennifer, it's so good to see you after you left a couple of weeks ago under regrettable circumstances. As you probably know by now, you have been reinstated," Dr. Sanderson said. "Please sit down. There's much to tell. This messenger or emissary has settled several major matters about our mission that we couldn't resolve. You can still see it on the monitor here from the ISS, where it has been since it downloaded the message over a day ago. The Messenger is undergoing some kind of metamorphosis."

They watched for a moment as it appeared to be disassembling itself. Swarms of tiny, metallic insectlike machines crawled all over the surface. They were eating away the shiny metal skin to reveal a complex skeleton of black, metal-like frames and unidentifiable boxes and wiring. For a while, it looked as if there would be nothing left in a couple of hours. But for now, there was more pressing business.

"What about the list of people invited on the mission?" Jennifer asked.

"There are more questions than answers," Dr. Franklin said. "The emissary somehow transmitted this list to every e-mail address in the world at the same time. There's no mistake about the names. Whoever is out there knows a lot about us. Here it is on the screen."

Greetings and peace to all the good people of Earth. You and your solar system are out of harm's way. There is so much to share with you and so little time. The following people are invited to make first contact at the interior rim of the Sphere. A special craft will meet them in forty days, noon, universal time, September 15, at your international space station for their two-week journey to the Rim. These people are

- Jennifer Bass, American astronomer, commander of the mission
- David Lopez, American biologist
  - Allison Bass, their daughter

- Vartan Bedevian, Armenian geophysicist
- Alice Cly, Navajo biochemist and geneticist
- Becky Ishulutak, Inuit electrical engineer and cyberneticist
  - Randy Ishulutak, her son
  - Andy Ishulutak, her son

- Timujin Ji, Mongolian mathematician
- Theodora Melas, Greek historian, musician, and poet
  - Anastasia Melas, her daughter

- Aprianoa Ngata, New Zealand-Maori ethnophysicist
- Maria Quaupucura, Chilean-Mapuche geographer
- Aizam Mat Sama, Philippino-Bajau linguist
- Fatima al-Tarabin, Israeli-Bedouin physician
- N!amce Xamseb, Koisan-Botswanian anthropologist
  - Toma Xamseb, his grandson
  - Kushe Xamseb, his granddaughter

"This list is astonishing." Dr. Franklin shook his head. "The only ones on here with a decent shot at going were you and David. None of the six finalists selected by the G-eight leaders were listed. The president is furious, as were the leaders of Russia, China, and western Europe. Our intelligence people are trying to make sense of the list."

"Where's everyone else?" David asked.

"They are being brought here by our military with the cooperation of their home countries," Dr. Franklin said. "With the exception of you, Jennifer, none of these are internationally known. They are all well-educated and competent practitioners in their fields of study. Something else strange is that all of them, yourself included, were off in remote places. One, Dr. Ngata, the New Zealander, was on a trans-Pacific canoe voyage with several dozen fellow Maori."

"When are they due here?" Jennifer asked.

"The best estimate is within twelve hours with the help of that special plane that General Morris has," Dr. Franklin said.

"Why the kids?" Allison asked.

Dr. Franklin looked at her. "No one knows. Maybe our friends on the Rim want to meet some younger humans. Every one of you has a parent or guardian on the list. What do you think?"

"I dunno." Allison shrugged her shoulders with wide eyes.

"Why forty days?" David asked.

"Again, we don't know," Dr. Franklin responded. "It gives us little time to prepare you for the mission. This is the reason I had you brought directly here from Ellington so we might brainstorm a little before the rest of the crew arrives tomorrow morning."

Jennifer stood and walked over to the window, staring out over the flat terrain as if an answer could be found there. "Well, for starters, it is essential that we get to know each other well and begin to build our team dynamics," Jennifer began. "And since they are providing the vessel, we won't need to worry about the normal mission logistics. It will be primarily on their terms. Maybe they will be the teachers, and we are their first class of students. We will have much to learn and millions of questions to ask. It's obvious they know much more about us.

Their technology is thousands, if not millions, of years ahead of ours. Perhaps they simply want the pleasure of our company."

"The disciplines of study seem to make sense," David said, "but why did they select people from such remote places? It's as if they wanted people from the farthest corners of the world."

"That makes another great question to ask," said Allison. She had grabbed her iPhone and was making notes on it. "I sure hope I can get this thing recharged out there. And what kind of signals will it get?"

The three adults looked at Allison with smiles on their faces.

"Well, the question of the mission will be our first order of business when the others arrive," Dr. Franklin said. "I am sorry we had to yank you away so quickly from your vacation. Why don't you head home to your condo for the night and rest up? I suspect you will need it. I have taken the liberty of providing high-level security for your home and transportation. For now, it will be best to insulate you from the press. They have already begun to show up here. Within a couple of days, this area will be as frantic as the Olympics. Anyway, I am glad you are back on the mission and look forward to working with you. We will do everything we can to prepare you for whatever awaits."

CHAPTER 9

Preparing for Mission Impossible

Jennifer and David arrived at half past seven in the morning on the top floor of Building One. It felt strange for Allison to be with them now, though both were delighted to have her involved in the most thrilling voyage anyone would ever take. The day before them was full of excitement and the unexpected. As tired as they were, with jet lag to boot, it was hard for them to sleep the night before, with the anticipation of meeting their fellow crewmembers. As they entered the conference room on the top floor, down the hall from Dr. Sanderson's office, they were surprised and pleased to see the other fifteen astronauts waiting in the first and second row of seats. Jennifer beamed and nodded at the crew. David gave a smile and a low-key wave. Allison looked and quickly averted her eyes in shyness. Dr. Sanderson came to Jennifer immediately, greeting her and leading her to the podium in the front of the room. There were a dozen other NASA and military officials in the room as well.

"Good morning, everyone!" he began. "I am Dr. Franklin Sanderson, director of NASA. We're glad you all got here so quickly and safely. We have already made arrangements for your housing and meals. All has been provided as a courtesy of our agency. It is a privilege to welcome you here to America's Johnson

Space Center. We will do everything we can to provide for your needs for the next forty days, before your departure for the International Space Station. We will also be here as a resource to train and equip you in preparation for your voyage. Now I want to introduce the leader of your expedition, Nobel Laureate Dr. Jennifer Bass, the astronomer who got all of the rest of us involved in this in the first place. Over the next few weeks, I know you will get to know and appreciate her as much as we do here at NASA. Dr. Bass, I'm sure you have some thoughts to share as we begin."

Jennifer stepped up to the podium, making eye contact, still smiling joyfully.

"Please, call me Jennifer," she began. "Like all of you, I haven't a clue why I have been called—chosen—by our friends out there, but I am thrilled beyond words at the extraordinary adventure we are about to share. It promises to be the greatest journey of all time. Maybe Columbus and Neil Armstrong had some of the same feelings you and I are experiencing right now. We know we and our world will never be the same. The invitation was clear on who, when, and what but with no explanation for why. We know nothing of why we were chosen from all over Earth eighteen from eight billion. There is no explanation of what will be expected of us, where we will go, and what we will do when we arrive at the Rim. There wasn't even a list for packing. The vehicle for transport is now being assembled by the emissary or messenger that came to Earth three days ago. It lies only a thousand meters outside the International Space Station, awaiting our arrival in thirty-nine days. Since the journey to the Rim is listed as two weeks, we know they will use technology far beyond our capabilities to attain that kind of speed. But for now, we have forty days to get ready for the impossible mission. Dr. Sanderson, other leaders from NASA, and I visited last night about how we can prepare ourselves for this amazing event. The invitation indicated I was to be your leader, so the next thing I want to do is for us to begin to get acquainted. This podium and the rows of seats are too formal. Let's rearrange our chairs into a circle where we can relax some and see each other at eye level."

The twelve adults and the two teenage girls quickly rearranged chairs in a circle after clearing away tables and other chairs. Petrus's two grandchildren sat at his feet, while the four-year-old twin boys sat on their mother's lap. The NASA officials then occupied chairs outside the circle, some seated behind tables with their laptops at the ready.

Jennifer looked around with a reassuring smile. "I have already been introduced to you. Please tell us something about yourself, your family, your field of study, and your life story if you wish."

Petrus sat to Jennifer's right. He gave a calm look and said, "I am N!amce Xamseb, and these are my grandchildren, Toma and Kushe. We are Khoisan, San Bushmen from Botswana. If you can pronounce my name, you must be one of us. Everyone calls me Petrus. I am a professor of cultural anthropology at the University of Botswana with a passion for hunter-gather societies like my own. Toma, Kushe, and I have been through some terrible times. I lost my wife, their grandmother, to cancer two years ago, and their parents, my son and daughter-in-law, were killed in a car accident a month ago. We were on a camping trip deep in the Kalahari Desert with some of our people when we got the call to come here. Toma and Kushe are shy, but when you get to know them, they will tell you all about themselves."

Next to Petrus sat a young man of slender build. His straight dark hair and deep-brown eyes accented his features. He looked down out of shyness and then found the courage to speak. "I am Aizam Mat Saman, age thirty from the Philippines. I am a linguist for my country, speaking fifteen languages. My people are Bejau, what some call sea gypsies. Until recent years, we made a living from the sea, seldom ever coming to land. My ancestors were born, lived, and died on their boats for generations beyond memory. I had gone home to visit and was out to sea on a fishing trip when the Philippine Coast Guard picked me up."

Next to Aizam sat Fatima. Even with a short, stocky build, she sat up straight, suggestive of self-confidence. Wearing western clothes except for the tarha to cover her hair, she spoke. "I am Dr. Fatima al-Tarabin from Israel. I work as a surgeon at the hospital in Rahat. My people are Bedouin. We have wandered with our herds in the desert since before time began. I was visiting with my uncle and his family in the Negev Desert when the prime minister drove up to tell us the news of my invitation."

Next to her sat an older man of stocky build with thick, wavy salt-and-pepper hair. He raised an eyebrow and said. "I am Vartan Bedevian. My children are grown, and my wife left me many years ago. I am a geophysicist who teaches at the university in Van, Armenia. I was doing field research, checking seismic instruments along some fault lines, when I was picked up by some people from my government who told me of this voyage and my invitation."

Next to him sat a young man of strong but slender build with epicanthic eye folds that betrayed his Asian origins. He looked around boldly and said, "I am Timujin Ji, an unemployed PhD in math from Mongolia. I finished my doctorate from the University of Bejing, but there's no demand for mathematicians among my people. We come from western Mongolia and are the direct descendants of Genghis Khan. Perhaps in his time, I could have found work counting horses and measuring the extent of his vast empire. Today, my people are losing their ancient way of life, herding camels, sheep, and horses out in the great valleys and mountains of our land. I was at a horse-racing contest when the government officials came to tell me of my invitation."

Next to him sat a broad-shouldered young man who could have been a wrestler. His short-sleeved shirt revealed tattoos of intricate design on his dark skin. His rounded face also sported a black-inked tattoo. Thick, curly hair grew in all directions, giving him a wild appearance. He smiled and averted his eyes as he spoke. "I am Apiranoa Ngata from Auckland, New Zealand, where I teach at the university. My field of study is ethnopsychology, a hybrid field between psychology and anthropology. My people are Maori, who came to New Zealand a thousand years ago after crossing the Pacific east all the way to South America and then turning southwest and discovering and settling in New Zealand. We crossed thousands of miles of ocean in open canoes, with only the stars, currents, and birds to guide us. Dr. Bass, since you brought us into this Sphere, the new stars are no help to us. Three days ago, I was two months out on one such canoe, retracing the voyage back to Hawaii, when a US submarine surfaced and picked me up to begin my journey here. I am ready to voyage with all of you to the Rim and beyond."

Next to him, contrasting Apiranoa's robust frame, was a petite young woman with long, flowing brown hair, an aquiline nose, and large brown eyes. She confidently surveyed the group and said, "I am Dr. Theodora Melas, a professor of classical and world history at the University of Athens. I also study and play ancient music and write poetry. My husband was lost in a boating accident ten years ago. Since then, I have had the immense joy of raising our amazing daughter, Anastasia. We were picked up while at a festival of ancient music in Thessaloniki. I am looking forward to making history and music with all of you."

Next to Theodora sat her daughter, a delicate beauty with features similar to her mother. She smiled, looked down, and said, "Hi. I am Anastasia Melas. I am fourteen. I am worried about missing my schoolwork in order to take this trip. Do you think I can get special credit for all of this?"

Everyone smiled and some chuckled. Jennifer nodded with a mother's understanding. Allison knew she and Anastasia would quickly become best friends.

Next was a white-haired woman with long braided hair crowned with a simple headband. Her denim dress was adorned with elaborate, handworked beads of turquoise and silver. Her dark, closely set eyes had great depth. Her wrinkled face seemed ancient. She showed no expression but simply waited her turn and said, "I am Alice Cly, now retired and living in Shiprock, New Mexico. I have studied biochemistry and genetics. My people are the Navajo. I had returned home to visit some of my kinfolk in a distant village of Oljato when a Bureau of Indian Affairs chopper picked me up on a mesa above the village."

Next to Alice was a young mother with two identical four-year-old boys nestled on her lap. They had round, smooth faces with narrow brown eyes. Their straight black hair hung down from their heads in disarray. She looked around with the hint of a grin and said, "I am Becky Ishulutak, and these are my twin boys, Randy and Andy. We are from Iqaluit, capital of Nunavut Territory in Canada. We are Inuit. I am an electrical engineer and cyberneticist and have been working for the diamond mines northeast of Yellowknife. We were picked up by the Canadian Coast Guard while on a whale hunt with my parents."

Andy and Randy looked around and smiled. Everyone returned their smiles, which encouraged them to descend from Becky's lap. They began to walk together holding hands as they briefly stopped to look at each person's eyes around the circle, earning nods, smiles, and simple words of greeting. They were finding their place as the mascots of the group.

Then all eyes turned to a middle-aged woman of medium-toned skin and dark-brown hair. She bore herself with a regal attitude. She looked up and said, with a slight Spanish accent, "I am Maria Quaupucura, a geographer from Santiago, Chile. When I am not working for the university there, I spend time exploring ancient settlement sites in the southern end of my country. My people are the Mapuche, the only native group to successfully resist the Spanish in colonial times. I was mapping out Yaghan archeological sites on Tierra del Fuego when people from my government found me."

Next, everyone looked to David, who said, "I am David Lopez, Jennifer's husband. We live here and at Fort Davis in far west Texas. I am a biologist with interests in exobiology and sociobiology as well as a passion for entomology. I like things that bug me. My people came to the new world from Spain, where we were the Basques, the oldest surviving ethnic group in Europe. We were kayaking in a glacial stream in Jennifer's ancestral home country of Iceland when an air force chopper came to pick us up."

Between David and Jennifer sat Allison. She took an uncertain quick look around the group and said, "I'm Allison Bass-Lopez, and I'm with them. Dad didn't tell you that we are direct descendants of Captain Juan Sebastián de Elcano, the only surviving leader of Ferdinand Magellan's five-year voyage around the world. I can hardly wait to take off on that vessel to the big unknown out there."

All eyes returned to Jennifer, who said, "I'm with them and you. My academic field is astrophysics. I love looking at the stars and miss them so much since the Sphere took us in two years ago. Something I hope to do when we reach the Rim is to see if we can travel to the outside surface to see where the Sphere has taken us. I am of Scotch-Irish and Icelandic descent. We were in Iceland visiting some cousins the day before yesterday. Today, we are now part of a new family that has just come together. I am thrilled to meet you and look forward to getting to know all of you better. We have so much to learn and do in very little time. I will need help from each of you. Since we were called to this mission for reasons and purposes unknown, with far more questions than answers, I believe the best thing we can do with the time we have before September fifteenth is to build our relationships with each other. I suggest we each take a day or so to teach something to the rest of us based on your life experiences and professional training. Along the way, let's keep the door open to any other options you believe would be helpful. We are open to any specialized training you feel would be useful. Dr. Sanderson and NASA are here to help us in any way they can. How do you feel about this for starters?"

There were some nods and a few soft yeses said around the group.

"Since this was my idea to begin with, I will conduct the first session this afternoon," Jennifer said. "I want to see if there are any questions you have of me or any of our NASA friends."

Theodora Melas spoke up. "Why us? Is there any indication why we were invited or chosen?"

Jennifer looked to Dr. Sanderson, who shrugged his shoulders. Then she said, "Your guess is as good as mine. Maybe there's a clue in our varied professions. I am intrigued by the highly diverse ethnic backgrounds we represent. It is as if they wanted people from all corners of the world."

David suggested, "Maybe they wanted people who were from the most adventurous of all of the peoples of our world. Our peoples are those who lived on the edge, out on the fringe, always ready to sail, walk, ride, or climb to the places no one had been before. This must be one of the questions we ask when we get there."

Becky Ishulutak posed, "Being an engineer, I need to understand how they intend to get us several billion miles in just two weeks. NASA's New Horizon mission took almost eight years to reach Pluto with a gravity assist from Jupiter. Even your experimental fusion engines would only reduce that time frame to over three years. But two weeks?"

Dr. Sanderson stepped up and said, "That has baffled our engineering people here too. They are probably using some kind of gravity drive. We still don't understand gravity enough to utilize it for our propulsion systems. With a two-week time frame for the journey, they may be using an acceleration curve that maintains 1 G. That means that midflight, the craft would turn 180° to begin deceleration to provide continuous 1 G all the way to the Rim."

Timujin Ji looked to Dr. Sanderson and asked, "Will we be coming back?"

Dr. Sanderson replied, "We don't know what you will find once there, how long you will stay, or even when or if you will be coming back. I would hope they would permit you to return to Earth to reunite with the rest of us."

"Just think of the pictures and stories we will have to tell," Allison said, then blushed when she remembered her place among all of these smart adults.

Aizam Mat Saman, the linguist, then asked, "What about recording our experiences, and, on a more crucial note, what about our communication linkage with Earth? Will we disappear into that vessel and take off, never to be heard from again?"

"Our tech people here at NASA are working on state-of-the-art video recording systems with lots of storage for years of real-time recording. As for the linkage of communication, it is up to our friends up there to connect to our systems in orbit and on Earth in order to maintain contact," Dr. Sanderson answered.

Jennifer added, "I believe our friends out there are most benevolent. Why else would they have bothered to go to all the trouble to rescue our entire solar system from a cosmic disaster? With technology as advanced as theirs, I suspect they will provide an excellent real-time connection with Earth."

Vartan Bedevian, the older geophysicist, said, "As someone who has travelled much in his lifetime, I want to know what we are to take along. What should we pack in our luggage, if anything? The nearest store will be a long way off."

Maria Quaupucura, the geographer, then asked, "What about gifts? Almost every culture on Earth has the custom of taking gifts when going on a visit. We are their guests. What should we take to give to them?"

"These are questions we will need to return to often," Jennifer said. "Now let's take a thirty-minute break for some snacks, restrooms, and a chance to call home to our families."

After the break, everyone reassembled. A video presentation was given to bring everyone up to speed on the events that had occurred since Jennifer's discovery of the loss of the star Sirius over two years earlier. The events of the past few days were covered in detail. Dr. Sanderson briefed the group on how NASA planned to deliver them to the International Space Station. The Aries rocket boosters, only on paper until recently, were being frantically assembled in Alabama. The Orion capsules were also being hastily built in California. He said these unproven systems would be ready by September 15, the date they would meet the sphere awaiting them in orbit. He told of the NASA tradition of naming each mission. The astronauts discussed numerous suggestions. Finally, it was decided to name it Odyssey after the epic voyage made by ancient Greeks as told by Homer. That name would be used as their moniker once the crew entered that spherical vessel.

They paused in awe as Dr. Sanderson showed them a real-time view of the morphing sphere outside the International Space Station. Within twelve hours, a much larger framework had been assembled, shaping a sphere of about one hundred meters in diameter. The tiny buglike machines were furiously working on every visible part of the new craft.

"We think these swarming things are some kind of miniature robots that are being directed by a centralized intelligence," said Dr. Sanderson. "Notice on the close-up that they are giants among even smaller robots that are almost microscopic. They remind me of ticks. At first, all of them were busy with the disassembly of the messenger, but now they are shaping and forming the vessel that will carry you to the Rim. With the basic skeleton in place, they are now forming the skin of the vessel. It is estimated that the exterior will be complete within half a day. Our view of their work will then be obscured. Who knows what will be done on the inside to build the habitat and propulsion sections. Maybe you will find out more once you're inside. We will deliver you to the

ISS, from which this view is situated. In just over a month, you will see it up close and personal."

"Once again," Jennifer began, "it begins. And now we have less than forty days to get ready for the most incredible journey any human has experienced. The people at NASA believe there a few things they can do for us that might be helpful. They want to put us through a crash course on basic astronaut training, including working in space suits, the medical challenges of spaceflight, hygiene, working under stress, and survival strategies. We will get time in the big pool and a couple of trips in the Vomit Comet to get exposure to low gravity."

"The Vomit Comet?" Aizam, the linguist, asked.

"Yes," Jennifer replied. "It's a specially designed jet with an empty, padded interior. The plane takes us to a high altitude and then makes a series of parabolic dives, simulating the experience of zero gravity for a few minutes. Some of the astronauts have had motion-sickness problems. We will have space-medicine physicians along to monitor us. David and I have already made eight of these flights in our previous training. Don't let the name scare you. It's really a lot of fun."

"As you plan your individual presentations for the rest of us," Jennifer went on, "think outside the box. We need the benefit of your fields of study, but we also need to be challenged to take on the unexpected and then cope, adjust, and improvise. Consider how you would prepare your ancestors from a thousand years ago if they were suddenly brought into our world today."

Alice Cly, the biochemist and geneticist, posed a startling question: "Jennifer, you said you would begin with the first presentation. Tell us from a personal perspective what it was like to make the discoveries you did and talk about how that affected your life.

Jennifer smiled, drew a breath, and began: "It has all happened so fast. Like the rest of you, before the disappearance of Sirius, my life was normal. Family life, my astronomy, and everything else were part of an everyday routine and predictable. Then, after our son and his friends first spotted the flickering light from Sirius that New Year's Eve two and half years ago, everything changed. My training in astrophysics and access to powerful telescopes helped me interpret and explain what I observed. Nothing could have prepared me for the tsunami of media attention and the whirlwind that drove me into a place of leadership. The spotting of the Dyson Sphere was a supernatural experience, a dreamlike vision sent from above. That discovery raised everything to a whole new order of magnitude. Then came the Nobel Prize in physics and the appointment to be an astronaut on this mission."

She paused, reflected, and then resumed. "It all went into slow motion about a month after moving here to begin training. As you recall, world leaders could not agree on anything about the mission. They fought over the crew, the vessel, and especially the cost, which was running into the trillions of dollars. The challenges of building and running a vessel large enough for any kind of crew for a time frame that appeared to be at least five years were daunting. As vast as the surface of the interior of the Rim is, we had no clue as to where to go. The surface area of the Rim is fourteen billion times that of our Earth. There are thousands of oceans, mountains, deserts, and other kinds of terrain we haven't even identified. And remember, we haven't gone beyond our own moon, and we knew we would have to take everything we needed with us for years. As time wore on, everything slowed to a crawl. Then a couple of weeks ago, President Barton announced a major change in the mission, with only six crew members from the richest nations—all of them political appointments. I was disappointed but also relieved. If I had gone on the Earth-created and Earth-supported mission as originally planned, David and I would have left our daughter behind for years, possibly forever."

Jennifer smiled and hugged Allison. She continued. "Then the emissary came with the invitation. I was on the list again, along with David, and Allison. It is another incredible, unexpected surprise. Now I find myself bewildered, as you must feel, to be invited by people of this advanced civilization to make first face-to-face contact as representatives of our world. Maybe it's a good thing we have less than forty days to think about it. Otherwise, I might find some excuses not to go."

With a wise look of a raised eyebrow, Petrus spoke up. "How do you feel about who or what we will meet out there?"

Jennifer looked around at everyone and then down with a perplexed look. "I believe we will be safe and secure. As for who we will meet and what they will be like, I haven't a clue. They know enough about our world to invite eighteen of us from among eight billion humans on Earth. The incredible part about it is that everyone has always dreamed about flying around the galaxy to visit other exotic worlds. Never did anyone expect them to come to us. The data from the atlas given by the emissary indicates that there may be several advanced civilizations on that Rim with room to spare. Who knows who else will be on the exterior surface of the Sphere or in the region between, which consists of over a half million miles of the most incredible engineered structure of all time. I feel like a kid about to start my first day of school. The best part is that we get to do this together."

Dr. Sanderson came over to the group. "Sorry to break in. If this is a good time to pause, the dieticians here have prepared a complete banquet with space food that would be served to our crews on the International Space Station."

Jennifer looked around at everyone and felt a consensus for a break. "Let's fuel up and take some time in pairs or trios with one another. Talk about whatever you want. When we resume, I will give you some basics on astronomy."

In the afternoon session, Jennifer began with a brief lecture and then guided everyone into a discussion about stars, planets, galaxies, and everything of a celestial matter. There was even a sharing of traditional stories and folklore about the heavens.

Even the kids got into the conversation. NASA had several video presentations that helped with the basic concepts, especially grasping the immense scale of the distance they were to travel and the enormous surface they would land on—like ants on a slightly concave continent of concrete. Many questions were unanswerable, but the rapport was building.

Around five, the energy levels were dropping, and Jennifer decided to close off the session. "David and I have made arrangements for a seafood banquet to be served at our condo. All of you are invited, and considering you have nowhere else important to go for thirty-nine days, we will see you there in an hour."

The caterers arrived on schedule and were stationed to serve the bounty from the Gulf of Mexico. David had also arranged for an earlier visit from their housekeeper to spruce up the place. Jennifer was checking a list to be sure all was ready for their fifteen guests when the minibus arrived from JSC. The doorman had been instructed to show them in and boarded them five at a time on the elevator, which opened directly into their thirtieth-floor condominium.

Jennifer turned to Allison. "I want you to be a hostess for the kids. You might want to take them to your room for games or karaoke, but please watch out for the younger ones, especially the twin four-year-olds, Randy and Andy. They will be fascinated with the balcony outside your window. That's fine, but just be sure no one climbs onto that railing. Let's not take them down to the pool tonight. It could get complicated with the need for adult supervision. They might be interested in the telescope later."

"Sure, Mom," answered Allison.

The intercom buzzed, and the doorman said, "The first group is on their way up."

Within a few minutes, everyone had arrived. Many were transfixed with the incredible view of Clear Lake, Galveston

Bay, and the surrounding area. Some were beginning to help themselves to the hors d' oeuvres. The boiled shrimp were a big hit. David gave everyone a tour of the abode. When everyone had returned to the big room, he gave thanks for the meal, the people gathered, and God's providence. The crew helped themselves to the food and then sat in groups of three or four in furniture clusters around the room. The kids ate lightly and quickly. They bonded well as they talked easily. Allison was already emerging as their leader. They followed her like the pied piper into her room. Many of the adults wondered at the contrast between their homes and Jennifer and David's sumptuous condo atop a luxury tower. As night fell, Jennifer decided to finish the evening with a viewing through her twenty-inch Meade telescope.

It was a great way to end the day's events since she had talked about astronomy. She explained about the symmetrical grid of one hundred twenty identical white dwarf stars hovering a couple of million miles above and across the Rim. They could barely make out the faintest of hints of terrain and water beneath the stars. Their discussion soon turned to what they might find there in less than two months. Several also mentioned missing the original version of the nighttime heavens.

The kids were fascinated with the views but coaxed Allison to turn the telescope toward earthly targets. They were excited to see the details of the patio and pool area at the Hilton a couple of miles away. Even the ice cubes in glasses could be discerned.

Jennifer interrupted their viewing before they thought of repositioning to view some of the rooms on that side of the hotel. Becky Ishulutak said she needed to return to their quarters at JSC because her twins were beginning to get tired. Everyone else followed suit and said their farewells. The caterers cleaned up quickly, and David, Jennifer, and Allison found their way to a nest of comfortable cushioned chairs.

"I'm sure glad today is over," Jennifer exclaimed. The other two nodded. "I believe we are off to a great start. Thank you two for all your help."

"The kids want to come back tomorrow," Allison said. "They want to swim in the pool and take a boat ride on the lake."

"That would be great fun," David responded, "but I'm not sure we will have enough time to get that in before we launch. By the way, your mom and I must visit your school to check you out for however long we will be gone. Tomorrow may be my only chance to get that done. School is scheduled to start in two days. Maybe I can get all your textbooks electronically, along with all your assignments. For the last two years, you begged us to let you quit or at least homeschool you. Now you will get the most unique educational experience ever."

"My friends will be so jealous." Allison smirked. "I wonder when or if I will be coming back."

"Allison," Jennifer started in a motherly tone. "It's vital you understand that this voyage is not some vacation junket to an exotic location. You, and all of us, have been chosen and invited for reasons we can't even guess. It is a great privilege that you are going. In a larger sense, you are a representative for all the young people who won't be going. You have been given a tremendous gift. That gift comes with great responsibility. If we can communicate back to Earth, you will need to take the lead in sharing and interpreting your experiences for all the kids back here."

"You're right, Mom," Allison said. "I'll need help from both of you to carry out my role in a responsible way."

"I don't know about you two," David interrupted, "but I am exhausted from tonight, earlier today, and our vacation. I need sleep, and tomorrow comes early."

They rose, said their prayers, hugged, and departed to prepare for bed.

CHAPTER 10

High Learning Curves

This was David's day to give biology instruction. He had made some advanced plans. When everyone gathered in the conference room, he presented a slideshow on the extreme scope and range of life-forms on Earth as well as a basic definition of life. He reminded them that they would encounter an even greater variation of species on the Rim. The talk was relatively brief because David had planned a couple of field trips. Everyone went to the first floor and boarded a minibus for the first expedition, a canoe trip on nearby Armand Bayou. When they arrived at the park, the six canoes were waiting, complete with oars and life jackets. The clammy summer heat was already making everyone damp. Steam was beginning to rise off the murky water in a few places.

"None of you originate from this kind of habitat," David began. "There will be a greater variety on the Rim. Today, we are going into an environment that is not always comfortable and sometimes even hostile to humans. There are alligators and poisonous snakes, not to mention an abundance of hungry insects. You are entering this place on their terms.

"Consider this a test of your observation skills. Pretend everything is out there on the Rim, and no one has any prior knowledge of what we may encounter. Engage the organisms you meet with all your senses. Out there, even small, seemingly innocuous creatures may be extremely dangerous or even sentient. Plants may be mobile. Animals may be capable of photosynthesis. Pay attention to your instincts and bodily responses, for they may be useful clues. Remember that most of the creatures here are smaller than can be seen with our unassisted vision. They are the true rulers of any environment.

"First, I want at least one adult in every canoe. There is room for three people in each one. Everyone will need to wear a life jacket. Do not stand up when waterborne, or you will capsize your canoe. Please try to stay close to the rest of us. Staying together is rule number one on any foray into other worlds. I will lead us for a mile or so to an island in the middle of the park that has seen little disturbance from people for several generations. It is almost pristine. Let's get started."

Everyone donned the jackets and stepped gingerly into the canoes, some at dock side and others nosed up on the shore. Slowly, every canoe launched and began to form a loose armada. David, Allison, and Anastasia occupied the lead canoe, with David paddling in the rear. The other five followed with varying degrees of skill. Aizam, Apiranoa, and Becky were experienced on the water and handled their three canoes like second nature. For a while, everyone was silent, as if in a vast green cathedral, taking in the holiness of the moment.

Then, while swatting a mosquito, Timujin Ji exclaimed, "I only wish I could have ridden a horse or camel instead of this!"

"Maybe we will only explore the deserts out there," said Fatima.

"Dad," Allison asked nervously, "what is that thing floating alongside our canoe? Is it a log or something?"

"It's clearly alive since there's no current here." David smiled. "It is a juvenile gator, about a year old. He's probably curious about us, just as we are about him. He's too small to cause us any trouble, but I wouldn't offer him a finger. Now that we're coming out from under the canopy, we can see his eyes. Isn't he a magnificent specimen?"

"Dad, I know that tone in your voice and the use of that word 'specimen,'" Allison said. "Are you thinking of catching him to take home?"

"Of course not. I couldn't care for him properly," David said. "On the Rim, we will collect nothing but photos and the microbes that climb on for the ride. Oh, good, here's the island we are going to explore in detail. Everyone, make for that bank to the right. There's enough room to beach all our canoes."

Within minutes, everyone had disembarked and listened carefully to David's further instructions. Then they dispersed in pairs or trios to explore the extent of the island sanctuary. After about an hour of poking and snooping around, complete with photos on smartphones or cameras, everyone returned to the landing site, anxious to return to civilization. After sharing and debriefing, the group headed back to the launch point at the pier.

Sack lunches were served on board the minibus as they travelled to their next destination, Herman Park Zoo near downtown Houston. Everyone's morale was given a boost with the thought of a more civilized encounter with animals, mostly of the cute variety, and all behind secure enclosures.

After entering the gates, everyone stayed together in a group. They journeyed to their right, where they studied various birds.

"Notice the messages these birds are sending," David said. "There's a lot they say with their postures, calls, and plumage. If we could smell acutely like dogs, who communicate with scent, then we'd have another sensory dimension of perception. Consider how they perceive you."

"This reminds me of an episode on that old sci-fi TV show, *Twilight Zone*," said Alice Cly. "Some of you may have seen it in reruns. It was the episode where an astronaut travels to another world full of people who look like us, only more advanced. He is treated well but soon finds himself confined inside a sealed house or cage. He is in despair, knowing that his fate is to remain on display as a human animal. It's something to think about for our journey."

Just beyond the avian exhibits were several enclosures for grazing animals. Opposite was a new exhibit irresistible to David—the bugs. He was impressed with their presentation and display. He was about to lose himself in describing the insects in detail when Allison and the other five kids interrupted him.

"Dad," Allison said frantically, "these antelopes are acting strange. Come and see!"

David and his attentive audience of adults turned around and crossed the walk to the other side, where all of the antelopes had stopped eating and were standing still, simply looking at the eighteen astronauts.

"I'm not sure this is anything unusual," David said. "Perhaps they picked up some kind of scent."

Allison, who had walked on a little further, came running back again. "Dad, the zebras and warthogs have also stopped to look at us. Is that normal?"

Everyone walked to that enclosure, not sure what it meant, if anything. They then walked to other exhibits and noticed all the larger animals stopped what they were doing and came to the front of their enclosures to silently stare at the astronauts. When the group moved on, the animals returned to previous activities. The lions even rose from resting positions to approach the barrier, as if paying respect. The chimps stopped their frolics and did the same, waiting for the group to move on before resuming previous behavior. By this time, keepers had noticed the unique responses of the animals, and one of the administrators approached the group.

"Excuse me," he said with a note of hesitation. "Our staff has noticed the unusual impact your presence has on our animals. Are any of you wearing an exotic perfume? Are you carrying any ultrasonic devices that are affecting them?"

David stepped up with a puzzled look on his face. "Hello, I'm Dr. David Lopez, a biologist from Sul Ross State University, and these are my colleagues. Quite frankly, we don't know what is causing their response to us. I am a specialist in animal behavior and have never seen anything like it."

"Wait a minute," the man said, squinting. "You are the crew of astronauts who have been invited on the mission to the Rim!"

When he said this, heads beyond the group began to turn. Cameras and smartphones snapped away as a crowd began to gather. Before long, people were asking for autographs and pictures with the crew, especially Jennifer, who was the most easily recognized. She looked to David, and he realized it would only get worse, so it was time to leave for the minibus.

"I'm sorry we've had a disruptive effect on the animals and your guests," David said. "We have a full schedule and must leave now for our next destination."

Back on the minibus, with a crowd beginning to gather again in a cloud around them, David told the driver to slowly drive out of the lot. He was not sure where to go, leaving the zoo earlier than planned. Allison suggested the Galleria, a major, high-end shopping center that was a few minutes' drive to the west.

"Wow, that was an unexpected response back at the zoo," David said to everyone. "The response of the people was understandable, but why would the animals act as they did? It reminds me of the strange animal behavior I observed on the day of Earth's envelopment two years ago. The animals all gathered to wait for that event, almost like some folk art image from the theme of the peaceable kingdom."

"What do you suggest for us at the Galleria?" Jennifer asked.

"It's a good thing we're in civilian clothing," David said with a thoughtful look. "When we get there, let's break up into smaller groups and scatter. The kids must stay with their parents or another adult. You may shop if you wish. Perhaps some will find a gift to take to the Rim. We all have the smartphones NASA gave us yesterday. Stay alert and in touch. Call if you have any problems. Be inconspicuous but also take advantage of this time. Pretend you are visitors from another world working undercover. Observe without staring. If someone engages you in conversation, keep it to small talk. Don't tell anyone why you are here in Houston other than you are looking for a job or are doing advanced studies. This celebrity thing is new. We had a little of that back when Jennifer discovered the Sphere, but people quickly forgot. Hopefully, you can blend in. Let's meet back at the garage elevators at five this evening."

Surprisingly, everyone managed to keep their identities concealed. Near five o'clock, they all began to reassemble at the designated location. Most of them had bags with purchased items. After boarding the minibus, they headed to Kenny & Ziggy's Deli for a sumptuous supper. Having entered in smaller groups, they were seated in six separate booths. Most of them ordered some of the famous kosher cuisine, while others tried Hungarian specialties. Again, they remained incognito.

After the zoo fiasco, David's confidence was returning, and he decided to make the final leg of their journey, a Houston Astros Baseball game at Minute Maid Park. NASA contractor Boeing had donated twenty field-box seats a few rows up from the first-base dugout. Before they arrived, David briefed them on what to expect to see at a baseball game. Most had never seen one before. He warned them about following the lead of the crowd to cheer. After being dropped off a block from the entrance with their reserved-seat tickets in hand, they again broke up into smaller groups, loosely clustered and following the gathering crowd. Once inside, most made their way to the seats. Jennifer stopped at the gift shop to buy an Astros hat and some dark glasses since she was by far the most recognizable member of the group. Just before the National Anthem, everyone had made it safely and quietly to their places. Many of them had acquired soda and hot dogs. Some had programs and were busy trying to learn more about the spectacle they were about to see. Everyone rose for the National Anthem and then the game began. Everything went smoothly until the seventh-inning stretch, when the view on the stadium's jumbotron showed a close-up view of all eighteen astronauts seated together. At first, several of them waved.

Then the stadium announcer said, "Ladies and gentlemen, I want to welcome some extraordinary visitors to tonight's game. The people you see on the jumbotron are none other than the eighteen astronauts invited to make the momentous trip to the Rim to make first contact. How about a big welcome for these incredible people!"

In an instant, everything changed. Cheers arose quickly from the crowd. For the past two days, the media had been giving extraordinary coverage to the upcoming mission. They had broadcast all the information they could find on the eighteen crew members. Now they were celebrities as well. People began to come to them with smartphones and cameras. Some wanted autographs. Many came from other parts of the stadium. The aisles were jamming with people. Even the Astros players in the dugout came out and were looking back at the new space celebrities. One of them even climbed over the railing to make his way to them in hopes of having them autograph his shirt. As the minutes passed, the game was not able to resume until the police began to disperse the crowd. The team's owner, Scott Rohloff, made his way to the astronauts. This, too, was broadcast on the jumbotron.

He walked up to the group with a wireless microphone and said, "We're honored to have you with us tonight. Please join us at my executive suite on the club level."

Jennifer stepped forward, removed her sunglasses, and said, "The honor is ours. We are all honored by your gracious invitation, but our schedule mandates that we must make an early evening of it. Perhaps we can accept your generous offer when we return from the Rim. Since we have only thirty-eight days before launch, it is time to return to JSC. May we please have a baseball to take with us?"

Mr. Rohloff agreed, and a baseball autographed by the key players was furnished for the occasion. As the crew departed, the crowd erupted in deafening cheers with a standing ovation. The driver had slipped out before the crowd had gathered. He met them at the main entrance with the minibus. Soon everyone was on board, and they were headed to the Johnson Space Center, relieved to be free again.

Inside the minibus, Jennifer stood up. Hanging onto a strap, she said, "That was nothing like any baseball game I've ever been to. Now it begins with our notoriety. We will need to be more careful about excursions off-site. Perhaps this is a preview of what we might encounter on the Rim. And then, when we return, the people here will overwhelm us. Brace yourselves. It is likely our lives will never be the same. May God give us the grace to handle it with wisdom and maturity. Tomorrow, several of the Apollo astronauts who went to the moon will be with us for an hour to talk about their experiences with this same thing. In the meantime, get a good rest tonight. Tomorrow is coming early."

After everyone had been dropped off at their quarters at JSC, David, Jennifer, and Allison began the short journey back to their condominium. They were surprised by heavy traffic on NASA Road One at the back entrance.

"There must have been a horrible accident," David said.

"No," said Allison. "This crowd is waiting for us. My friend, Marleigh, has just texted me that our appearance at the game was breaking news all over. People down here figured we would return home. Marleigh and the other girls want to know if they can come on up to our place when we get home. They're in the crowd waiting near the driveway."

"Absolutely not," Jennifer snapped. "Not tonight. We have to get up early tomorrow to keep training."

Just then, a police car pulled in front of them at the exit gate to escort their vehicle the one mile back to their condo tower. TV cameras and flashes from smartphones and cameras were lighting their way, as if they were royalty. The mob was cheering and waving, hoping for the fleeting view of one of their faces.

"Mom," Allison said with irritation, "when am I going to have time with my friends? It's so unfair I have to work all the time now."

Jennifer turned from the front seat and looked her almost-grown daughter in the eye and said, "Allison, I don't know when we will ever have time again for anything. None of us chose to be on this mission, you least of all. But it is a great honor and responsibility that has been given to us, and we will have to adjust and grow to meet the demands of it. Your friends will understand."

"Sometimes I wish this had never happened," Allison said, pining.

"Us too," David said. "Life was much easier back in Fort Davis. And it was a good life too."

Jennifer smiled at Allison and said, "I know this is very hard for you. It is for all of us; all this intense training, the short time frame, and the uncertainty of what will happen when we leave the International Space Station. And the hardest part for now is all this unwanted fame. I had the thought that our launch in thirty-eight days can't come soon enough."

Soon they drove into the condo property, which had been secured by the police. Jennifer wondered how much longer they would be able to stay in their own home. When they stepped off the elevator on their floor, the spotlights of hovering media helicopters were shining in on them. David wanted to call the FAA to ban the choppers from the sky around their condo, but for now, only closed blinds would help. They got ready for bed, prayed, and adjourned to the bedrooms for a fitful night's sleep.

For the next week, the Odyssey astronauts underwent intense briefing and training on site at JSC. The fourteen-hour days were varied in content, as each one of the crew shared his or her own expertise. One of the highlights was an afternoon in the moon pool, the giant indoor water tank where they were fully suited up for extra-vehicular activity training to get accustomed to working in space suits. The kids had more fun than anyone.

Early Monday morning, everyone made an outing to Galveston beach to share MREs (meals ready to eat) on the beach while watching the sun rise in glorious oranges. Shortly afterward, they boarded a Coast Guard cutter for a day trip to the Flower Gardens Banks National Marine Sanctuary. There they would test their new space suits and skills while diving onto Stetson Bank. As they put on their suits, casual conversation arose among the group.

Vartan Bedevian gave a mischievous look at Jennifer and said, "Jennifer, do you think we will miss the paparazzi out here?"

"If they come, they will have to dive to find us," Jennifer replied.

"Maybe we can feed them to the fish." He smirked.

"Dr. Bass," asked Anastasia with trepidation, "what kind of animals will we find down here?"

Jennifer responded, "My husband will be better able to answer that," looking to David.

"There will be plenty of plants and animals that make their home here," David stated. "In addition to the microbial life like plankton, there are also algae as the main representative of plants. The animals range from millions of tiny critters, like copepods, to larger salt water fish, like sharks and rays."

"How large?" Toma asked.

"Most will be smaller than you," David said reassuringly.

Within minutes, everyone was in the water, fully suited and wired up with full com links. Most of them uttered "ooh"s and "ah"s as they descended onto the top of the bank. Everyone was immersed in a world of blues. They were welcomed and inspected first by the barracudas. Then a hawksbill sea turtle made an approach, as if seeking a lost child. All around were sponges, algae, and coral in a dazzling array of colors scattered across the rocky ridges. Urchins and starfish moved across the rocky surface at a slow pace, each in different directions. Thousands of smaller fish of many varieties swam around them as if they, too, were rock outcroppings. Amberbellied Creole fish moved about in schools, like clouds passing over the crew.

Everyone's silent reverie was shattered by squeals from Andy and Randy as they swam in pursuit of an octopus.

"Look up toward the top of the ridge next to us!" Apiranoa Ngata said. "There's a large manta ray coming our way."

Silently, a massive ray with a ten-foot span glided over them, as if on wing. It never indicated any awareness of their presence.

"Well, what could we have said or done to make first contact with that ray?" asked Becky Ishulutak.

"A fresh fish held out as a food offering might have meant something," said Aizam Mat Saman. "It had places to go and things to do. It's probably old enough to have seen plenty of humans. This is another intrusion by the harmless aliens from another world."

"We are as out of place in their world as they would be in ours," said Maria Quaupucura. "When we get out there, it should be even more bizarre. Will we even have a frame of reference?"

"I would hope our hosts will consider the strangeness we will see and make efforts to prepare us," Jennifer said.

"You don't have to look far, even in our world, to find life in environments and organisms challenging our definitions of life-forms," David said. "Just think of what these animals make of us."

All too soon, their time was up and the dive master signaled for everyone to begin the slow return to the surface. For a moment, the world above the surface seemed strange after a couple of hours down in the blue sanctuary. After everyone had climbed aboard the cutter for its journey back to Galveston, Jennifer took a call from Dr. Sanderson. Her happy face turned serious at the news.

"I see," she said. "I'll tell everyone right away. We're headed back now."

After concluding her cell conversation, Jennifer said, "Listen, everyone. Dr. Sanderson just told me that President Barton will be with us tomorrow morning at ten for an important visit and a major announcement about the mission. I'm sure he will want to know about our progress."

After returning to Galveston, everyone enjoyed a fresh seafood dinner in a private dining room at Gaido's. Jokes were made about eating the creatures they had visited only hours before. On the drive back to JSC, everyone was lost in thought about all they had experienced in the past ten days. Some were also anxious about the next morning's presidential visit.

CHAPTER 11

Unwelcome Visitors and Escape to Freedom

In the utter darkness of a place below and beyond time and space dwelt a beautifully hideous being of nearly infinite ability, whose seething rage drove him on relentless wantonness. Since the time before time when he had rebelled against the one who created him, the obsessive desire to mar and destroy all of creation had devoured his supreme intellect and craftiness. Time and again, through wreaking havoc in world after world and life after life, his efforts had fallen short thanks to the relentless grace of the Creator, who had dealt him a mortal blow at the very moment of his greatest triumph—the voluntary death of the most beloved part of the Creator thousands of years ago on a beautiful world gone so wrong. He thought for sure that the empty meaninglessness of that torturous death would result in his final ascension against his ancient foe. Then came the impossible, the violation of all natural laws written by the Creator himself—the Resurrection. This dark one had underestimated the astonishing power of the helpless, sacrificial love that had overturned everything he had worked for during timeless ages. Everything was forever changed through that peculiar event on such a remote, insignificant world. In his searing heart, he knew that it foretold the eclipse of his power as well as his transformation to mortality. It was a trick of the grandest kind, even more shocking than anything he had concocted in his most devious imagination.

The dark one knew not the timing or means of his end, but the arrival of the Sphere had marked a major threat to his plans for that little world he had hoped to destroy for so long. His hatred blazed into a fury he had not known for millennia. With the coming of the Sphere, almost all of Earth had turned their thoughts from ancient hatreds and violence toward a peaceful shaping of a bright and hopeful future. It was now time for him to arise from his dark brooding into immediate action to counter and undo any good that had been accomplished. In that world, he had many faithful minions that were nearly as dark of heart as he was. They craved the same kind of divine power that he had suffered to grasp for himself. Many had worked their way to powerful political positions. They would prove useful.

Back at the Johnson Space Center, briefing and discussion for ninety minutes, the astronauts went to the big auditorium in Building Two at nine in the morning, where preparations were well underway for the presidential press conference. They were thoroughly searched and cleared through security. The media, who had been severely restricted in access to the astronauts, were a major component of the crowd. The rest were NASA personnel and White House staff. Only three TV cameras were permitted and carefully set by White House staff, who also oversaw the placement of the teleprompters. The White House members also oversaw the NASA staff who handled the sound and video systems. The whole place was a beehive of activity. The Odyssey astronauts enjoyed being spectators of the purposeful event. They were seated as a group several rows back from the first row, with some White House staff seated at the ends, as if to contain them.

The designated ten o'clock time for the president came and went without the president or any explanation for the delay. At twenty after, a senior White House staff member came to the podium. She was a stocky, confident woman in her late fifties with a piercing look. Initially, Jennifer felt as if she were staring directly at her with malice.

"Silence!" the woman said with force that could be felt in the chairs. "I'm Judy Macy, President Barton's chief advisor for space and science. You are privileged to be in the presence of the president. He is momentarily delayed but will arrive within ten minutes. President Barton has an important announcement to make. Due to his unusually heavy workload, he will not be taking any questions, even from the press. When the president arrives on the stage, you are to rise and applaud enthusiastically. Wait until he raises both hands to wave you down to slow the applause and for you to be seated. During the course of his speech, there will be pauses. Watch me for cues on the far left side of the stage. When I stand, you are to stand and begin applauding and cheering with great enthusiasm. At no time will catcalls or boos be tolerated. We have many of our staff people here today and are watching for any negative or unenthusiastic behavior."

Ms. Macy then walked to her post on the stage. Jennifer looked at David with a concerned expression.

"What's going on here?" she whispered. "Is this a pep rally or a press conference? Why did they need to set it up in this way?"

Before David could answer, he noticed two of the White House minders staring directly at him threateningly. He simply shrugged his shoulders.

A loud voice came over the sound system, saying, "Everyone rise! Ladies and gentlemen, William Barton, the president of the United States!"

As instructed, every one rose and applauded. White House staff were cheering even louder. The president, a tall, slender man in his late forties, walked in with swagger, waving with his right hand and smiling at the crowd. He stepped to the podium as if to possess it. His confident bearing spoke of arrogance. Jennifer thought she detected a slight red light from the center of his eyes.

He let the applause linger for a moment while waving with the same right hand. The applause seemed to inflate him. Finally, he waved the crowd to silence with both hands in a grand gesture.

"Thank you, my friends. How great it is to be back here in Houston on this great historical occasion. People will remember the events of these days for millennia to come, and you and I are alive to experience it all. I can't emphasize enough the importance of this mission that our friends on the Rim have provided. Like many of you, I would love to make the trip as your representative, but my responsibilities here prevent that. So, like most of the people of our world, I will simply support those who go with our blessings."

He paused with a big smile. Off camera, Ms. Macy cued the crowd, and everyone rose, applauded, and cheered. Jennifer looked to David with a raised eyebrow. Other crew members glanced at one another, not sure what to expect next. Suddenly, two people appeared on stage near the president. Jennifer recognized them as George Sharkos, a multibillionaire, and his significant other, the CNN anchor, Millicent Grant. They were both dressed in NASA flight suits. Even more glances were exchanged among the astronauts. Then they realized that their minders, the White House staff around them, were all staring with hostility. The spell was broken when the president again waved the crowd down with his hands and shining smile.

He resumed his speech. "Thank you again. I have come here today to fulfill a promise I made a month ago when I assigned the honorable George Sharkos and Millicent Grant to represent our nation on this important mission. Now that our friends from the Rim will be providing the transportation, much to the relief of the budget-minded bean counters in Congress, I now assign them to head up the Odyssey mission and to determine who will accompany them on the voyage to the Rim. George and Millicent, in addition to being longtime personal friends of mine, are two of the finest and most capable representatives we could send out there to that big world in the sky. I want you to welcome them and then they will have something to say to all of you."

Again, Ms. Macy prompted everyone to rise and applaud. This time she sat down a little sooner, as did the crowd.

Millicent Grant, a well-known media celebrity with "the look," stepped up first and said, "I am so honored to be a part of the Odyssey mission and am looking forward to working with all of you here on the NASA team as we prepare for this trip. I will also be reporting regularly back to CNN for exclusive news as it happens. Many of you will be sharing this mission with the world."

With a perfect smile and a wave, she stepped aside to let George Sharkos step to the podium. The applause became lighter, and Ms. Macy sat down quickly. Sharkos was a hulking figure with a full head of black hair sprinkled with hints of grey. His quick eyes spoke of intensity and attention to detail. He looked around the room as if he owned it all.

"I look forward to this trip," he said, oozing with confidence. "This will be my fourth trip to space after visiting the ISS at my own expense. Everything is old hat to me. We have only a month until launch. It wouldn't be good to keep those people out there waiting. Let's get back to work."

Sharkos shot a quick glance of menace at the Odyssey astronauts, waved, and stepped back with Grant and the president. Then, arm in arm, they walked off the stage. The cameras were immediately turned off, and the applause was replaced with the soft sound of quiet conversations.

Sharkos came over to the seating area where the astronauts had been confined. He looked at them with an angry gaze and said, "I expect to see you in thirty minutes upstairs in Building One where you have been meeting. It's time to set a lot of things straight."

Jennifer saw another glimpse of the red light—this time in Sharkos's eyes.

Jennifer and the other astronauts returned directly to their conference and training center on the top floor of Building One. They were stunned and surprised by the presidential announcement. Even Dr. Sanderson was without explanation. They were dumbfounded as to what this meant for the mission and their preparations.

Ten minutes late, Sharkos and Grant walked in with Andre Volper, all with angry, determined expressions on their faces. Jennifer was even more surprised to see an old adversary from her time at the observatory. The trio made their way to the front of the room and took the podium.

"Everyone get your chairs in a row here in front," Sharkos ordered. "It's time to get things cleaned up."

The crew members looked to Jennifer, who simply picked up a chair from one of the circles and moved it to the area in front of the raised platform, which held the podium and the three visitors. After everyone was seated, Sharkos looked around, glowering.

"Now that the president has put me in charge of this Odyssey mission," he began with an imperious tone, "it is now time to change our mission roster. Bass, you, your husband, and daughter are off of the mission and will need to leave JSC immediately. Your services are no longer required here. As Donald Trump would say, 'You're fired!'"

Sharkos smirked while a gasp arose among the astronauts. Everyone looked at Jennifer and Dr. Sanderson.

With Andre Volper in the room, Jennifer's mind flashed back to their encounters at the observatory two years earlier. She calmly rose and walked straight up to the podium, standing a few feet in front of Sharkos. The words began to come to her as she opened her mouth: "Mr. Sharkos, your presence and statements come as a surprise, and I am sure that was the intention. But as far as I and the other astronauts are concerned, there is no way I am off the mission, nor am I leaving the site or this room. My place on the Odyssey mission was clearly indicated in the invitation. It could be dangerous to defy the people of the Rim who issued it."

Millicent Grant stepped up with a vicious look that seemed to break the perfect appearance of her face. The same red light flashed for an instant in her eyes. Grant hissed, "You have a lot of problems to attend to here on Earth. There's no way you will be able to go on the mission. The president told us that the IRS is conducting a comprehensive inquiry into your financial affairs. The attorney general considers you both to be a flight risk and, as we speak, is seeking a court order to have you both confined for the duration of the investigation."

Again, Jennifer felt the blast of surprise but prayed silently for the leading of the Spirit. She then asked, "What investigation? On what charges?"

Sharkos again showed his gnashed teeth in a menacing grin as he said, "You and your husband are the greatest frauds of all time. Dr. Andre Volper, your former boss, helped us piece the picture together. We are still trying to figure out how you managed to carry out the trick of sending a probe into the NSA's center and posting that bogus invitation list to everyone's e-mail inbox. By the time we finish with you, the only trip you will make will be to a federal penitentiary. I suggest you shut up and leave now before I have security take you away."

Dr. Sanderson stood and came forward with a distressed look. "Mr. Sharkos, I'm sure you've got it all wrong. I've worked with Jennifer and her husband for two years, and there's no way any of these accusations have merit. I insist on discussing this with you further in private."

Sharkos raised an eyebrow and narrowed his eyes at the NASA director and said, "Sanderson, your time here is limited too. The president has given me unlimited authority. I'm in charge here, and all of you will do as I tell you!"

Sanderson drew in a deep breath and said, "Until I hear directly from the president and Congress, I will not allow you to take over. The security personnel follow my orders, and I say we will wait until this is sorted out to my satisfaction. If that is not satisfactory with you, then you may leave, with or without a security escort."

Sharkos began to falter but caught himself. He turned back to Grant and Volper, and they whispered for a few moments. He then returned to the podium to stare down at Dr. Sanderson and Jennifer. "We will be back, and you will regret this!"

The trio then left.

Jennifer and the crew were still in a state of shock when her cell phone rang. She moved toward the windows to answer it.

"Mom, this is Justin," said the image on her FaceTime app. "Sarah and I have been detained and questioned by government agents. This started late last night. They won't give any ID, but they have grilled us on all kinds of details about you and Dad and your work at home and at NASA. We are not allowed to leave our apartment here in Austin. An agent was assigned to keep watch on us while the others left, but he smoked a joint and then popped some pills, so he's unconscious for now. What's going on? Are you and Dad okay?"

Jennifer responded with an effort to keep from choking. "Justin, I don't know what's going on yet but just remain calm. We've been through the mill as well. It seems the president's friends, George Sharkos and Millicent Grant, were upset that their names were not on the invitation. The president decided to reinstate them and give them complete control of the Odyssey mission. In addition, in order to keep us here on Earth, they must have decided to exploit executive power to harass your dad and myself and remove us from the crew. Give it some time, and I think help will come. Please stay in touch. Give our love to Sarah. You both are in our prayers."

Jennifer went to David and told him what had happened to their son in Austin. David was clearly upset. They were joined by Dr. Sanderson, Allison, and the other fifteen astronauts.

"We will get to the bottom of this," Dr. Sanderson said, trying to reassure everyone.

"All that happened this morning reminds me of my teen years back home when Armenia was still a part of the Soviet Union," said Vartan Bedevian.

"With all that's at stake here," said Theodora Melas, "it is not surprising some would do anything to go in our place. Humans have often behaved poorly when there is so much opportunity for power and wealth. They would find it irresistible."

Jennifer composed herself and said, "What's important for us is to keep on with our preparations. We were meant to make this voyage, and I don't believe anyone can stop that. I now would like for all of us to join hands and pray, silently at first, and then I will close."

Everyone calmly circled, joined hands, and bowed their heads.

After a few moments, Jennifer prayed, "Dear God, we are scared and confused, but you are involved in all of this, working for good. Help us to proceed with wisdom and calm. Protect us and our families from evil. Confuse the proud in the imaginations of their hearts. May your will be done in all matters related to this mission. In the name of all that is holy—amen."

Jennifer then said, "Let's take a break and come back together in half an hour."

During the break, Dr. Sanderson, Jennifer, and several others made calls to family and friends to check on safety and to seek assistance. When they returned, it was decided to proceed forward with the original plans for the day. Dr. Petrus Xamseb, the Khoisan anthropologist, began his time of instruction, integrating the morning experience into his presentation.

Near six in the evening, the crew took a break to walk to the cafeteria building for supper. It had been good to get back into their studies to get their minds off the anxiety of the morning. Jennifer was even more concerned. As they sat at their table, David ate, but she only dabbled, occasionally checking her cell phone.

"David, I'm worried about Justin," Jennifer said tensely. "I haven't gotten anything from him since this morning. No texts, no nothing. What are they doing with him and why?"

David pulled out his phone and tried to call Sarah's number. "That's odd," he said. "I can't even get a signal, and I know signal strength here is fine. Is someone jamming our phones?"

Jennifer checked hers again. "Mine shows a signal, but there's no connection on any call I've tried. I'm worried about Mom. You remember how scared she was two years ago when those agents were vetting me for the Cabinet position. Maybe we should just quit and leave. If you and I are out of the way, maybe they will stop this harassment and leave us alone."

David looked at her with that wonderful serenity that had seen her through the scary times after the Sirius disappearance and the black-hole discovery. He held her hands and looked reassuringly into her eyes.

"I don't know how, or why, or even what," he said. "But I have this deep feeling that everything is going to be all right."

He then began to eat his space-style ice-cream drops and looked into her eyes again. "We've come too far to quit now. Allison and the other fifteen need us to stay with it. We were all invited, so we will all go. The Lord will make a way in spite of all this IRS trouble. He's bigger and smarter than all of that."

Shortly thereafter, they all returned for the four-hour evening session. At the conclusion, when the others were leaving to go to their quarters on site, Dr. Sanderson asked Jennifer and David into his office. Allison followed and sat in a chair in the corner.

"Jennifer, I don't know how to tell you this," began Dr. Sanderson gravely. "Things have gotten worse. The White House is working hard on this situation. My people here have informed me that your condo tower is under surveillance by government vehicles, probably FBI, so you should stay here for the night.

What's more, some of these agents have tried to come on site, but I have instructed our security to keep them at bay. They have all our gates covered with unmarked vehicles. We're under level-four lockdown—no one admitted in without special clearance. It's only a matter of time before they get warrants to get in. I have also received a stream of intense e-mails from Washington. There have been calls from the White House I have not taken or returned. Your time here is short for now. I will do everything I can to clear this matter up, but it looks like we are running out of options."

Jennifer looked at David with great anxiety and then back to Dr. Sanderson. "Franklin, I don't understand all that's going on here. What have we done to merit this kind of hostile attention, and from our own government and president?"

"Jennifer, I don't know any more than you do. I'm so sorry all of this is happening," he said.

Just then, that small, special phone began to honk. It was the one that had surprised them at the airport in Iceland a couple of weeks ago. This was the specially issued phone for Jennifer's responsibilities during the crisis of the Sphere's appearance.

"Hello," said Jennifer with trepidation. She put it on speaker so David and Dr. Sanderson could hear it.

"Dr. Bass, this is General Morris," the voice said. "I understand you and your family are in a little trouble. Don't worry. There's a plan in the works. One of my people will be there shortly. Do as he tells you. I will see you later tonight. Bye."

Jennifer looked at David and Dr. Sanderson with wonder.

"What's he up to now?" she said.

"Maybe that's one part of the reason I said that everything will be all right," David replied.

Dr. Sanderson was handed a note from a staff person.

"You are to leave your regular cell phones in your office here and proceed downstairs to the cafeteria using the utility tunnel system and report to Charlie in the recycling room," he said with a puzzled look.

Jennifer, David, and Allison left and went to the basement as instructed. Then they travelled the long, white corridor underground to the cafeteria a quarter of a mile away. Before they could enter the stairway to go up to the main floor, a man in standard janitorial scrubs came out from behind a steel door and motioned them inside a room filled with bins for sorting and numerous trash receptacles.

"Are you Charlie?" David asked.

"Yes, there's no time for explanations," the man said. "Put on these jumpsuit uniforms and caps. Jennifer, you and your daughter climb into that trash canister over there. It's as clean as we could make it on short notice. Once you're inside, make no sound whatsoever. I'm sorry for any difficulties you will experience. Whatever happens, remain calm and act normal."

They quickly did as instructed, and soon David was rolling the canister outside the cafeteria, where he and Charlie hoisted it by machine into a garbage truck. Charlie motioned to David to climb into the cab. They got in, started up, and began to drive off toward one of the back entrances. Several miles down the road, Charlie pulled into a restaurant parking lot and stopped at the rear near a trash dumpster.

"This is where I get out," he said. "We've made a good getaway from JSC and are in the clear. Proceed on to your destination at normal speed, and you will get further instructions there. Godspeed, Dr. Lopez."

Charlie handed him a tightly folded note. David moved over to the driver's seat and read the note. It was a simple map with directions to a sanitation site near Hobby Airport. He worried about Jennifer and Allison in the back of the truck but knew he couldn't address that now. Within twenty minutes, David pulled the truck into a parking lot full of trucks and canisters. There was a large metal building for truck maintenance toward the back of the property. The door was opening as he drove in. A man at the lit entryway motioned him inside. David stopped the truck at the designated place and got out. There were two men who met him. They also wore sanitation uniforms.

The taller one said, "Dr. Lopez, let's get your wife and daughter out of the back now."

These were the best words David had heard all day. Jennifer and Allison were okay, if not a little stinky.

"I sure hope our trip to the Rim won't be like this," Allison quipped.

"What's next?" Jennifer asked of the men, who were now helping them out of their jumpers.

The shorter one said, "Put on these polo shirts and caps and climb into that catering van."

Soon the taller man was driving the van with the three of them in the back. This trip was much shorter as they drove into the airport and out to a hangar, where they carried food containers inside to a waiting, unmarked 737 jet.

After the last of the food was loaded into the plane's galley inside the empty plane, the man turned to Jennifer and said, "Pick your seats, buckle up, and enjoy some food. Sorry we don't have any in-flight movies. Godspeed, Dr. Bass."

They did as instructed, and soon the plane was moved out in front of the hangar and prepped for takeoff. In five minutes, they were airborne, headed into the dark of night to an unknown destination. After a few minutes, the plane leveled off at high altitude. Jennifer knew they would be aloft for some time, so she unbuckled, and they helped themselves to the food they had packed only minutes before.

"Well, David," Jennifer said, "we've changed from astronauts, to sanitation workers, to caterers. Talk about career changes. What's next?"

Just then, the cockpit door opened and out stepped General Morris. He looked gravely serious as he sat down to join them in the leather-covered swivel seats.

"We got you out in the nick of time," he said. "Another hour or so, and the Attorney General would have gotten those warrants to the agents at the gates, and you would have been in their custody and en route to some undisclosed destination for an extended time."

Jennifer wrinkled her face and said, "General Morris, thank you ever so much for saving us. But why was any of this necessary? What's going on here?"

"I never thought it would come to this," he said with gravity, "but our country is in deep crisis, and few even know anything about it. Ever since his election, President Barton has been acting way beyond his constitutional authority. What has happened to you and your family is a small part of a larger problem. Many of us in Washington, both military and civilian from both parties, are very worried. First of all, his election is suspect. It appears to have been carefully and electronically managed to make it appear that he carried districts in crucial swing states. Ever since his inauguration, President Barton has had very little connection with the normal channels of power in Congress and Washington. He has locked the military out of all major policy discussions. The executive orders he has issued are increasingly troubling in their scope and nature. He even ignores federal court orders that have declared some of his executive orders unconstitutional."

"But what can be done?" David asked. "Isn't the media making a big stink over his behavior?"

"First of all, most of the media has given him a pass until recently," General Morris said. "But in the last month, agents and minders have been stationed in all the major media headquarters. All news items must meet their approval. Fox is under special scrutiny. They have been warned that they all face arrest and the network shut down for good if they cross the line the administration has drawn."

Jennifer's eyes got big as she said, "Aren't you sworn to obey the president in your military oath? You have taken a terrible risk removing us like you did. When they get a hold of Dr. Sanderson, won't they trace it all to you?"

"I've known Franklin for a long time," General Morris said reassuringly. "He's loyal to the America we used to know. They won't get anything out of him. My oath is not to the president, though he is my commander in chief. I am sworn to uphold and defend the Constitution, which is now under attack like never before."

"But why?" David asked.

"With this mission to the Rim, to make first contact with an advanced civilization," General Morris replied, "There is so much at stake. It is an unprecedented opportunity for power and control. Imagine the power that would come to anyone who could mediate Earth's relationship with them, not to mention the sole access to such advanced technology. It's sort of like having ownership of all the patents to the airplane, the car, the computer, and the TV. It's already apparent that the people on the Rim have some kind of mind-reading and even mind-control abilities. Whoever could possess all of this would control everything and everyone on Earth."

Allison was entranced by the conversation, her mind fully engaged. "Can anything be done to stop them?"

General Morris looked at Allison and smiled. "You have your mom's ability to cut right to the chase. Not yet, but soon. This is not the first time America has been threatened by a half-mad, tyrannical president. The last time was over a generation ago in the last days of the Nixon administration. In the summer of 1974, President Nixon had a psychotic episode and had to be relieved of office by the provisions of the twenty-fifth amendment. This was a week before his official resignation. All this was hidden from the American people. The good news is that the political and military leaders of that day made the right call. We are not far from that same point today. The difference today is that the general public knows little or nothing of the grave crisis we are facing. It will be much harder to respond now. Rest assured that the vast majority of our military and civilian leaders are loyal and can be trusted. We are waiting for the right moment to act."

Jennifer returned to her earlier question. "General, what now? What's to become of us while all of this is working its way through?"

"We are now flying to Wright-Patterson Air Force Base. where you will change planes," he said. "You are, for the time being, Wes and April Welch, with your daughter, Kayla. David, you an army major who was severely wounded from action in Afghanistan, with burns over most of your body. Jennifer, you and Allison will have a complete makeover. After prepping, you will be transferred to a military transport plane and flown to a base in San Antonio, where we will move you to a secure, high-level quarantine isolation ward at Brooke Army Medical Center. It's unlikely Barton and his people will ever find you there."

Within six hours, Jennifer, David, and Allison were safely settled in an isolation burn ward in the most secure area of BAMC. Jennifer's hair had been trimmed and dyed black. She was fitted with window glasses of a contemporary style. Allison had been radically restyled as well, with spiked hair, fake tattoos, black clothing, and several fake body piercings.

"Mom," said Allison as she poked at a metal ring in her nose, "how long are we supposed to do this? I hate my redesign. My friends will never recognize me. I don't even recognize me!"

"If you think you have it bad," David said in muffled tones from his hospital bed, "I'm wrapped up in about forty pounds of bandages with tubes poked into places all over me. I'm now a living pincushion, and I can't even get up to go to the bathroom."

"At least we're safe, which is more than I can say for our country or even Justin and Sarah," lamented Jennifer. "I am scared to even think of what might happen to them after the administration finds out that we're gone."

Just then, a familiar face showed herself at the door. It was Sarah.

"Mrs. Welch?" she asked.

Jennifer ran to grab her in an embrace. "Sarah, it's a miracle to see you." She then choked up with tears.

"Mrs. Welch," Sarah continued, "I'm not sure you remember me. I'm Jennifer Bradford, and my husband, Captain Christian Bradford, was injured in the same attack as your husband. He's next door in the same kind of set up as Dad, I mean Major Welch. The staff said you would want to know how we are doing and that everything will be okay."

Allison closed the door behind Sarah as she took a chair beside the bed. Jennifer was overcome with tearful relief. Allison, crying, found the tissue box and placed it next to Jennifer, who began to pray aloud with thanksgiving. David could only watch while constrained with straps and tubes.

Jennifer composed herself enough to say, "I have to see him, my boy, I mean Captain Bradford."

Sarah led her to the adjoining room along, with Allison. David was perturbed at not being able to join them.

As they entered the room, Jennifer ran to Justin's bed, grabbed him in a hug, and began to sob again. "Thank God" is all she could say.

Justin, just as tied up as his dad, said, "Come on, Mom, I mean Mrs. Welch. Is this any way to treat a severely burned man? Just think of what the nurses would say if they could see you."

"I think what Mom will want to know," said Allison, "is how did you get here?"

"Some military people showed up at our apartment late last night," Sarah said, "and they showed papers to the agents who were holding us. They told them the White House had ordered our transfer to an undisclosed location. Justin and I were terrified."

"But then while we were being driven in an unmarked SUV, I got a phone message from General Morris explaining what we were supposed to do," Justin continued. "I knew we would be fine when he mentioned seeing you. I want to know when I can get out of this crazy disguise."

Jennifer composed herself. "I'm so thankful you both are okay. It's one of the greatest joys of my life to see you here, even if you are all wrapped up in fake bandages.

"Is Dad, I mean the major, okay?" Justin asked.

"Of course," said Jennifer. "He's as tied up as you are, but for now, you must act your parts well. All of the personnel here should be trustworthy, but we must do all we can to help make it work. Even the smallest leak from some unexpected source could blow our cover and make everything much worse. I think we should lie low for now and wait."

Everyone played their parts well, and the next two days passed without event. There was no hint of any crisis on the TV news. Even Fox news didn't give any indication of the trouble in Washington that General Morris had talked about. David and Justin complained regularly about their confinement. Jennifer was beginning to doubt they would ever get back to NASA, much less leave the hospital. Then, in the evening, a doctor dressed in an isolation suit walked into David's room with a chart and closed the door for privacy. It was General Morris.

He took off the biohazard hood and said with a big smile, "I see the patient has made a remarkable recovery and is now ready to go home."

"What do you mean, General?" Jennifer asked.

"The threat to you and your family is over," he said. "Our sources in the White House think the president got a call from the King of Saudi Arabia and then ordered his agents to back off and leave you alone. You are now free to return to JSC and resume preparation for the mission. You have also been reinstated as the commander of Odyssey. What we don't know is why."

"What about the other astronauts and Dr. Sanderson?" David asked.

"The others are fine. They weren't targeted. But Dr. Sanderson was under intense pressure and house arrest," said General Morris. "I'm proud to say that Franklin never gave us away. He even made up a wild story about you fleeing to Antarctica. There are probably agents still hunting for you among the penguins. I'm also happy to report that they left your mother alone, Jennifer."

Jennifer rose and hugged him. "General Morris, I don't know how we can ever thank you for all you have done for us. You probably saved our lives."

"It's all in the line of duty," he said with modesty. "I know you would have done the same for me if I was in need. It's been a pleasure serving you. Now you have less than two weeks to get ready for the mission. As your doctor, I'm now signing your release. I will see you again shortly before you leave Earth. There's one more surprise I have in store before you launch."

Within an hour, Jennifer and her family were free and on their way back to Houston. Justin and Sarah returned to their apartment and university studies in Austin. It was as if nothing had happened. Jennifer and David found their condo as they had left it four days earlier, even after federal agent searches. But they remained uneasy, never sure when things could suddenly change again. Fearing listening devices, they were careful to discuss the experiences of the past few days in writing alone.

CHAPTER 12

Getting On with It

The next morning, Jennifer, Allison, and David returned to their training area on the top floor of Building One to enthusiastic applause and hugs from the staff and fellow Odyssey astronauts. There was no sign of Sharkos, Grant, or Volper. It was back to normal, or so it seemed.

"We have missed all of you so much," Jennifer said, choking back tears. "I'm so thankful you are all okay. And, Franklin, thank you for all you did to protect and help us."

"We were even more concerned about each of you," Petrus said. "We were like meerkats without their lead female. Now we can get back to the business of forging ahead in preparation for the mission."

"Some of you may have heard that President Barton reversed himself on his plan to alter the Odyssey mission," Jennifer said. "Our help came from the strangest of places. I am told that the King of Saudi Arabia called him and made him change his mind. Why? I don't know."

"I do," said Fatima al-Tarabin, the Bedouin physician. "When we found out the nature of the troubles you were having, I called my uncle, Abdullah bin Hassan. His wife is a sister, a full and favorite sister, of King Salman of Saudi Arabia. She made the call and so did her brother, the king. He gave over two hundred million dollars to help finance President Barton's election and has offered another one hundred million to pay for his presidential library. The King told Barton he would not only go public with the story but would also impose an immediate oil embargo on the United States if Barton did not reverse himself, call off his agents, and let you resume your leadership on the mission. How is it that you say? 'He yanked Barton's chain.'"

"Oh, thank you, Fatima," Jennifer said, walking over to hug her. "You have saved our lives and the mission. You are indeed a wonderful doctor."

"I thought everyone would like a change of pace today to take our minds off what we've been through," said Dr. Sanderson, "so I have arranged a flight for all of you on the 'Vomit Comet.' It awaits you at Ellington, and the minibus will take you over as soon as you are ready."

Soon, all in flight suits, the astronauts boarded a large white Boeing 727 with the words "G-Force One" emblazoned on the side. The interior was padded on all surfaces except the windows. They strapped down during takeoff and the climb to thirty-eight thousand feet. The straps came off before the first parabolic dive, when the plane matched their rate of fall, giving the feeling of weightlessness. Everyone smiled. Some laughed or giggled nervously. The kids took to it easily, squealing with delight as they propelled themselves across the cabin, bouncing off walls, ceiling, and the floor. The NASA staff, who had come along, passed out food and drink pouches to give the astronauts a feel for eating in microgravity. For the first several dives, everyone seemed to enjoy themselves, but the effects of motion began to take its toll after the tenth dive. Ironically, none of the astronauts needed the air-sickness bags, diminishing the aura of the name "Vomit Comet." They returned to JSC to undergo intense medical checkups.

Late in the afternoon, the briefings and teachings continued. It was noted that the vessel being constructed outside the ISS was now entirely enclosed and impervious to radar scans. There was no response to multispectral radio transmissions from the space station. It could only be guessed as to what was happening inside. The outer skin shimmered with a pearly luster similar to the effect observed on the great Sphere before it enveloped the solar system. No seams, cracks, windows, writing, or features of any kind could be seen. Everyone felt a mix of curiosity and fear at the thought of spending two weeks inside a huge silver ball. The remaining weekdays were full from dawn to dusk with a mix of rigorous physical training and briefings. The last weekend before the scheduled launch on September 15, everyone boarded a 737 and flew out to Fort Davis, landing at the base that had been hastily developed two years earlier.

David and Jennifer hosted everyone, rooming them at the Indian Lodge at the Davis Mountains State Park, which had been entirely reserved for the crew. On Friday night, they were given a tour of the McDonald Observatory, getting to look through the great telescopes and see the details of the inner surface of the Sphere with greater clarity. Cities could be seen. Networks of lines indicated transport systems, like the rail or highways. Of great interest was the periodic occultation of each of the white dwarf stars that gave darkness to the surface beneath. The astronomers at the observatory talked about the changes in their work, focusing now on cartography. Solar astronomy, however, continued as before but with the incredible cessation of solar flares and storms. It was thought that the Sphere had somehow balanced the turbulent magnetic forces in and on the sun. Jennifer's colleagues also noted that the constant bombardment of cosmic rays had ceased completely after entering the Sphere. There was also talk about what one might see if standing on the outside surface of the Sphere. All the old star patterns in constellations known to humanity for millennia were gone with the movement to a different position in the galaxy. The question was how far the solar system had been moved. Late into the night, everyone travelled to the Indian Lodge for rest. David, Allison, and Jennifer hurried home to put the final touches on brunch for the next morning. Friends had cleaned up their Fort Davis home the previous week since it had been closed for two years while they trained in Houston. It seemed so natural to be back in their own home again. When Jennifer finally hit the pillow, she half expected to wake up in the morning and discover that the past two years were simply a dream.

Morning came, and Jennifer woke up to the same reality she and her family had been living. She was proud to share her home with the fellow crew members. They had become close in the previous four weeks. It felt like family to be together. Conversations, both serious and casual, were heard as they enjoyed the meal. The people of Fort Davis had worked hard to help Jennifer and David prepare a great experience for the astronauts on their final weekend. The media had been fooled into thinking the crew had headed to Las Vegas for their final fling before flight, so their activities were quiet and low key, free of reporters. By midday, they were transported by a school bus to Sam and Ida Wilson's ranch, where Jennifer, David, and their kids had enjoyed so many hours together. The local ranchers provided the horses and tack for a trail ride for the entire group. They spent the afternoon riding into and around the south end of the Davis Mountains. David was enjoying himself immensely, telling everyone about the plants and animals they were seeing. Vartan Bedevian joined in to enhance the geological aspects of the experience. The kids simply enjoyed the ride.

By the time they returned to the ranch house, everyone was getting tired and saddle sore. As they approached, the aroma of barbeque filled the air. Sam and friends from the community had put together a traditional Texas feast, complete with all the fixings. Justin and Sarah surprised their parents by driving in from Austin. Sarah's mother and sister joined them as well. Several kinds of cobbler were also offered, complete with homemade ice cream. They finished the day with a bonfire and s'mores for the kids. The adults preferred watching the glorious sunset from the great porch on the western side of the house. The bus returned them all to their lodgings in the deepening twilight.

The next morning, the entire crew decided to join David, Jennifer, and Allison for the Sunday worship service at the First United Methodist Church. The church was packed with friends and neighbors. Hymns were sung with feeling, prayers were prayed with fervor, and the message focused on Psalm 139, the topic being that there is no place anyone can get away from our wonderful God. The congregation had furnished a lavish covered-dish dinner afterward, and everyone lingered for a couple of hours. Jennifer and David hugged and thanked all their friends. Then the group headed for a tour of the historic Fort Davis, an outstanding restoration of a nineteenth century frontier fort. All too quickly, it was time to fly back to Houston. Most of the town came to the base to bid them Godspeed.

The last few days were frantic as everyone scrambled to pull together last-minute details of training and packing. NASA worked tirelessly to assemble the next-generation space suits that were nimble yet protective against the harsh environment of space. Every suit included the latest in communication and recording technology. Molecular-level storage systems allowed for years of recording, powered by newly developed batteries that could hold a strong charge for a decade. Some food, water, and medical supplies were to be carried along in compact caissons. A high-density storage device contained digital images of most of the books of the Library of Congress and the Oxford Library, in addition to all works of the major artists and composers. There were also extensive image collections of Earth's landscapes and various kinds of maps, all digitalized. Greetings from all the heads of state from every nation were also included. Most interesting was a moon rock, the first one collected by the astronauts from Apollo 11.

The closer the day of launch came, the more unreal it seemed. The Odyssey astronauts were to be delivered to the ISS by means of three new Orion capsules mounted atop untested Aries boosters. Training for piloting this new generation of launch vehicle had been intense. Even the kids knew some of the basics of emergency procedures. The spherical vessel still had no apparent port of access, so the astronauts were going to be launched in full space suits, dock with the ISS, enter with cargo, and then exit near the designated time of noon, universal time, to travel by tether and rocket pack to the surface of the vessel.

On the day before the launch, everyone had personal time to make a last communication with family. Justin and Sarah had brought Jennifer's mom from Midland, and they shared a quiet farewell breakfast at their condo. The early afternoon was busy with a worldwide press conference and speeches. Finally, the crew made one last expedition to Houston. They shared the last supper together at Mama Ninfa's on Navigation Street near downtown. Then they traveled to Jones Hall for the world premiere of a symphony composed in their honor by John Williams, who conducted the Houston Symphony Orchestra. It was a grand evening with exhilarating music. Jennifer didn't want it to end, but they would have to leave right after the concert for the flight to the Cape in Florida for the launch the next morning. It was just as well because no one would have slept that night.

The minibus took the crew to Ellington Field, where they disembarked with suits and luggage before a strangely familiar aviation artifact, the SST Concorde. One had been taken out of mothballs in Europe, flown to Ellington, and was ready to deliver them to the launch site. Soon they were aboard and aloft, on their way to Florida, or so they thought. Many of the crew were lost in thought, reading, or busy texting friends or family. The younger kids slept. Allison and Anastasia were playing a smartphone app together.

Jennifer turned to David and said, "Well, your optimism was right. After all we've been through, we're on the way now. In less than twelve hours, we will be on our way to space, to return who knows when. It all seems so unreal."

David listened carefully, as always. "And it's only the beginning. Just think of what we will tell our grandchildren."

Jennifer shot an inquisitive look at David. "Did Justin and Sarah tell you something that I should know?"

"Of course not," David said quickly. "I was thinking about twenty years from now. Consider what it will all look like in the rearview mirror. Maybe that will help us remember it better."

Jennifer paused to peer out her window. After a few moments of careful study, she turned to David with a concerned look and said, "David, I don't think we are headed east to Florida and the Kennedy Space Center. I'm still seeing the lights of towns, cities, and highways, with no hint of the darkness of water we should see if over the Gulf of Mexico. With this Concorde, we should get to Florida in under an hour, and we've been airborne for seventy-five minutes now. I would guess we are headed west."

David stared blankly and offered, "Do you want me to go to the cockpit to make sure?"

"No," she said. "I'm jumpy after all we've been through."

Just then, the cockpit door opened and out stepped General Morris. He looked directly at Jennifer with a big smile and said, "I promised you one more surprise before you left, Jennifer."

Jennifer looked puzzled. "This Concorde flight?"

"No," he said, laughing. "We are headed west, deep into the Pacific Ocean. Several of my sources warned me that there was a bomb on the first rocket to launch tomorrow. It was set to detonate only a thousand feet above the launch pad, killing everyone on board. That would have been your capsule, Jennifer. Of course that 'tragic accident' would have caused the other two launches to be scrubbed indefinitely. After hearing of the plan, I decided to send you a different way to get you safely up to the ISS."

He sat down in an open seat across the aisle from David and resumed. "We are taking you to where DARPA has maintained a fleet of space shuttles identical to the ones recently retired. These are top-secret versions that continue to serve the space transport needs of our country. Four of them will launch and carry you and your luggage to the ISS."

"Are we headed to Area 51?" David asked.

"No," General Morris said. "That place is too public. It has served as a decoy for the last several decades—the perfect diversion for a curious public. The real action was taking place at Johnston Atoll, a tiny coral island about eight hundred miles west south west of Hawaii. It's about one and a half miles long and about seven hundred yards across. Johnston Atoll has been the perfect place for all kinds of black projects, far from prying eyes. We are due there in about an hour. That will be about eight in the evening, local time. Enjoy the flight."

He got up and returned to the cockpit.

CHAPTER 13

Launch Day

Allison leaned back in her seat in front of David and Jennifer. She said, "Look, Mom, the sunrise. We must be getting close to Cape Canaveral."

"No, dear," said Jennifer with a grin. "What you are seeing is today's sunset. The Concorde is flying at twelve hundred miles per hour and has caught up with the evening over the middle of the Pacific. The plans have changed. We're launching from another place in another way from the original plan."

Allison looked hard at her mom and said, "Let me guess. General Morris's doing."

Soon they were slowing and descending ever lower toward the trackless waters of the Pacific. No land or ship was in sight anywhere. Landing gear was deployed with a bump and slight drag. The astronauts began to wonder if they were about to ditch in the ocean. Descent and deceleration continued. They could see the spray from the waves and fish jumping up from the water. Suddenly, the plane passed over a rocky breakwater and the tires squealed on touchdown a second later. They were thrown forward as the flaps, thrust reversers, and brakes kicked in. Outside the windows was a view dominated by ocean water. Everyone wondered how far the runway extended. There was a collective sigh of relief when the plane finally stopped, and they were still on solid ground. General Morris came out of the cockpit again and motioned to the attendant to open the rear stairway.

"We're here!" he said. "No time to lose. Everyone, get your suits, gear, and luggage. I'm due back in Washington in several hours, and you are due up there about the same time."

Everyone blinked at the brilliance of the setting sun over the western side of the thin strip of land. They and all their gear were moved to a paved area at the side of the runway. It looked like a building may have been there at one time. There was little else to the island except for a few seabirds and the skeletal remains of some storm-battered buildings.

"Godspeed to you all!" General Morris said, as he and the attendant returned to the stairway. They climbed into the Concorde. The stairway retracted, and the plane taxied around, readying for takeoff. Much to the crew's shock, the Concorde's engines screamed to life. It roared down the runway and slowly lifted off and away.

Everyone looked at Jennifer for answers.

"This wasn't in the plans, Jennifer," said Alice Cly. "And now here we are, stranded in the middle of the Pacific Ocean. We have a ride to catch in less than ten hours. How are we going to get there?"

"I wish we had a couple of our great canoes," said Apiranoa Ngata. "Even if we missed our ride to the Rim, I could get us back to civilization."

"Can you imagine what the people at the Cape are doing about now?" said Becky Ishulutak. "They will probably assume that our plane went down somewhere over the Gulf."

"Yes, and imagine their surprise when we show up at the ISS," David said.

"But how, Dad?" Allison asked. "It's a long way up there, and I don't see anything down here but water, rocks, and a few seagulls. You wanted to get away from it all. Now you have really done it."

Jennifer broke her silence. "I know General Morris, and he won't leave us abandoned and deserted. He said there was another surprise. I get the feeling it is coming soon."

As the minutes passed, some sat on their luggage. Others walked to various points on the deserted atoll, inspecting the ruined remains of old buildings and docks. The cool breeze of the Pacific picked up as the sun set below the horizon, filling the sky with a varied palette of yellows, oranges, and reds. No one appreciated the grand beauty. Despair was beginning to set in with the darkness. David and several others broke out some flashlights from among their gear. Allison gave the other kids some snacks from their provisions.

Without warning, a tremor began to shake what land there was.

"Great!" exclaimed Aizam. "First we are dropped off in the most remote place on Earth, and now we will suffer a massive earthquake."

"Just be glad there are no structures or hillsides to fall on us," said Vartan.

"Look over there, in the middle of the runway!" shouted Anastasia.

The younger kids screamed as a large square of the runway dropped away, much like the elevator on an aircraft carrier. Light came from the growing gap. Just as they approached the opening, it rose to close again. Several uniformed men and some carts were on top. When the great door closed, they came and welcomed the crew, picked up their luggage and gear, and moved everyone and everything to the middle of the great square, which, once again, began to descend into the depths below the island. Everyone was astonished at the depth and massive scale of what was a huge, subterranean base, full of activity, machinery, aircraft, and equipment of every description. It looked as if the bottom of the massive base extended at least twenty stories or more. The base was shaped like a giant bell, expanding ever wider the lower the level. The lowest levels they could make out seemed to extend for over half a mile in all directions. The seamount supporting the Atoll had been radically re-engineered to accommodate this—the most secret of America's military bases.

Lower down, the sight of seven shuttles came into view. Four of them were mounted on mobile launch platforms. Streams of vapor indicated they were being fueled up for immediate launch. These shuttles were about thirty percent larger than the ones recently retired from NASA. They lacked the brilliant white color on the upper surfaces of the fuselages and wings. Like the X-53 that Jennifer, David, and Allison had flown in almost two months ago, their upper surfaces were covered with the same electronic stealth cloaking material that made them shimmer and fade, almost like dull flames.

"They are larger than the civilian shuttles," Jennifer noted.

An air force officer who escorted them turned and said, "Yes, they have been enhanced with the extra power needed to reach high orbit, a feature helpful in deploying satellites in geostationary orbit. We could even use one to get to the moon. Orbit, that is. Landing there would not allow a takeoff. Notice the enhanced boosters, including a larger liquid-fuel tank and two more solid rocket boosters."

The elevator stopped at a level even with the cockpits of the upright shuttles.

"Come with us," he said. "We must get you ready and inside for launch in thirty minutes."

Uniformed airmen assisted the crew with getting into their space suits. The luggage and gear had already been stowed aboard when the crew was divided into groups of five, with the exception of David, Allison, and Jennifer. They were led to the shuttles, where they entered and settled into their seats in the crew sections. Each shuttle already had a pair of pilot astronauts, who were aboard to fly the crew to the ISS and then return the shuttles back to the base.

As soon as everyone was securely fastened in, the hatches were closed. The first shuttle, which held Jennifer, David, and Allison, was moved out onto the massive elevator and raised to the surface. The mobile platform moved it a few hundred yards down the runway and off to a large square, concrete pad to the side. Jennifer, David, and Allison couldn't see much from their vantage point in the crew cabin below the flight deck where the pilots sat, but the video monitor changed camera views and gave them perspective on what was happening. The next shuttle, on its mobile platform, was already emerging from the great opening in the runway when they heard the launch status check being called off. Each systems controller reported to the NASA test director their "go" response in proper sequence. They could hear his voice call to the launch director, "We are go for launch." Then the countdown resumed from T minus twenty seconds and counting, soon reaching zero.

"This is it!" said Jennifer with giddy excitement. She reached out to hold David and Allison's hands. They were seated on either side of her.

"Wow!" said Allison. "If my friends could see me now."

"I wonder what Juan Sebastián de Elcano would make of this," David said.

As the full thrust of the booster and shuttle engines roared forth, the entire shuttle rattled and shook like an old train going way too fast on loose tracks. Allison looked at her parents in panic. Jennifer gave her a reassuring smile and whispered, "Love you, kid." David was grinning like a child in a candy store. At first, the shuttle seemed to hover, but soon it began its ascent and rolled over, steadily climbing ever upward into the night sky. The shuttle flew on its back at this part of the climb. The earth began to fall beneath them. The dawn's early light welcomed them as the shuttle climbed eastward toward orbit. All three of them were startled when the shuttle jettisoned the solid rocket boosters and again when the liquid-fuel tank separated. Allison was the first to notice that the sky was now black, with the blue atmosphere falling behind them to the west.

"Wow!" exclaimed Allison. "We're off again and out of this world."

"What a trip! said David, rapt in wonder.

Jennifer tightened her grip on each of their hands and said, "Let's pray. Lord, thank you for this awesome moment and the miraculous life you have given us. We know you are already making a way for us in this incredible journey. Use us to serve you and your people in all we do. In Jesus's name. Amen."

The special phone Jennifer had guarded for the past two years honked to life again. She quickly pulled it out of a suit pocket and synchronized it with her suit com system.

"Hello, Jennifer," said General Morris. "I'm sorry to have left you so suddenly back there at Johnston Atoll. Your arrival at the ISS will come as a big surprise.

"There are two pilots in every shuttle—one from NASA, who knows how to dock at the ISS, and one of ours, who can land them back at Johnston Atoll," he said. "You are in very capable hands. Once you arrive at the ISS, you will be able to make full contact with Mission Control in Houston. Soon the world will know more about one of the military's greatest secrets, but it was for a good cause. Godspeed to you and yours. I look forward to seeing you again when you return."

"Thanks again, General," Jennifer said. "We'll try to bring you a gift from the Rim. Jennifer out."

The other three shuttles followed in succession on their journeys to deliver more of the Odyssey crew to the ISS. Everyone experienced an awe-filled mix of wonder and fear as they rushed to join the first shuttle, now well into orbit and on its way to the station and the future of humanity.

Meanwhile, there was worldwide concern over the failure of the Odyssey astronauts' Concorde to arrive at the Kennedy Space Center. Hundreds of planes frantically searched the Gulf of Mexico in the early hours of the morning. The media was hinting at the worst-case scenario.

CHAPTER 14

It Begins

Millicent Grant was dressed in an orlan, a Russian space suit, minus the helmet. She was broadcasting live from the International Space Station. The previous day, she and George Sharkos had arrived courtesy of the American taxpayer and the Russian Soyuz capsule to record the beginning of their intended journey aboard the sphere outside the station. She attached her camera to the wall of the cupola, where Alexi Bugarin, one of the station's cosmonauts, was trying to control routine station operations. Millicent positioned the camera to get the best angle of her face and also show the Earth view through the top window.

"As you can see from the split-screen shot," she continued, "things are pretty somber at the Kennedy Space Center, where the Odyssey crew of eighteen invitees were due to arrive over nine hours ago. We can only assume that their plane was lost somewhere over the Gulf of Mexico last night. Ships and planes are furiously searching the waters, as are satellites high above, for any sign of survivors. It is a terrible loss."

She began to show hints of a grin but caught herself. Bugarin got excited and began to speak in Russian. Then, realizing he was on international television, he said, "I just received a request from a shuttle to dock at PMA number two. What shuttle? They have all gone to museums." He looked at Grant in confusion.

She was equally confused and asked, "Alexi, what is a PMA?"

"It is a pressurized mating adapter, or docking port," he said.

Outside the window, a distant shuttle could be seen rapidly approaching. Its cargo-bay hatch was opened, revealing a docking adapter in the front end of the bay where the crew could transfer into the station once docked.

"You are go for docking," Alexi said, with concern.

"There will be three more shuttles after this one," the voice on the com said. "We will dock for a few minutes to transfer our three passengers. There are fifteen more coming. Make room for them and their cargo. Their stay will be brief."

Millicent instantly realized who the upcoming visitors were. She cursed under her breath and then regained her professional composure, remembering that she was live before several billion people back on Earth.

"This is incredible!" she said. "It looks like the eighteen Odyssey astronauts were not lost after all. Four space shuttles are about to deliver them here to the International Space Station. Let's see if I can get you a shot of the first one coming in."

The shuttle conducted several elegant maneuvers as it drew nearer to PMA number two. The Canada Arm 2 was deployed to assist with its final approach. Grant and Bugarin both felt the gentle bump as the docking was completed. Lights flashed on the consoles, indicating success.

Within a few minutes, the hatch was opened, and Jennifer emerged in her streamlined extravehicular mobility unit (EMU) minus the life support subsystem (LSS). Her helmet visor was open, revealing a radiant smile. Tied to her and trailing behind was her LSS. Grant was shooting the entire scene while several feet away. Off camera, Sharkos gnashed his teeth.

"Welcome aboard, Dr. Bass," said one of the American ISS crew members.

"What a story!" Millicent tried to sound excited. "Jennifer, how did you get here? And why this way?"

Just inside the hatch opening, Jennifer paused, opened her helmet, and reset her com system. She chose to ignore Grant's question. "Houston," she said. "Do you read me now? Odyssey here. This is Dr. Jennifer Bass. I have just arrived at the ISS with two other crew members. The other fifteen will be here shortly."

There was a brief gasp as the flight director composed herself. "Jennifer! Odyssey! How wonderful to hear from you and now see you. How did you get up here? Where did those shuttles come from?"

"I can't explain much right now," Jennifer interrupted. "We must hustle to prepare for our EVA over to the Sphere. I'm sorry we gave all of you such a shock."

Jennifer began to float by the camera as she worked her way toward the Harmony node number two, being directed by a station crew member to continue on to the Destiny Lab. She only smiled, nodded, and waved at Millicent and her camera. Allison soon followed, also suited up in her EMU. She lost her smile when she spotted Grant, recalling their time together at JSC several weeks earlier. David came last, lingering to help off-load gear and luggage for the crew. Before long, the first shuttle was finished, undocked, and headed home. As soon as it had left, the second one docked. The same process was repeated for the other two shuttles.

Within an hour, all eighteen Odyssey astronauts had been delivered, along with all of their necessary gear. Mission control in Houston was in full contact, and Jennifer explained their unusual arrival. They gave her a green light to proceed with the mission. Movement around the station was difficult with the mission astronauts in EMUs, the six ISS crew members, and Grant and Sharkos. Grant continued to try and get video feed and ask questions. Sharkos was demanding answers. Jennifer and the members of her crew were busy getting fully rigged for their extravehicular activity (EVA) by tether to the waiting sphere. There was still no change in the sphere, nor was there any message as to procedures for the astronaut transfer process. In less than an hour, all eighteen crew members had to be outside and moving toward the Sphere with their gear in tow. There were no plans from that point on. No one knew what would happen at noon. Jennifer even joked that she intended to knock loudly on the skin of the vessel.

It was time for them to begin exiting the station two at a time through the Quest airlock. A queue had formed through the Unity node number one and into three other parts of the station. Jennifer was set to enter the lock when she began to look for the tether.

"Where's the tether?" she asked over the com.

"I know it was transferred in from the shuttle," David said firmly. "Where could it have gone?"

The rest of the Odyssey mission crew and the station crew began to look around. Their intensity and concern rose as the moments passed. Sharkos shot a knowing look at Grant and winked with a smile.

"I need to speak to Dr. Bugarin," Jennifer said with a hint of panic.

Alexi worked his way through to the Unity node.

"Our people have looked everywhere," he said nervously.

"Is there anything we can use in place of the tether?" Jennifer asked.

"Nothing that could take all eighteen of you over the distance needed to reach the sphere," he said.

"I am open to suggestions, people," Jennifer said.

"What about the Canada Arm 2?" Becky Ishulutak asked.

"No way it could reach," said one of the station crew members.

Grant, who was transmitting the proceedings with limited comment, spoke up and asked, "Well, what are you going to do now, Dr. Bass?"

"Dr. Bugarin," Jennifer said. "Please return to the control center and try hailing the sphere again. Let them know we're ready over here."

"Sorry, Dr. Bass," said Alexi over the com. "There's still no response, and the Sphere just hovers there like it has for the last forty days. It hasn't changed position, matching our maneuvers precisely when we had to activate thrusters to climb to a higher orbit."

Silence fell over everyone as they looked back and forth at one another, the clock ticking down the last few seconds to noon. Jennifer closed her eyes in silent prayer.

Precisely at noon, the sphere slowly drew closer to the ISS.

"Look!" shouted Alexi over the com. "It's coming to us!"

Everyone looked at the monitors placed throughout the station. The sphere halted only five meters from the docking port recently used by the shuttles. Then a long white tube, which looked like the siphon on a clam, emerged from the closest point and attached to the PMA.

Jennifer made her way through the crush of crew members and through three sections back to the PMA, where she had entered only an hour before. The others quickly reversed their lineup and readied their gear. As Jennifer approached the hatch, it opened by itself. A mild, sweet fragrance, like a rose, wafted past her. Closing her helmet, she turned to the others and said, "This is it! Let's go!"

As Jennifer moved into the passageway headfirst, she began to feel gravity and stopped. She pulled back, grasped the handlebars at the mouth of the hatch, and swung her legs inside. She entered feet first, sliding like a child through the tube and into a large, open chamber of uncertain size. Jennifer felt the pull of normal gravity and was able to stand after having slid in on her behind.

"That may have been one small step for Neil Armstrong," Jennifer mused aloud, "but it was one big slide for me."

She began to look around at the surprisingly large chamber. There were no windows, controls, furniture, or fixtures of any kind. White light suffused the area, which seemed to stretch a great distance from the portal she had entered. Jennifer was burning with curiosity but also felt an overwhelming feeling of calm.

She turned back to the opening and said through her com, "What are you waiting for? Come on in!"

Allison came sliding in next, soon joined by Aizam, Fatima, and Vartan. Each of them rose and stood transfixed in wonder. Then the luggage began to slide in. Vartan and Aizam began to stack it off to the side. Within minutes, everyone else had joined them, with David bringing up the rear.

"Alexi," Jennifer said over her com, "we're all aboard. Everything's fine over here. Somehow they have synthetic gravity."

Just then, an angry scream and cursing could be heard from the station's end of the tube. It was Grant and Sharkos, fully suited up. She was trying to enter the hatch, only to find herself unable to move into position to enter. In her struggle, she broke her camera, and the network feed was lost. Sharkos found himself moving helplessly in slow motion. Their muscles were not responding to their brains. The hatch began to close on its own, leaving them behind. Only the invited would make the journey. When it was sealed, the tube was retracted back into the sphere, and it returned to its previous position a couple of hundred meters forward of the station.

Jennifer and the others were relieved to hear that they still had contact with the station and Mission Control in Houston.

"Houston," Jennifer said. "Odyssey here. We're fine. Give our thanks to Commander Bugarin and the crew of the ISS for their hospitality. Everyone is accounted for. The next step is up to our friends from the Rim. Now it begins."

CHAPTER 15

The Messenger Speaks

All the astronauts stared at their surroundings. Their recording and transmission systems were fully operational. Their com from Houston was quiet. David was the first to notice that the atmospheric analyzer on his wrist indicated normal, earthlike conditions. He boldly opened and took off his helmet. Jennifer looked at him with concern.

"It's fine," David said. "The air even smells better than what was over there in the ISS."

The rest of the crew began to open their helmets. Some removed theirs. Randy, Andy, Toma, and Kushe started to scamper off. Their elders quickly called them back to the group. They began to huddle together in a circle, some facing in, while others were turned out, still trying to understand what they were seeing.

"What do you make of it, Jennifer?" Petrus asked.

"It's not what I expected," she said. "I thought there would be a highly structured and confined place like the ISS."

"Odyssey, this is Houston," said the com signal. "We can't make out anything through your video feeds other than you, your gear, and the white light. Can you see anything else?"

"Houston, Jennifer here," she said. "Nothing so far. This chamber appears to occupy almost all the inside of the sphere, except there is a flat, firm surface beneath our feet. The air is fine, so we have opened up. There's no sign of any fixtures, panels, or controls."

"Mom, maybe we should try speaking to it, or them, or whoever," Allison suggested.

Jennifer smiled at her insightful daughter, grateful that she had come along. She closed her eyes again for a brief, silent prayer.

Jennifer began. "Hello to whoever is here with us. We come in peace. All of those you invited are now here. We are reporting for duty."

There was a pause for a few seconds and then a still, small voice said, "Welcome. It is wonderful that you came."

"Where are you?" Theodora asked as everyone looked around, not sure of the direction of the voice.

"I am the sphere that you have entered," the voice replied. "I will now take you out to the Rim of the Great Sphere. The trip will take about two of your weeks."

"Are you a biological life-form or silicon based?" Timujin Ji asked.

"I am what you would consider a machine, though I also have some manufactured biological components," the voice said.

Alice said, "We understand that you know who we are. Who are you? Or what should we call you?"

"Whatever you like, Alice," the voice said.

"How about 'Messenger'?" offered Jennifer.

"That is fine," Messenger said.

"So what's next, Messenger?" Jennifer asked.

"We must get underway on our journey," it said. "In front of you is the view outside. It has been rotated up to eye level so you will not be disoriented."

The area in front of the crew became as clear as if they were outside. The ISS was to their left, and the Earth to the right.

"What would it look like in the real view?" Becky asked.

Suddenly, the entire interior became transparent with no visible structure. The black sky surrounded them except for the

ISS floating behind them at a thousand meters, and the Earth was below their feet. The sun shone brightly in opposition to the Earth. The kids began stomping their feet against the invisible floor. Everyone began to feel agoraphobic hovering in midspace. The view then returned to the original one.

"We are now accelerating," Messenger said. "You will feel no discomfort. Synthetic gravity is energy intensive and challenging to sustain at these levels in objects of mass as small as this. So the acceleration curve will continue at one G until midway, where this vessel will rotate and decelerate at the same rate."

The ISS began to slowly fall into the distance. The Earth seemed to hold its full size a while longer, but gradually, it, too, began to shrink.

"How are you driving this sphere?" Becky asked.

"It is what you might call gravitic drive," Messenger replied. "It uses the select focusing of several larger subatomic-particle streams of dark matter in near-absolute-zero conditions. These streams bend the contours of the seventh and eighth dimensions, resulting in an enormous attractive force that is easily controlled. Think of it like the effect of the wind on a sailing ship."

"What do you mean 'seventh and eighth dimensions'?" Vartan asked.

"Those are a few of the higher dimensions that are parallel or accessible on the quantum level," Messenger continued. "When they are distorted, there is an enormous quantity of energy available to bend and manipulate time-space."

The crew was beginning to feel like six-year-olds in a calculus class.

"Please make yourselves comfortable," said Messenger.

There was a cluster of couches and soft chairs that materialized in front of them. Some jumped back at the sudden appearance.

"How did you do that?" Aizam asked.

"There are many things I can do through the manipulation of dark matter and the higher dimensions," said Messenger. "I anticipated your need to sit down as you ask questions."

"We have so many questions," David said. "I don't know if we have time to ask them all in two weeks."

"You will feel more relaxed if you take off your EMUs," it said.

At that invitation, they began to doff their cumbersome suits, leaving the single-piece jumpsuit-style flight suits. They all retained their headsets with their com systems and video cameras. Soon most were seated in the plush chairs. Allison and Anastasia walked away to find walls. At fifty meters, they stopped, not wanting to lose sight of the others.

"How far does this go?" Allison asked.

"As far as it needs to," said Messenger.

"How far is that?" Anastasia queried.

"It can be thousands of kilometers or just a centimeter. I am capable of expanding and contracting space with a similar technology to that which drives this vessel," it said.

They looked at each other with wide eyes and made their way back to the rest of the crew.

"Why did you choose us over all the other people on Earth?" Jennifer asked.

"You were chosen by the people who sent me," Messenger replied. "It took a long time of careful study and discussion to select you. There are many others who could have come too. Your professions, personalities, and character were key components. There were over a thousand variables that were used. We gathered information on you through millions of microprobes that were sent to Earth when you entered the Great Sphere."

"Why did you invite children?" Allison asked.

"We did not want to separate you from your parents or guardians," it said. "You and your younger colleagues may be the most interesting of your crew."

"What do you intend to do with us?" Petrus asked.

"Nothing without your permission," Messenger said. "You want to make first contact with the people on the Rim, so I was sent to bring you back. You will be taken to a hovering space station a thousand kilometers above the surface, where you will meet these people. What you do from that point on is up to you."

"You call them 'people,'" said Maria. "Are they similar to us?"

Messenger paused, as if in thought, and then said, "In many ways, yes. But they are also quite different. That is all I can tell you."

"Did they build and drive the Great Sphere?" David asked.

"No," it said. "They were taken on board thousands of years ago."

"Who, then, built and flies this Great Sphere?" Becky asked.

"I do not know," Messenger said. "It was constructed over a period of tens of thousands of years by someone unknown to me. It is about six billion years old and comes from the other side of this galaxy."

"Are the builders still living here?" she continued.

"I was built only a few months ago," it said. "That information is not in my programming."

"What is the purpose of the Great Sphere?" Jennifer asked.

"It travels the galaxy in search of sentient creatures on worlds that are in trouble," it said. "That trouble can be natural or self-inflicted social disasters. Your world faces two threats. The first one was the cosmic threat from the black hole. That was easy to fix with the envelopment and relocation of your solar system using the technology we have to expand and contract space-time. The second one is common to worlds of your level of development—self-inflicted trauma from ceaseless conflict and warfare. The major factors causing social and political instability are at dangerous levels. The fix for that is far more complicated. The prognosis for the midterm, the next five years, is grim. The Sphere may have come too late."

The crew was stunned to hear this news. They had been so busy preparing for the Odyssey mission that world news and trends had eluded their attention. They immediately thought of their families and friends back home on Earth.

"As you would say, it is time for a break," Messenger said. "From your memories, I have synthesized many of your favorite foods. Help yourself."

A long table with dozens of platters full of a wide variety of cuisines appeared next to the chairs. Plates and utensils were laid on one end. When everyone walked over to begin to serve themselves, Jennifer offered to return thanks for the food. Everyone joined hands.

She closed her eyes, paused for a moment, and prayed, "Lord, thank you for our safe arrival in this vessel. Thank you for the wonderful food we are about to enjoy. Please help us do our best to carry out our responsibilities. Bless and protect our families back home. Please bless those who are working for peace and good in our world. And please bless the people and creatures on the Rim. In Jesus's name we ask."

"Amen," said Messenger.

Everyone opened their eyes in surprise, but the attraction of the food was irresistible, so they began loading up their plates. They ate well, not having had food for over twelve hours. Several remarked that it was the best they had ever had. There was little conversation during the meal. When everyone had finished, the table vanished, along with their empty plates, which were scattered around the seating area.

"That's going to take some getting used to," Alice said.

"I like this food much better than the space food NASA gave us," Anastasia responded.

"It's sure wonderful not to worry about cleaning up or washing dishes," Allison added.

"What about our living quarters?" Theodora wondered aloud. "Are we supposed to sleep here in these chairs?"

"As the mother of two four year olds," Becky said, "what about bathroom facilities? Has anyone seen anything like a toilet?"

"Let's ask Messenger," Vartan suggested.

"What about it, Messenger?" David asked.

"Your sleeping quarters will materialize as needed," it replied. "Toilet facilities are not needed. Your food contained nanorobots that will establish themselves in your lower colons and bladders. All waste products will be transported away through microscopic subspace passages. You may have already noticed that none of you has felt the need for a bathroom."

"What about the long-term effects on our urinary and alimentary systems?" Fatima asked. "Are those nanorobots removable? What about atrophy in our sphincter muscles?"

"There are no long-term problems," Messenger said. "When you return to Earth, they are small enough to be eliminated without any trouble. If you prefer, you may return to the diapers, catheters, catchment bags, and odors found on your ISS."

Everyone looked around, and a general consensus was quickly reached that they would prefer to take the risks with the new technology.

"You may also become worried about microbes," said Messenger. "There is another set of nanorobots that have entered your bloodstream and cleansed your bodies of viruses and harmful bacteria. You will never have a cold or flu again. Your immune systems are also being fine-tuned to prevent cancer, lupus, and even allergies. There are no biohazards in those you will meet on the Rim."

"What will Messenger think of next?" Jennifer remarked. "What are we to do now?"

"Anything you like," Messenger replied. "May I suggest further decor to make you feel at home here? First, I will arrange this area like a control center, with video feeds from spots on the outside of the vessel. I will add readouts for velocity, rate of acceleration, and distances from Earth and to the Rim. A chart marking our progress from start to finish will be helpful. Here is a screen giving live video from NASA. They have been able to see you; now you can see them." All the equipment appeared as Messenger spoke.

The people at Mission Control in Houston all waved. The crew waved back.

"What are we going to do about the time lag once we have gone some distance from Earth?" Becky asked.

"I have left a transceiver in orbit with direct links to NASA and other communication links," Messenger said. "The rest of that transceiver is on board with us. It is linked together through a higher dimension that allows us to have real-time, instant communication with Earth all the way to the Rim, with no time lag. Personal communication is available in addition to official connections to Mission Control. So, Allison, you will be able to text message your friends back in Houston."

Allison beamed and pulled out her smartphone. "It's got a full signal, Mom!" she said with glee. Immediately, she began texting and sending pictures.

"As for your living quarters," Messenger said, "I will create them on a level above this one. Each of you will have a spacious room similar to what you enjoyed at home. Children will room with their parents. A shower and sink are provided in each room. Every room will also have a window with a view to the outside that can be changed in perspective and magnification."

A ceiling appeared three meters above their heads. A couple of stairways leading upward materialized at either end of the room where they were seated.

"Perhaps you would like to see your quarters and unpack your personal belongings. If you desire any changes, call me by name and ask," said Messenger. "When you feel settled in, you would be welcome to return here to resume our discussion."

Everyone retrieved personal luggage from among the baggage and left for the upstairs quarters. When they got to the top of the stairs, it felt very familiar. Everyone already knew the way to their own rooms. Jennifer and David were delighted to find their suite to be a close replica of their home back in Fort Davis, complete with French doors that opened onto the porch. The room was accurate in every detail, even with the familiar smells. There was a view beyond the porch that seemed real.

"David!" said Jennifer with excitement. "This is amazing! How did Messenger get this so real? Wait! My office and bookshelves are in the guest room at home. Here, they're right in that corner. Remember that you and I had talked about moving it someday."

Allison opened the closet door in her parent's room to be surprised that it led directly into her room. "It's not like this at home," she said. "But it will do. Maybe Messenger can make some changes I've always wanted, like painting the room a different color."

"Messenger," David said, "thanks. This is wonderful. You've thought of everything."

"You are most welcome," it said.

There was a large screen above Jennifer's desk. It was similar to the ones in the control room downstairs.

"Messenger," Jennifer said. "Can you connect us to my mother and our kids in Austin?"

"No problem," it said. "Give me about three minutes.

David, Jennifer, and Allison pulled up chairs around the desk. A second screen appeared. Soon Jennifer's mom had answered the hail on her computer at home in Midland and appeared on the screen to the right.

"Jennifer, is that you?" she asked.

"Yes, Mom, it sure is," Jennifer responded. "David and Allison are here too."

"What's been going on with you?" her mom asked. "The TV said you were lost and then found at the station coming in on strange ships. Are you okay?"

"Of course, Mom," Jennifer said. "In fact, we're inside the spherical vessel that is already on its way to the surface of the Rim. Can you see Sarah? She's on our other screen now."

"Yes, my computer screen split the view," she replied.

"Hey, y'all," Sarah said, leaning closer to her computer's camera, then turning back. "Hey, Justin, get in here! Mom, Dad, and Allison are linked up, along with your grandmother."

Soon Justin was seated next to Sarah. "Wow! It's really you," Justin exclaimed. "How's it going out there?"

"We're just fine, Son," David said. "The vessel is well underway. We decided to call it 'Messenger.' The place is very comfortable."

"It looks like you're back home," Justin replied. "Have you played a trick on everyone?"

"No, Messenger has replicated everything in great detail," said Jennifer.

"Watch this," Allison said. "Messenger, change our room to be the inside of our condo in Houston."

Just then, their entire surroundings changed instantly to their living area inside of the Endeavor at Clear Lake.

"That's incredible," remarked Sarah. "How does Messenger do that?"

"It's using advanced technology that is centuries ahead of our understanding," David said. "We wish you were with us out here."

"Messenger tells us that we will be able to have real-time visits like this all the way to the Rim," Allison said. "It's something to do with a transceiver in orbit and on this ship with a connection through a higher dimension that allows instant communication."

"You're getting pretty good at explaining things, kid," said Justin with a hint of pride in his younger sister. "We've followed most of what you've been doing inside of Messenger through the NASA channel and website. It's incredible what's happening to you out there. I want to hear more about specifics on engineering. It might impress my professors."

"Can we call you?" Jennifer's mom asked.

"I'm not sure," Jennifer answered. "Messenger, how can they contact us?"

"I have loaded special apps into their computers and smartphones," it said. "All they need to do is turn those devices on and then ask to speak to you. I will make the connection here instantly."

"Messenger," Justin asked, "can I visit with you and ask questions like the astronauts do?"

"Like you, Justin, my attention is limited," Messenger replied. "It would be complicated for me with all the tasks I have here. My primary responsibility is to be available to the crew to meet their needs. I will not be able to instruct you on advanced engineering because the demands here are too great."

"Justin, you will have to learn like the rest of us did," said David. "Maybe you and Sarah will be on a future mission."

"We need to sign off for now," Jennifer said. "I want to get back to the control room and check in with Mission Control in Houston. Let's talk again soon. We love y'all. J, T, and A out."

A couple of hours later, they returned downstairs, others were also leaving their quarters. Many had made contact with their families back home as well. Some had changed to casual clothes with Messenger's ability to create things on demand. Randy and Andy had enjoyed a good nap and ran down the stairs to the loungelike seating area. In the center of the ring of chairs was a huge pile of Lego blocks waiting for the kids. The chairs and blocks were all atop a large, soft rug. The twins, Kushe, and Toma squealed with delight and instantly began to make things.

"Nice touch, Messenger," Jennifer said.

"I anticipated their needs," it said. "If I miss something, do not be afraid to ask."

Jennifer walked over to the large central screen with the image of Mission Control back in Houston.

"Houston, Odyssey here," she said. "Everything couldn't have gone better. Everyone is well and excited to be on board. Is there anything you require of us?"

"Negative, Odyssey," the Flight director said. "Everyone has enjoyed watching and learning along with you. Your host has even provided complete telemetry on your medical conditions and environment. Like you, we feel we have gone back to school to learn. We'll let you know if something comes up. Your questions are similar to ones we would have asked. Great work. We'll talk again soon. Over."

"Copy that, Houston," Jennifer said. "Odyssey out."

Jennifer returned to the seating area and took a seat among the crew.

"How are you doing?" she asked. "Is everyone comfortable?"

Everyone nodded or gave short answers indicating a high level of satisfaction.

"Shall we resume questions?" Jennifer asked.

There were more nods and general assent.

"Messenger," Aizam asked, "do we need to learn a new language to communicate with the 'people' we meet on the Rim?"

"No, they are telepathic and capable of speaking in your language already," it said.

Everyone looked a little concerned at this revelation.

"How much of our minds can they read?" asked Vartan. "For that matter, how much can you read?"

"It is more art than science," Messenger said. "We are not able to fathom the entire scope and depth of your minds. Feelings and thoughts that are near the surface are apparent. For those on the Rim, it is a natural, inborn capacity. For me, it involves a wide variety of our advanced technologies and requires a great deal of my processing capacity to read the larger codas. There is much that I miss."

"Can we learn to read minds?" Anastasia asked.

"Yes, in time," Messenger said. "It takes a lot of training and discipline, but your minds do have that capacity. Those on the Rim may decide to teach you. It is beyond my programming."

Toma looked up from his work constructing a Lego castle. He and the other young ones had been listening.

"Messenger, will we ever go back home to Earth again?" he asked.

The older crew members perked up at this question.

"Yes," said Messenger. "I will return any and all who choose to go. The length of your stay is up to you. Some may decide to stay on the Rim."

"Being a geophysicist," Vartan said, "I would like to know if the land masses we saw in the atlas you downloaded are dynamic. Are there plate tectonics?"

"In places where volcanism is essential to the ecology, yes," said Messenger.

"Then I must also know about gravity," Vartan continued. "The Great Sphere is so massive that if the same laws of physics apply there as on Earth, the gravity would crush any life-forms like us. Is that not so?"

"You are correct," it said. "The Great Sphere is capable of attenuating gravity to the level needed in that area of the interior surface. The region where we are headed is tuned to what you would call 'one gravity.'"

"How do you attenuate gravity?" he continued.

"Beneath the surface of the Rim's interior are vast regions with energy intensive, cryogenic mechanisms that focus, channel, and regulate the intensity of the gravitational force," Messenger replied. "Near the ground state of matter, approaching absolute zero, gravity loses its attraction. Strata of super-chilled, compressed helium II is the central material in this process. It is not only unaffected by gravity but also acts as a barrier or shield against the gravitational forces of the deeper mass of the Great Sphere. When the attractive power is focused into the interior, stars and planets like yours can be moved without the least disturbance. If you like, I can furnish the details."

"No, thanks," Vartan said. "I get the idea."

"Please tell us about the route you are taking," Jennifer asked. "On the high screen over there, it appears that we will pass near Mars, Saturn, and Neptune, along the solar ecliptic."

"Yes," it said. "Though our final destination is about thirty degrees above the plane of the ecliptic, I want you to have the chance to see some of your planets up close. It added a day and a half to our journey, but when you see them, you will agree it was worth the detour."

"You told us earlier that this Sphere was been constructed over six billion years ago and rescues civilizations in trouble," David said. "How many worlds have been rescued in the past?"

"Thirty-seven," Messenger said.

"Are they still here?" Apiranoa asked. "And will we get to meet them?"

"There are millions from each group still living out there in thirty-seven distinct regions," it said. "Most of the Rim, however, is uninhabited. There is only one species of people you will meet when you arrive. They will decide if you are to meet any of the others."

"May we see pictures of them and begin to learn about their civilizations?" he asked.

"No. The ones you will meet must decide if and when that is appropriate," Messenger said.

"Has the Great Sphere traveled beyond this galaxy?" Maria asked. "Are there other Spheres?"

"No, to both questions," Messenger answered.

"Has the Great Sphere come to Earth before?" Theodora asked. "If so, when and why did it come and then go?"

"Yes," it said. "I am not permitted to tell you anymore."

Everyone looked at each other in wonder. Jennifer noticed that everyone was rapt with attention toward the conversation. Even the children were listening carefully, engaged in thought as they worked with their hands.

"What are the levels of civilization above ours?" Petrus asked. "How do we develop to those levels, and will you share scientific and cultural information to help us advance?"

"Nearly all of them are much older than yours and also more mature," Messenger replied. "Again, the ones you will meet are to determine what is appropriate for you to receive in the ways of knowledge and information."

"How long will Earth be inside this Sphere?" Allison asked. "And if the Earth's solar system is to be left outside, can any of us stay here on the Rim?"

"The duration of Earth's stay is yet to be determined," it said. "That could be months, years, or even centuries. When it is time to leave, your solar system will be returned to its original position. It depends on what happens on Earth in the near future. As for staying on the Rim, that will be decided by the ones you will meet."

"How common is life in our galaxy?" David asked. "For that matter, how common is sentient life and civilization?"

"Life is not as common as you may have hoped," Messenger answered. "Where it is found, life is abundant, diverse, and robust. Sentient life is extremely rare for a wide variety of factors. Most of the life-forms out there are represented here in specially adapted sectors of the Rim."

"What can you tell us about God?" Toma asked, surprising everyone.

"There is much I am not permitted to say," it said. "But I will say that the One many of you worship in your world is well known out there."

Everyone paused to reflect for a while on the magnitude of what they had heard. Jennifer looked up at the central monitor to see that Mission Control was still connected. Earth had been listening as well. She then stood up, stretched, and looked toward the screens.

"I feel like we've started first grade all over again," said Allison. "And now we have been given a taste of advanced college subjects. How will we ever catch up?"

"Do we need to catch up?" Petrus wondered aloud. "Like Jennifer said, everything has changed now. Like Neolithic people who walked into a city with modern conveniences like grocery stores, malls, and libraries, we can never go back to the way it was. Humans are no longer the top dogs in the universe, and we know it. The challenge for us now is where do we go from here?"

"Messenger, I believe we need to take a break soon to ponder what you have told us, but first, I have several questions," Jennifer said. "Can we travel to the exterior surface of the Great Sphere? And does anyone live out there?"

"Yes, you can and will travel to the exterior surface," it said. "And no, there is no settlement out there apart from scientific observatories. With sensors across the entire exterior surface, a composite, multispectral telescope is created with highly detailed views across the entire sky."

Jennifer beamed at the news, realizing she would get to see the familiar stars again, even if in different perspectives. "My final question is what do you want to know from us?"

"We know a great deal already," Messenger said. "I do want to know how each of you are doing and if you need anything. If there are other things I need to know, like you, I will ask. Now I will provide some snack food for a break. After half an hour, I suggest you may want to attend to the latest news from Earth. Though your mission has dominated coverage, there are other events that may interest and concern you."

A food and drink table, generously adorned, appeared close to the seating area. Soon everyone was eating, drinking, and talking.

They gradually returned to their seats and asked Messenger to display headlines on their tablet computers so they could catch up on the latest news. It was not good. Like wildfires during a hot drought, conflicts were popping up in troubled areas around the globe. Their mission had become the subject of controversy. Sharkos and Grant had returned to Earth, and with help from President Barton, launched a media attack on the integrity of the mission, charging the astronauts with fraud and conspiracy. The news in general and this story in particular depressed the crew. After an hour, they began to turn off their tablets and became restless.

"I sense your unease," Messenger said. "Let me give you a refreshing diversion."

Everything around them changed in an instant to a deep, verdant forest with a well-worn trail that invited them to follow it. Beethoven's sixth symphony played quietly. The temperature was in the low seventies with a gentle breeze.

"Very nice, Messenger," Jennifer said.

Soon they were walking in small clusters at a brisk pace. Wildlife and blooming flowers were easily seen in the various vistas they passed. It was the perfect antidote for the bad news from home. Messenger provided supper for them at an opening in the canopy, complete with a campfire. When the sun set, stars began to peep out between the branches overhead. They shared small talk and stories of their childhoods. Then they decided to retire for the night, and the stairway to the upper level quarters appeared off to the side. It was a good night, and they all had a great sleep.

CHAPTER 16

Adventures Remembered

The next morning, everyone awoke refreshed. They gathered in the lounge area for breakfast. Messenger had provided another wide variety of foods and beverages. They noticed they had passed the distance from the Earth to the moon, setting a new record for human travel.

"Look at that," Jennifer said. "We have surpassed the Apollo astronauts in distance and are still accelerating."

"You have also broken the all-time speed record," Messenger said. "It was also held by the Apollo astronauts at forty thousand kilometers an hour. We are well over seventy thousand and going ever faster."

"How long until we pass Mars?" Kushe asked.

"Late tomorrow afternoon," it said.

"What should we do next?" David asked.

"We are just passengers along for the ride," said Aizam.

"Maybe we could do some creative things, like painting, composing, or writing," suggested Theodora.

"Did anyone ever think we would come out here just to sit and do nothing?" Alice asked with a hint of sarcasm.

"May I make a suggestion?" Messenger said. "Since there are thirteen days left until arrival and only three planetary flybys, perhaps you would enjoy living recreated moments from each of your own ethnic heritages."

Everyone paused and looked at one another, seeking input.

"I'm up for it," said Vartan.

"Why not?" said Maria. "Otherwise, we will have to stare out the windows and into these screens for almost two weeks."

"Messenger, how would you do this?" Becky asked.

"Like with these living quarters and control room, I would recreate each of twelve distinct situations from somewhere in your histories, using historical and physical geographic sources," it said. "Let us start with a great moment in Basque and world history."

Suddenly, they were all aboard the *Victoria*, one of the Spanish carracks that had set off with four other tiny sailing vessels in 1519 under the command of Ferdinand Magellan. They were alone on a battered, leaking ship somewhere in ultramarine ocean waters. There was no land in sight. High in the azure sky, the sun beat down. The limp sails were tattered, as were their clothes. David was wearing clothing suggestive of a higher rank, possibly captain.

"David," Jennifer said, "I think you are now Juan Sebastián de Elcano. Do you have any idea where we are on the voyage?"

The rest of the crew gathered around, searching for direction.

"Jennifer," he said, "there must be some charts, a compass, and an astrolabe in the captain's cabin in the back of the ship. Since you are the astronomer, I suggest you take those tools and figure out where we are."

"What about the rest of us?" Petrus asked. "What should we do?"

"Apiranoa and Aizam, you have considerable experience at sea," David said. "I want you to guide the rest of us on managing this ship. Alice, you take the tiller and keep the ship on a steady course until we can determine where to go next. Allison, you and Anastasia climb up to the crow's nest and look to see if there's land in any direction.

"First, you will want to check the captain's cabin for a spy glass. The rest of you need to assess the condition of our ship.

Fatima, you and Petrus check for food and water supplies in the galley. Becky, you and Vartan go below and inspect the integrity of the hull. We need to know how bad the leaks are. Please keep your kids close to you. The young ones should not climb the riggings. The rest of you join them or take on some other task that you think would be helpful."

Jennifer returned with the instruments. Theodora was helping with the charts.

"I would judge from the angle of the sun and the time of day on my watch that we are about thirty-six degrees latitude, north," Jennifer said. "I won't know more till the sun sets, and I can see the stars."

"Knowing the history of their voyage," David said, "I suspect we're on the latter part of the journey, maybe somewhere off the northwest coast of Africa. Elcano completed their circumnavigation with only one ship and a total of eighteen crew members after three years at sea. They had set out from Spain, heading west across the Atlantic. Near the east coast of South America, they sailed south to Cape Horn and headed northwestward into the Pacific. After many problems, including mutiny, they arrived in the Philippines, where Magellan was killed. Elcano took command and sailed further west into the Indian Ocean and around southern Africa at the Cape of Good Hope. The final leg was the journey up the west coast of Africa and then back to Spain at the port of Seville. We need to determine where we are on that trip."

"David," said Maria, who had climbed up from the deck below. "The decks below us are loaded with casks full of what I assume to be spices. That would explain why the ship is riding somewhat low in the water."

"Dad!" Allison shouted from the crow's nest thirty feet above his head. "I think we've spotted a coastline ahead, way off to the left. It runs a long way in either direction on our port side."

"Great work, girls," David said.

"I can't keep this tiller steady," Alice said. "I think there are some pulleys and ropes to help steer. They're down on the quarter deck beneath me."

"Aizam, you and Timujin Ji figure out the steering system and help Alice with the rudder," David asked.

"David," Becky said after scrambling back up on deck, "Vartan has gone looking for some kind of pump. The hull is leaking water like a melting iceberg. If we don't start pumping right away, this ship won't make it to the coastline, and I don't see any lifeboats."

"Found it, I think," Vartan said from below deck.

Becky went below to help set it up. Fatima and Petrus soon emerged. Fortunately, Kushe, Toma, Randy, and Andy had stayed close to their adults, content to watch the action.

"The water is septic, and most of the food is spoiled or rancid," Fatima reported. "I would recommend fasting until we get to shore. It is a miracle that eighteen made it home, considering the food and sanitation conditions."

"Thanks, Fatima," said David. "We have a bigger problem right now. Becky reported that the hull is leaking badly. Would you and Petrus go below and render assistance to their work?"

They departed to join the pumping and bailing. Apiranoa and Aizam came up to David with hopeful looks.

"Except for the leaks, this ship is very seaworthy," Apiranoa said. "The sails are slack and not turned in the right direction for the wind."

"We've figured out how to re-rig them to give a lot more speed," Aizam said. "Do you want to get to the shore over there?"

"Please make it so," David said. "If my guess is correct, the coast is a couple of miles to the port side. It might be the southwest coast of Spain. The latitude is right, and I say we make for it and sail offshore until we reach a port of some kind, assuming that this is 1522."

"That sounds logical to me," said Jennifer, standing behind David. "Do you see anything out there, girls?"

Two faces appeared over the rim of the crow's nest.

"All we can see is the land continuing out of sight!" Anastasia shouted. "We don't see any buildings, ships, or harbors. Wait! Allison has spotted a break in the shoreline."

The few who were not occupied with steering or pumping went up to the forecastle to get a better vantage point of the approaching land. Apiranoa and Aizam had retied and tightened the riggings, making the sails taut against the wind, which blew toward the shore. Alice and her helpers were able to steer hard to the right to maintain a half-mile distance from the shore. As they came closer to the break in the shoreline, another shoreline appeared in the distance ahead, running southward to the right and out of sight. They were about to enter the mouth of a river.

"This could be the Rio Guadalquivir," said Theodora, fumbling with a sheaf of charts.

"Dad!" Allison shouted from above, "we see buildings and ships off to the right! It's probably about three miles over there. It looks like a port."

David looked at Jennifer. "What do you think?" he asked.

"I say we try to head to it if we can get this ship turned that way," she said.

"Alice, you and your helpers try turning the rudder even more to the right, which is your left," David said. "Let's see if we can turn enough to head down that far coastline to the town."

Theodora squinted again at the chart on the top of her bundle. "That could be Sanlúcar de Barrameda, if this chart can be trusted."

"I see a Spanish royal flag flying over some small fortification!" Anastasia shouted from her perch above. "You will see it soon."

Before long, they were in sight of the port. Aizam and Apiranoa frantically furled the sails. Others joined in their efforts so the ship might coast into the docks. Alice and her helmsmen labored to pull alongside the open area of the docks. They were still moving too fast and about to pass by. Apiranoa threw the lasso of a heavy rope at a large post on the dock in a desperate attempt. Like a cowboy, he nailed it. The other end was fast to the ship. When the line played out, the ship bumped against the dock and came to a halt. Aizam jumped onto the dock and took a second line, making the ship fast to the dock.

The pumping crew came from below, the girls from above, and the steering team from the back. They joined everyone on deck. The crew was astonished that no one in the town paid much notice to their arrival. To the townspeople, this was just another battered, old ship that had come with a cargo for the crown.

"David," Jennifer said, "I hope your Spanish is good enough to get us by."

David looked around at his ragtag crew and said, "I'm not sure they will understand my twenty-first century, new-world Spanish. Besides, Elcano and his crew sailed up the river to the city of Seville to finish where they had started three years earlier."

"I don't think we should try that leg of the journey," Petrus said. "We were lucky to make it to this dock before running aground."

"What should we do now?" Jennifer asked, searching for suggestions.

Before anyone could answer, a short, portly man dressed in clothing suggesting importance came walking down the dock with a look of concern.

Looking straight up at David, the apparent captain, he said in archaic Spanish, "You should move that awful wreck from this dock at once! Another ship is due any time. Get out and go somewhere else!"

"I humbly beg your pardon, sir," David replied. "I am Juan Sebastián de Elcano. We have returned from India and the Far East."

"Of course you did," said the official, "and I am the Holy Roman Emperor!"

David noticed some soldiers emerging from the barracks coming to join the official. This did not look good. David figured they thought he was a smuggler or pirate.

"We left here three years ago," David tried, mustering his courage. "This is the only surviving ship from the five that left here under the command of Ferdinand Magellan. He was killed by the natives in the East Indies."

"I will have to inspect your papers and cargo before I can let you stay," the man barked. "Some of your crew look suspicious. You even have women on board. Not everyone looks Spanish. I must detain you for further questions."

The official and soldiers approached the side of the ship at the dock to climb the short distance to the opening on the side.

David had enough. "Messenger," he said, "it's time to conclude our little experience."

"Yes, of course, David," it said.

Instantly, they were back in the control room and in their flight suits.

"I hope you found that trip interesting," Messenger said.

"Odyssey crew, Houston here," the capsule communicator (CAPCOM) said, "Everyone okay?"

Jennifer looked around and said, "None the worse for wear. Did you see all of that, Houston?"

"Affirmative, Odyssey, and when you return to Earth, we will train all of you on how to sail a ship properly," the voice said with a chuckle. "Maybe you can get jobs on a cruise ship."

"We will debrief, Houston," said Jennifer. "Is there anything you want us to attend to here?"

"Negative, Odyssey," CAPCOM said. "Houston out."

"Jennifer," said Messenger. "May I suggest that you and the crew refresh yourselves with some food and drink?"

"Thanks, Messenger," replied Jennifer. "Let's chow down, everyone."

The table full of food and beverages reappeared near the seating area. Thanks was given, and everyone was soon feasting on Asian food. Allison and Anastasia were texting friends back on Earth as well as updating their Facebook pages, which now had a couple of billion followers.

"Mom," Allison said in alarm. "My friends are telling me that some of the media and the president are now saying that our trip is a fake, and we have defrauded America!"

Everyone paused from eating to process this latest news. Several pulled out their tablets to check news websites and found it to be true.

"Well, what are we to do about it?" asked David, speaking the same question on the minds of the others.

"I'm not sure," Jennifer said. "Everyone saw us leave the ISS and is still getting a live feed from what we're doing, even now. We've become a living reality show."

"Maybe they're being fooled by the instant communications link provided by the transceiver," Timujin Ji said.

"May I offer a suggestion?" Messenger asked. "Tomorrow afternoon, we are due to fly by Mars. I have enough energy reserves to make a landing for a couple of hours and then launch to resume our journey. See if Mission Control will permit the landing."

"That's a great idea, Messenger," Jennifer said. "I'm not sure our EMUs are safe for Martian EVA, but it doesn't hurt to ask."

She got up and walked over to the central screen that showed Mission Control.

"Houston, Odyssey here," Jennifer said.

"Odyssey, we read you," CAPCOM said.

"Our host has offered to land us on Mars tomorrow afternoon," she said. "I need to know if our EMUs are good for an EVA on the Martian surface. Are we go for a Martian landing?"

There was a pause as the controllers looked around at one another. Then Dr. Sanderson stepped up to the camera in Houston.

"Jennifer, normally something this big would have to be cleared with Washington," he said. "But under the present circumstances, I give a green light. Just be sure to bring back some rocks and take some pictures. You are go for Martian landing and EVA!"

"Thanks, Franklin and Houston," Jennifer said. "Odyssey out."

She returned to the seating area and the rest of the crew.

"This was not in our training," Jennifer said. "What do we need to do to prep for this? And where do we land?"

"I suggest landing near Mt. Sharp on the borders of Elysium Planitia and Terra Cimmeria," Messenger said. "It would be within a hundred meters of the Curiosity rover."

"Perfect," said Vartan. "Just wait till the people out at the Jet Propulsion Lab in Pasadena see us walk up to their rover!"

"If you like, I can give you an overview of Martian climate, geology, and natural history to begin your preparation," Messenger said.

"Let's do it," Jennifer said.

A couple of large screens appeared, hovering on either end of the seating area and came to life with the presentation. A larger assortment of toys appeared in the center for the four younger children. After a couple of hours of viewing and discussion, the crew took personal time to return to their quarters. Jennifer made contact with Chris Wallace of Fox News. After supper, he conducted an extended live interview with the entire crew. After the show concluded, Chris told them that the Nielsen numbers were the highest ever. He reassured them that most of the people back on Earth believed in the reality of their mission. Later, for fun, several crew members requested to watch *The War of the Worlds*. Becky snuck off in order to get her twins to bed. Before the movie began, Messenger provided popcorn and soft drinks. It played a recording of the "Mars" movement of Gustav Holtz's *The Planets*.

After an early breakfast the next morning, the crew relived the crossing of Beringia in 10,000 BC with a band of hunters. They worked their way along the seacoast in search of woolly mammoths in the area now submerged by the Bering Straits. Maria, Alice, and Becky all felt a kinship to their Neolithic ancestors who made one of the first migrations into the new world. After they had helped bring down a mammoth, the scene changed, and they were on jagged sea ice, trekking with skis and dog sleds and following Admiral Robert Peary and Matthew Henson on the final leg of their 1909 North Pole expedition. It proved to be arduous as they had to climb over and around pressure ridges. Peary drove them on relentlessly until he was satisfied he had attained the Pole. He stopped, took a sextant reading, and entered the feat into his journal. After finding that the primitive camera was broken, Peary ordered the expedition to begin the return journey. Fortunately, Messenger ended the recreation in time for lunch. Mars was now close enough to see surface features. Its face occupied the bulk of one of the screens over the control center.

In the early afternoon, Messenger entered orbit and continued deceleration in preparation for landing. Half the wall was illuminated with the view of the passing Martian terrain. The crew quickly donned their EMUs. They were in awe of the passing scenes of Olympus Mons, the highest mountain in the solar system and an extinct volcano. Gasps of wonder were uttered at the sight of Valles Marineris, the great gash of a canyon scarring the face of the western hemisphere. The polar ice caps were hidden from view because of the closeness of the orbit. Messenger mentioned and indicated on the view the sites of previous landings from Viking 1 to the Spirit and Opportunity rovers. Everyone was astonished at how monochromatic it all was in contrast to the living colors of Earth.

Time came for the landing descent. Messenger provided a complete set of custom-sized and belted couches for entry and landing. With everyone strapped in, the vessel began to descend. An invisible energy field of great magnitude shielded the outer skin but glowed red with the friction in the Martian atmosphere. Their descent continued for what seemed like an eternity. The G force diminished as they slowed and then gently touched down near a prominence they recognized as Mt. Sharp.

"Houston, Odyssey has landed," Jennifer said.

"We copy, Odyssey," CAPCOM said. "Well done."

From the distance, a few dozen meters away sat the Curiosity rover. Its artificial intelligence had turned its cameras and instruments toward Messenger, and it slowly ambled forward for a closer look.

"Remember to bring the sample containers," Jennifer said. "Everyone, be sure to check your com and video systems."

"Does anyone have anything to plant on the surface, like a flag?" David asked.

"How about a platinum column with all the flags of Earth and your names engraved on it?" Messenger asked.

"Again, you've thought of everything, Messenger," Alice said.

She stooped to pick it up after the column materialized on the floor in front of her.

"What's the inscription on this column?" Theodora asked.

"It says, 'We come in peace for all humanity,'" Allison said.

"That will do fine," Maria said.

"I hate to ask this, but who goes first?" Apiranoa asked.

There was a brief silence as everyone looked up and around at each other.

"I think Jennifer should be the first to step down on the surface," said Fatima. "After all, she's our leader, and we never would have made it without her."

"Hurrah, I say," said Apiranoa. "Go for it, Dr. Bass! Shall I lead us in a Maori warrior dance?"

"No thanks, Apiranoa," Jennifer said. "Let's go."

Just then, a passageway opened to one side, revealing a descending stairwell. It was long enough to hold everyone. David and Vartan carried the column between them. When the last one had entered, it closed, and the air was evacuated, replaced by Martian atmosphere. Everyone deployed their solar visors inside their helmets. At the lower end of the passageway, the hatch opened to reveal a flat metal plate that served as a landing. It was a meter in length. The ruddy Martian soil surrounded it. Jennifer stepped out onto the landing and looked around at the world no one had seen in person before. She prayed a silent prayer of praise and gratitude.

"We come in peace, and in peace may you always remain, Mars. And may we not be the last of our kind to visit here," Jennifer said, as everyone back on Earth watched.

Jennifer was about to step onto the surface when she stopped and turned around to face the others.

"Becky, pass your boys down here to me," she said.

Becky, who was five places back in line, passed Randy and Andy like packages to Jennifer. When she had both boys in her arms, Jennifer lowered them down to the Martian soil.

At first, Randy and Andy hesitated. Then they looked at each other and kicked some of the soil into the air. They began to squeal with joy and ran off as much as their EMUs would permit.

"Okay, pass Kushe and Toma next," said Jennifer. "And then I want Anastasia and Allison to go after that."

When all six of the kids had made it to the Martian surface, Jennifer said to them, "You are the future here with us today. May you return here as men and women to lead more of us back to this world and beyond."

Soon the entire crew was out on the surface and moving around, surveying the view in wonder. Curiosity was slowly coming closer as David and Vartan raised the column and rammed its long, spiked foot into the soil. Everyone stepped up, and many saluted.

"Okay, who's going to take pictures?" Jennifer asked.

"Remember, all of us are taking pictures all the time," David reminded her.

"Houston here," CAPCOM said over their com systems. "Your host has you covered as well. It's going to take about thirty-five minutes for the signal from Curiosity to reach Pasadena, but those will be the greatest shots a rover ever got."

Everyone moved from the column to cluster around the Curiosity rover, which was scanning them and taking their pictures. Andy started to touch its arm.

"Leave it alone, son," Becky said. "We don't know how delicate it is. Just look, but don't touch."

"Houston, is there anything you would like for us to do for or with Curiosity?" Jennifer asked.

"Negative on that, Odyssey," CAPCOM said. "JPL said it's self-sufficient, but you are welcome to stand around it for group pictures. And don't forget to take some rock samples. Our geologists are begging for some samples from the various strata you can see on the slope of Mt. Sharp to your east about a tenth of a kilometer."

"Vartan, would you, Maria, and David collect and record those samples?" Jennifer asked.

Toma bent over, picked up a rock, and threw it. He was amazed at the distance it travelled.

"Remember," said Petrus, "this world is less than half the size of Earth."

"I wouldn't want to live here for long," Allison said. "There's no beach, and shopping is a world away."

"Just think," Theodora said. "People have dreamed of setting foot here for millennia, and we are the first ones to get the privilege."

"Let's hope we're not the last," Alice said. "The coloration and terrain reminds me a little of my home back in Monument Valley."

The magnitude and unreality of the moment drove everyone into silent reverie.

Their solitude was broken by Messenger, who said, "The time to launch is drawing near. Please return and reboard."

Before long, everyone was back on board, strapped in to the couches for launch, and on their way again.

Thirty-five minutes later, the striking images of the spherical vessel and its quaint crew of astronauts ambling about were received in Pasadena, California, at the Jet Propulsion Lab. Messenger had already left Mars orbit and was rapidly accelerating on its outward journey.

A few hours after their Martian landing, the crew found themselves in oceangoing canoes similar to the one Apiranoa had left behind to ride the submarine over a month earlier. This time, they were part of an armada of two dozen laden canoes on their way westward across the trackless Pacific. The time was over one thousand years ago, during the final great Polynesian oceanic migration. Apiranoa directed the entire flotilla. Within an hour, they spotted land and made landfall on the northern end of the North Island of New Zealand. As the first humans to visit, they had the incredible wonder of seeing the fauna and flora in pristine condition. The Great Moas, the largest birds ever, long extinct in modern times, were abundant and had no fear of the newly arrived humans. They enjoyed several hours of exploration, seeing long-lost plant and animal species flourishing in the lush environment.

The next experience was with Fatima's Bedouin people over 3,200 years ago. Much like some modern Bedouin, they were tending their herds deep in the Negev Desert when they beheld a huge column of smoke, followed by an oncoming mass of people moving their way from the south. It was the Israelites being led by the Levites, carrying a large ornamented box that David identified as the Ark of the Covenant. After spotting Moses and Aaron near the front, the crew joined the procession further back, trying to fit in. Among the swarm of people were livestock that included cattle, sheep, and goats. When the Israelites made camp, Fatima realized that they were at Kadesh Barnea, where the Israelites would spend most of their forty years in the desert wilderness. Thanks to Messenger, they were able to understand the ancient form of Hebrew and had been dressed in appropriate attire that helped them blend in. After pitching their tents, they were able to spend time listening to one of the elders repeat the story of the Exodus and God's covenant, with the children around a campfire.

The next day was completely different. Messenger had brought the vessel into orbit around Saturn, within a hundred meters of the A ring, not far from the Cassini division. The astronauts were all suited up in their EMUs and tethered to a special propulsion probe. When they cleared the airlock, the probe led them down into the ring.

"Who'd a thought?" David exclaimed, "that anyone would ever get to do this?"

"Houston, Odyssey here," Jennifer said. "Do you want us to take samples? The chunks vary widely in size but are almost completely made of ice. I'm not sure we can get them back to you in pristine condition."

"Odyssey, we copy," CAPCOM replied. "Give it a try. Your host will be able to store them somehow, perhaps in a higher dimension, until you return. We'd love to study them in detail. Your video images are great. Please turn one of your cameras back toward Earth. We'd like to see how far you've gone."

"Copy that, Houston," Jennifer said as she spun slightly on the tether. She faced her headset toward the bright, starlike object only five degrees to the left of the now diminished BB-sized ball of the Sun. "Got it! Hello back there."

Kushe grabbed a baseball-sized piece and, while holding herself steady with one hand on the tether, chucked the ice ball with the other hand at her brother. It hit his helmet dead on.

"What was that?" Toma shouted, turning to look around.

"Careful," said Becky. "If you had hit him on the front of the helmet, it might have cracked the visor and caused a rapid decompression."

"No more ice-ball fights," Petrus ordered.

"Sorry," Kushe said.

"It's all so beautiful," Theodora said softly. "I am overwhelmed with the majestic beauty out here. It's enough to make me cry while writing a violin concerto. I can hear the music now."

"Too bad we can't land down there," Anastasia said.

"Too much hydrogen," Vartan said. "We see only the outer gaseous atmosphere. Below are layers of liquid hydrogen, metallic hydrogen, and a rocky core. It would be fascinating to see, but the temperature deep down rises over eleven thousand degrees."

"This beats even sailing the Pacific in a great canoe," said Apiranoa.

"I think I would still prefer riding my horse," Timujin Ji said.

"So all we can do is float out here and look?" Aizam said.

"It's enough," Maria replied. "More than enough."

The crew became silent, lost in the moment. It seemed like they had been hovering above Saturn forever. They were jolted back to reality when Messenger began to retract their tether. It was like reeling in a fish. Within short order, everyone was inside, unsuited, and ready for the next adventure. Messenger resumed the outward journey, only one-fifth of the way to the Rim.

Midway on the journey, Messenger flew by Neptune, using its gravity to help steer upward toward a target thirty degrees above the solar ecliptic (the plane of the solar system). The great, featureless blue ball slowly moved across the screen as they passed at high velocity. Messenger executed a turnabout and began the slow deceleration toward the Rim, which was now becoming easier to see. It was clearest straight ahead, slowly fading away in all directions across millions of miles of highly varied terrain.

After the Neptune flyby, the final days were spent studying the latest information from Earth from the digital atlas that Messenger had delivered. Special attention was given to the region immediately below the hovering space station, their destination. It showed up like a collection of metallic cylinders all fastened together. There were no visible markings, windows, or docking ports. Unlike the ISS, there was no solar-power array to be seen. No other vessels were detectable. As the time drew closer, sleep became more difficult for the adults on the crew. They were fully aware of the great responsibility they bore. The political situation back on Earth continued to deteriorate as well. Reports came in about the collapse of Wall Street, followed in rapid succession by other world financial markets. Russia launched invasions of all of the former Soviet republics. China invaded and occupied Taiwan. India and Pakistan opened fullscale war against each other. The Middle East erupted in widespread chaos, with Iran annexing Iraq and Afghanistan, while savagely fighting radical Sunni factions. The Palestinian territories went into full attack mode against Israel.

Even the United States was not immune from trouble. The Mexican border overflowed with an unprecedented influx of desperate people from Central America. The president was enraged by the military's surprise launch of the secret space shuttles. He accused military leaders of trying to overthrow the government. Simultaneously, the media revealed widespread corruption scandals in his administration at the highest levels. Most interesting was the discovery that the gold at Fort Knox had been replaced with gold-painted lead ingots. The last bit of news indicated that the president had declared martial law, ordering the arrest of all military leaders of command rank as well as congressional members of the opposing party. Covertly, over several years, he had infiltrated the ranks of several federal law enforcement agencies with operatives loyal to him. Even while all of this was taking place, NASA continued to monitor the mission. Worry was beginning to show on their faces when they communicated with the crew. For the time being, their families back on Earth were still okay.

CHAPTER 17

Journey's End

It was now one day before their arrival. The entire crew was gathered in the seating area, looking at the screens and monitors. The surface of the Rim now filled well over half of their entire field of view. The Rim was so large that the surface appeared completely level, though their minds knew it was ever so slightly concave, running for billions of kilometers before returning to the same place. Though they were still millions of kilometers away, it gave the appearance of being only a few thousand meters below them. Everyone was restive about who or what they would meet the next day.

"Messenger," Jennifer said. "Tell us again about what will happen tomorrow."

"My mission is nearly complete," it said. "Midday tomorrow, your time, we will have slowed to a stop and then will dock with a space station that is hovering a thousand kilometers above the surface of the Rim. There you will meet those who sent me."

"Why can't you tell us more about them?" David asked.

"They were very specific in my programming," Messenger said. "They imposed severe restrictions on any information I could share with you. I can tell you that you will not be harmed in any way, nor will anything happen to you without your full understanding and consent. For example, even now, I am prepared to take you back to Earth if you request it."

"No, we are excited about meeting them, whoever they are," said Jennifer. "We've come all this way. It would be rude to turn around and go home because we are feeling nervous."

"It would also be the biggest act of cowardice in human history," said Maria.

"Just think, most of the people back on Earth would give anything to be here with us," Anastasia said.

"Messenger, is there anything we should know about behavior, customs, or taboos that could cause misunderstandings?" Petrus asked.

"No, you will find them very accommodating," it said. "Besides, they already know a great deal about you and your world."

"Will we need to wear our EMUs?" Kushe asked.

"No, their atmosphere is identical to yours," Messenger said. "You may wear any clothing you choose. I can fabricate anything you do not already have in your quarters."

"Is there any special protocol or ceremonies we need to prepare for?" Theodora asked.

"Nothing is planned to my knowledge," it said. "You have brought some gifts to present. Perhaps you would like to share those at the first meeting."

"Does the space station have microgravity like our ISS?" Vartan asked.

"No, it is similar in design to me," Messenger replied. "You will experience one G."

"What happens after we meet them on the station?" Allison asked. "Will we then go down to the surface?"

"That will depend on what you and your hosts decide after your meeting," it said.

"Houston, are you getting all of this?" Jennifer asked, looking at the center screen.

"Odyssey, we copy," CAPCOM said. "As far as we are concerned, you are go for first contact tomorrow at noon, universal time. Just follow the guidelines we went over during your training. Nearly everyone back here on Earth will be watching. Godspeed to you all."

"Thanks. Odyssey out," Jennifer replied. "I think we need to take some personal time after supper to visit with our families back home and reflect on what we will face tomorrow. I suggest that tomorrow morning, we rise and reconvene at six for a time of prayer, then have breakfast and finish with a review and discussion of our guidelines. Is that okay with everyone?"

She looked around and saw agreement from everyone.

They broke for supper and lighter conversation. Then everyone retired to their quarters for Skype sessions with family and friends back on Earth.

At about midnight, David and Jennifer found themselves awakened by being stood up, in flight suits, and in a dark, featureless room. Everyone else was there as well, looking bewildered. Randy and Andy were rubbing their eyes.

"Messenger, what are you up to?" Jennifer asked. "Is this another relived experience?"

No answer.

"Messenger, please respond!" David shouted.

Still no answer.

"This is not the control room or anything we recognize," Alice said.

"Is anyone sensing anything unusual?" Fatima asked. "Check your vitals and your senses."

Everyone's vitals were normal, and they felt fine.

"Houston, Odyssey here," Jennifer said. "Do you read us?"

No answer.

"I'm getting no signal on my iPhone," Allison said.

A light appeared to one side and grew in brilliance, making it almost painful to look at. At the same time, the crew experienced a feeling of calm. Inside the light, even brighter still, was a man dressed in white garments with a dark-brown beard and long hair. His eyes seemed to be looking at each one of them. He was familiar yet different than anyone they had ever met.

"Peace be with you," he said. "You have nothing to fear."

"Are you one of the people we are to meet?" Jennifer asked.

"No, Jennifer," he said, with a reassuring smile.

"Are you part of Messenger's programmed experiences?" David asked.

"No, David," he replied. "Messenger has nothing to do with our meeting."

"Are we asleep and dreaming?" Toma asked

"No, Toma," he said. "This is all very real."

"Who are you?" asked Alice. "And what do you want with us?"

"Deep in your hearts, you know," he said as he breathed upon them.

Everyone gave a deep sigh, filled with deep serenity and happiness. The adults and teens entered a gradual realization and dropped to their knees, some even prostrate on the floor. Several crossed themselves. Toma, Kushe, Andy, and Randy ran up to him, softly giggling, and embraced him.

"You are Jesus," said Andy, beaming.

"Can we stay with you?" Kushe asked.

Jesus had already dropped to his knees to take the kids into his arms. He looked deeply into their eyes with profound love.

"Yes, I am Jesus," he said. "And Kushe, I will stay with you, and Toma, and everyone else forever. I have already been with you all your life."

"Jesus, can you bring our mommy and daddy back from the dead?" Toma asked.

Jesus looked into Toma's eyes, only inches away. Tears began to run down Jesus's cheeks. Kushe began to cry. She reached up and touched Jesus's face and wiped some of his tears, then kissed her fingers. Kushe smiled through her tears.

"Will we see them again?" Kushe asked.

"Of course," Jesus said. "They live with me."

"Are they okay?" Toma asked.

"They are more than okay," Jesus replied. "They are very aware of all that has gone on in your lives and love you very much."

"Why did they have to die like they did, so young?" Toma asked.

"All of you live in a broken world where sad and even terrible things happen," he said. "I am working to make good come out of all bad things, even the death of your parents. I was the same age as your father when I was killed. At first, it was a terrible thing too. Then our Father changed it into something wonderful that began to change everything else in the world."

Jesus then showed them the nail holes in his hands and feet. Kushe leaned her head against his shoulder. She felt a deep peace, still not fully understanding, but now her heart was healed. Toma leaned forward and hugged Jesus's neck, crying until he, too, felt that same peace. Randy and Andy began to dance about and sing. Their joy was effusive.

"Lord, why have you come to us?" Jennifer asked softly, still kneeling, her head slightly bowed.

"Jennifer, I have come to tell you two things," Jesus answered. "First, the ones you will meet tomorrow are innocent. Though they have extensive knowledge of your world, they have no understanding of selfishness, fear, anger, jealousy, envy, or any of the other problems that make your world such a troubled place. Their minds are advanced, but their hearts are tender. You must treat them with the greatest love and care. They have much to teach you. Second, your world is in great peril from its continued sinful ways. You have followed the news during your voyage and know that conditions are deteriorating rapidly. You have been brought out here to prepare for your mission. Here you will see how your people can live well in peace, truth, and love."

The adults and teens looked up from their reverential awe.

"Lord, is it not our mission to come out here and make first contact?" David asked.

"This is just the preparation for your true mission," Jesus said. "Your vessel has been named 'Messenger.' Now you will become messengers who will carry my message back to your world; first David, Jennifer, and Allison, and later, the rest of you."

"Don't we have that already in the gospel?" Vartan asked.

"Yes," Jesus said. "Your trip out here will amplify and clarify much that is in the Word. You and some others will return and share that message."

"Will you be visibly with us like this?" Maria asked.

"No, not yet. But you will feel my presence in the Spirit, which I have given you," he said.

Fatima, Aizam, and Timujin Ji arose and slowly approached Jesus. Toma and Kushe returned to Petrus, who embraced them tightly.

Timujin Ji said, "I was raised a Buddhist, but my schooling removed all religion, teaching that it was all false. What now? I know you are real. Help my unbelief."

As he lowered his head in shame, Jesus reached out and lifted Timujin Ji's chin with his hand.

"I once had a follower like you," Jesus said. "He was also very bright and struggled with his belief. His name was Thomas. Once he saw me risen, Thomas never doubted again. Your faith will serve you and me well, Timujin Ji."

"Aizam and I are Muslim," said Fatima. "We know now that you are real and much more than the prophet that the Koran says you were. What about our faith? What are we to believe now that we have met you?"

Aizam was silenced by his sense of wonder but nodded in agreement with Fatima.

"Fatima and Aizam," Jesus replied. "You are two people of good hearts, keen minds, and passion for truth. Mohammed was a great man. He had a heart for God and received some revelations. However, when he sought help in interpreting those experiences, he was gravely misled by false teachers, like Sergius of Damascus. You may know him by the name, Bahira. Mohammad's heart was deeply wounded over the years that followed, and it lead to a distortion that was further abused by some of his early followers. I loved, lived, and died for him, all who follow his teachings, and for both of you. Now that you know the full truth, you are messengers to the Muslim part of my family."

Fatima looked in Jesus's eyes, took his hand, and kissed it. She then hugged him. Aizam knelt and bowed before Jesus, who placed his hand on Aizam's head. Aizam then rose, smiling, and hugged Jesus. The three then rejoined the others.

"It is time for you to return," Jesus said. "I am with you always, even to the close of the age."

As suddenly as he had come, Jesus's visible image was gone. They were all back in the control room. The clock indicated the exact instant that they had left their quarters.

"Messenger, what has happened?" Jennifer asked.

"I am not sure," it said. "You were removed from your quarters and instantly set here, downstairs. I have no explanation."

"I think we had a collective spiritual vision," David said. "Jesus has spoken to us all, and it may take some time for us to process what it means."

"Wonderful," said Messenger. "He is often seen across the Rim. The ones you will meet tomorrow know him well."

Everyone was energized by their experience. Sleep was out of the question for a while, so the adults snacked and talked about their spiritual journeys as the kids played with toys and blocks. After a couple of hours, everyone had unwound to where they were able to retire and get a few hours of fitful sleep.

CHAPTER 18

First Contact

Morning came quickly. Messenger had told them to dress comfortably. The EMUs wouldn't be needed again. Jennifer, David, and Allison dressed and shared in a brief time of prayer before exiting their quarters to join the others downstairs in the control room. Everyone had chosen to wear their Odyssey flight suits. The headsets were adorning every head, including Andy and Randy. David had brought the case that held all of the gifts for first contact. Before breakfast, Jennifer asked them to join hands in a prayer circle. Several prayed heartfelt prayers.

With a slight tremor in her voice, Jennifer concluded, "Lord, we are grateful for the wonderful journey. Soon we will step forth to meet the first people from beyond our world; we feel anxiety and great responsibility. Please help us to get it right, to represent the best of our world, and to not offend our hosts. May your Spirit guide our steps, words, and deeds all the way. In the name of all that is holy. Amen."

Messenger provided a generous breakfast, but only the younger children ate well. Everyone else was too tense to enjoy the food. Some only had coffee. Silence ruled the meal since everyone was lost in thought. When it was over, Jennifer and the others approached the control monitors, which showed the space station drawing near.

"Messenger," Jennifer said, "are you sure we have covered all the details? Are we ready to meet our hosts?"

"There is no need to worry," it said. "Your arrival has been anticipated with great joy. Your hosts will be able to read your thoughts, even when words fail you."

"Houston, Odyssey here," Jennifer said. "Do you read?"

"Yes, Odyssey, we copy," CAPCOM replied. "All of your telemetry is coming through fine, including the feeds from everyone's headsets. The flight director says that you are go for first contact."

"Houston, Messenger says we are about five minutes from docking," Jennifer said. "We will keep you appraised as we are able."

"Odyssey, copy that," CAPCOM said. "Godspeed."

Everyone moved toward the part of the room where they had entered two weeks earlier. Apiranoa and Aizam carried the caisson of gifts. A large hatch appeared before them. It was large enough to walk through upright.

Jennifer took David's hand and looked into his eyes. "I'm more nervous than when we married."

"Me too," he said. "Though the births of Allison and Justin had me wound up just as much."

Allison came to David's other side and wrapped her arm around his waist. He reached his arm around her shoulder and gave her a reassuring hug.

"Dad, I'm scared," she said. "Do the great moments like this terrify people?"

"I don't know, sweet one," David said. "If people weren't pumped up, they probably didn't fully realize what they were doing."

"Everyone remember to breathe," Fatima reminded them.

A glance back at the screen of the outside view showed the surfaces of Messenger and the station coming together. There was a subtle, gentle bump. A hissing sound indicated that a secure connection had been made and that the door was about to open. It slid open to the right, disappearing into a hidden slot. Beyond was a short entry hall that led into a well-lit gallery. There were two figures standing near the opposite side.

"This is it, everyone," stammered Jennifer. "Now everything changes forever for us all. Godspeed to us and to them."

She led the way through the door as the others quickly followed in order. A strong feeling of calm and happiness came over the crew, washing away their anxiety. As they entered the gallery, they could see it was sparsely decorated with a cluster of two dozen soft chairs off to one side. The light came from transparent walls on either side that afforded breathtaking vistas of the surface of the Rim a thousand kilometers below. Almost immediately, the crew's attention was riveted on the two who quietly awaited them. They appeared humanlike but taller, at about two meters. The clothing they wore was simple and modest. Their skin was a bright bronze. The hair on their heads resembled the nappy, peppercorn hair on Petrus' head. Their bodily forms suggested that they were male and female in gender, like humans. The overall facial appearance gave the impression of agelessness with a hint of many years. Most striking were the engaging pale blue eyes surrounded by epicanthic eye folds. They wore easy smiles that conveyed a warm welcome. Jennifer began to feel that they were the most beautiful people she had ever seen.

"Hello," Jennifer began, hoping English would suffice. "We come in peace for all of the people of Earth. Our minds and hearts are open to share whatever we can with you and yours."

"Welcome home," the man said. "We are very happy to have you here. I am Seth, and this is my wife, Deborah."

His words came haltingly but with a musical inflection. The English was clean, and the accent resembled Welsh.

"Please forgive our slow speech," Deborah said, smiling. "We use our voices for singing and talk with one another through what you call 'telepathy.'"

"Are you human?" David asked.

"Yes," said Seth. "There will be time later for your many questions. First, we want to express our love and best wishes to you and everyone watching back on Earth. May the One bless and keep you all. Now we would like to meet each of you."

He stepped forward, then took and held Jennifer's hand.

"You are the leader, Jennifer Bass," he said. "How wonderful to meet you in person. And this is your husband, David, and your daughter, Allison."

Seth and Deborah came to each person in turn, taking their hands, looking warmly into their eyes, and calling them by name, as if they had known them forever. Kushe, Toma, Andy, and Randy were shy until they made hand contact, at which point, each of them broke into unguarded smiles. The crew then stood before their hosts in a loose cluster as Jennifer lifted and opened the case of gifts.

"We have some modest gifts to offer to you," Jennifer said. "I will let the individuals give you their own gifts."

David lifted a small, round instrument from the case. "Here's a compass used by Juan Sebastián de Elcano, the first mariner to circumnavigate our world. It helped him find his way home."

He then removed a sizable locket from his neck. It opened to reveal two old Spanish silver coins. At first glance, they appeared identical, with the king of Spain on the face and the pillars of Hercules on the reverse.

David passed them on to Seth. "These are Spanish coins from the late fifteenth century; they are identical, but one is a couple of years older. It depicts the monarch, King Ferdinand, on the obverse and the twin pillars of Hercules on the reverse. Those pillars mark the Strait of Gibraltar between the Atlantic Ocean and the Mediterranean Sea. The older one has the label, 'ne plus ultra,' meaning 'no more beyond.' After the discoveries of Columbus, it was reissued with the words 'plus ultra,' meaning 'more beyond.' Because of you, we know that there is much beyond."

Vartan presented a shard of time-worn wood embedded in Lucite. "This is a fragment from the ruins of Noah's Ark on Mt. Ararat from my homeland," he said.

Fatima stepped up and said, "Here's a gold bracelet and a bridal headband of silk and silver that has been in my family for over six thousand years."

Alice Cly presented a Navajo sand painting of the cosmos, showing the four directions and the sacred mountain.

Theodora gave them one of the last surviving icons from Hagia Sophia in Constantinople. It had been quietly passed down through her family since 1453.

Aizam and Becky presented fishing implements from their people.

Petrus offered Khoisan fire sticks, a bow and arrow, and a finger harp. The harp was supplemented by a Mongolian banjo from Timujin Ji.

Apiranoa shared an ancient way-finding star chart made from a network of woven sticks used by his Maori ancestors when crossing the Pacific.

Maria gave them a handwoven blanket of Alpaca wool in a unique Mapuche pattern.

Jennifer then handed Seth and Deborah a molecular scale storage device that contained nearly all of the written works, art, and music of Earth, displayable on a screen. She finished with the most unique gift.

"Here is the first moon rock collected by Neil Armstrong, the first human to walk on the moon a half century ago," Jennifer said.

Seth and Deborah's faces radiated gratitude and joy at the presentation of each gift. "We are deeply touched by your remarkable kindness," they said. "Now we offer you our love, goodwill, and hospitality in return."

They laid the gifts on a newly materialized table and walked toward the cluster of chairs, beckoning the crew to follow. As everyone gathered by the window wall, Seth motioned for them to be seated. The terrain below stretched out for thousands of kilometers before them. There were wide, open savannahs nestling shining rivers that drained into a vast ocean off to the left. Great snow-covered mountains punctuated the region to the right. Deep-green forests blanketed their flanks and flowed down to the edges of the grass lands. Cultivation was not evident in the area within their field of sight. Randy and Andy remained at the window, faces pressed to the glass, staring down in wonder. The others turned their attention back to their hosts.

"How do you know to speak English?" Aizam asked.

"We have studied it diligently in preparation for your arrival," said Deborah. "Please forgive any clumsiness in our speech. We do not mean to offend."

"Your English is excellent," Aizam responded. "There's almost no hint of dialect. It's as if you were native speakers."

"What do you mean when you say the 'One'?" Theodora asked.

"The One is the being who made everything," began Deborah, searching for words. "You call him 'God,' 'Jesus,' or the 'Holy Spirit.' We know him well in all three persons, the One. Jesus came to us shortly before you arrived. He told us of the trauma in your world and how we are to prepare you for your mission when you return. The Holy Spirit is within us, and we follow his leading."

"Why did you say 'home' when we first arrived?" asked Allison, blushing slightly from self-consciousness.

"Oh, young one, you have asked a big question," Seth answered. "We say 'home' because your people were here with us long ago. Seventy thousand years ago, a super volcano you call Tobu erupted before this sphere could come to help. By the time it arrived and enveloped your solar system, the damage was extreme. Most larger life-forms were dead. Less than a thousand of us survived in a remote region of east central Africa in what you today call Tanzania. Everyone was evacuated off Earth to the region out here that you see below you. It was reengineered to provide a safe sanctuary for all of the survivors and samples of larger plants and animals. Work began to restore Earth. We humans lived out here on this Rim for over five thousand years until it came time to return the solar system to its original place and move on to rescue another world. At that time, there arose dissent and rebellion. Many did not want any closeness to the One. The rebels chose to return to Earth and be left behind. It was very painful. We are the ones who stayed here."

"You say 'we,'" noted Fatima. "Who do you mean?"

"Deborah, several thousand others, and I are among those who were alive at the time of separation sixty-five thousand years ago," Seth said.

The crew gasped at the implied age of their hosts, still trying to process the meaning of this extraordinary news.

"How can you be seventy-five thousand years old?" Fatima asked.

"We are free from all disease," Deborah said. "Even the genes in our cells don't deteriorate when they go through mitosis. There is no aging. No one dies, even from accidents. We can heal any injury."

"Then your population must number in the hundreds of billions," Alice said.

"We bear a small number of children within the period of a century in our earlier years," Seth said. "The total human population here is now around eighty billion. There is no death or dying. As you can see, we have plenty of room, with almost fifteen billion times the surface area as Earth."

"Are you the only intelligent creatures out here on the Rim?" Alice asked.

"No, there are thirty-six other civilizations from other worlds," Seth replied.

"Will we be able to meet them and learn from them?" Theodora asked.

"Not at this time," Seth responded in a guarded tone.

"Do you have any children?" asked Anastasia.

"Yes, there are four," replied Deborah. "Perhaps you will meet them when we go down to the surface."

"When will that be?" asked Jennifer.

"Anytime you would like," she said.

"How will we get down there?" Becky asked.

"Your vessel will take us all down, like at Mars," Seth said.

"I say we go now," said Jennifer with excitement. "I wonder what incredible surprises await us down there. Houston, are we go for surface landing?"

"Copy that, Odyssey," CAPCOM replied. "You are go for surface landing on the Rim. Godspeed. Houston over and out."

She looked around, saw eager agreement, and nodded to their smiling hosts.

Soon all twenty were aboard Messenger and on their way for the final leg of the journey. All that they had dreamed about for years was coming true.

CHAPTER 19

Home Again for the First Time

After Messenger landed, the passageway opened as it had on Mars. This time, no one was suited up in EMUs. Wearing only their flight suits and headset communicators, the crew stepped out onto the surface of the Rim. The sky was as blue as any on Earth. There was a bright, white star nearly overhead. Six others, all fixed in place, could be seen in the distant horizon, almost like the evening star, Venus. The air was slightly cool and refreshing. A gentle breeze caressed their faces. The soft grass beneath their feet invited them to go barefoot. Andy and Randy immediately took off their boots and socks and began to run about, joyfully giggling. They stood in an immense meadow that was sprinkled with blooming flowers of many hues and varieties. The hum of bees could be heard. In the distance were formidable snow-capped, jagged mountains that rose great distances into the sky. In between the meadow and the foothills below the mountains were vast stretches of forest that had never been cut. On a low hill in the opposite direction stood a large open-sided pavilion, the first structure they had seen. There were other people similar in appearance and dress to Seth and Deborah entering from several directions.

"Come, we have prepared a feast in celebration of your arrival," Seth said, leading the way.

As the crew entered the pavilion, the hundreds of people of all ages gathered turned, looking at them, and began to sing a song of welcome. Its tonal quality immediately lifted their spirits, conveying a sense of joy and deep peace. The harmonies were intricate and flawless. Though the words were unknown to them, the crew understood the feelings conveyed by the sincerity and happiness on every face. Soon the focus shifted, suggesting an anthem of praise and gratitude to God for their guests and the banquet. It was so tender that several crew members began to cry for joy. Their hearts longed to join in. Some of them hummed along. All too soon, the music ended. Jennifer felt her heart ache for more, wishing the song could have gone on for hours.

"It is now time for feasting and honoring our guests, our brothers and sisters from Earth who have come such a long way," announced Seth.

Like with the tables and food aboard Messenger, dozens of tables appeared, full of sumptuous food of wide varieties. Chairs appeared, and the others began to seat themselves. A row of tables on a raised area appeared near Seth, Deborah, and the crew, with seats for them all. As Jennifer and David sat next to Seth and Deborah, Jennifer noticed the lack of utensils or individual plates. As soon as she thought it, a beautiful china plate appeared in front of her, complete with the familiar fork, knife, and spoon.

"David!" she exclaimed. "This is our china pattern and flatware from home. How is this possible?"

"You thought of it, and it came to be," Deborah said with a sweet smile.

Jennifer was too astonished to say anything, but her hunger led her to serve her plate from the platters of food within reach. A platter of barbecued ribs appeared in front of David, catching him by surprise.

"This is incredible!" he said. "I thought how good some pork ribs would be right now, and they just appeared. Would you like to try some, Seth?"

"Gladly," he said. "I look forward to sharing more food with you. Help yourself to ours as well. You will soon find them irresistible."

Allison was seated on the other side of David, next to Anastasia. She had a large glass of a dark, bubbling liquid appear before her plate. Allison gingerly tasted it.

"Dad!" she said. "It's Dr. Pepper. I haven't had one since our last supper back in Houston. This is best one I've ever tasted. I wonder what their ice cream will be like."

"How can we create these things by thought?" Jennifer asked Deborah.

"Here on Eden, we have our God-given powers unhindered," she replied. "You will learn much more about the gifts he has given you. It is essential that you use them only for doing good. Otherwise, the One will take them away or inhibit your ability to use them."

"Deborah, again you surprise me," Jennifer said. "You call this place Eden. Is it the Garden of Eden from the Bible?"

"Yes and no," Deborah replied. "It is free from the troubles and evil that may kill your world. But those of us who first came here named it Eden after an even earlier place the One had made for our very first people long ago. We call ourselves 'Edena.'"

"Messenger has told us that we all have telepathic abilities as well," Jennifer said. "I've already had a deep sense of connection and understanding with you and everyone here on an emotional level. I can 'hear' thoughts coming from many directions, much like listening to conversations in a crowded room. Is this what it is like?"

"Yes," Deborah said. "In the days to come, you will learn to focus and discipline your mind to receive and send these thoughts."

"Will all of my thoughts be open to everyone?" Jennifer asked.

"No," she responded. "Only those that you wish to reveal to others. However, they will sense your feelings if you hold something back. It will all become clearer as time goes on, much like a blind person suddenly being healed and learning to interpret what he or she sees."

Jennifer turned to David with a warm smile.

He looked back with a quirky grin and said, "I love you too!" and kissed her.

"It looks like you two will pick it up easily," Deborah said. "It's all powered by a loving heart."

As the meal progressed, the crew sampled many of the exotic dishes available. They also reveled in materializing and sharing their own favorite Earth dishes. The biggest hit of the meal was the ice cream that appeared in a few dozen varieties with all kinds of toppings. The Edena were especially excited about the chocolate varieties. Coffee was also extremely popular. Some were even beginning to sing about its qualities.

"Jennifer," David said, "do you think you should make a speech since we are the guests of honor?"

"No, but pass the word down the table to the rest of the crew to fill their minds and hearts with gratitude and love for the people here," Jennifer said. "I believe that they will receive it well."

No sooner had the word been passed and the crew focused their thoughts, that a hush came over the entire assembly, as they all turned their attention to the crew. Joy radiated from every face. Soon another song began, richer and more complex than the one before the meal. The crew members were so enthralled that they were surprised when the fading light indicated the approaching evening. Their hearts soared like eagles as the rhapsodic music proceeded forward. Time had passed and stood still as they were lost in the music. As twilight enveloped everyone and their land, the Edena began dispersing to go to their homes in the forest.

Seth, Deborah, and the crew left the pavilion and walked back toward Messenger.

"Is this as dark as it gets at night?" asked Jennifer.

"Yes," said Seth. "The star above our region is occulted with a huge piece of subspace for eight to fourteen hours every cycle, giving the effect of night and day as well as the seasons. With other fixed stars at a distance, the nights are never as dark as they are on Earth."

"Where does everyone go at night?" Allison asked. "Do they sleep like we do? Do you have homes to dwell in?"

"Yes, we sleep like you do," Deborah said. "Most of us choose to dwell in the forests. Our homes are modest structures and blend well into their ecosystems. Tomorrow, you are welcome to come to ours. It is just beyond the pavilion where we shared the banquet."

"How long are we to stay here?" David asked. "Jesus told us to prepare for our return voyage and mission back on Earth. What are we to do here?"

"We have been told that you are to stay for forty days, as each of you will be tutored by scholars among us who share similar interests to each of your respective specialties," Seth said. "We have been preparing for this time for years, even before your solar system was enveloped. The One told us that you, Jennifer, were chosen for your role in all that has happened; and you and the others will be prepared for all that lies ahead. For now, I hope you will have a restful night's sleep. We look forward to seeing you in the morning. You will know the way to our home when you leave Messenger near dawn. Good night, and may you rest in the Spirit."

The crew reentered Messenger and quickly checked in with Mission Control in Houston. Everything they had experienced had been transmitted back and recorded. The controllers were in awe and wonder like the crew. Billions of others across the Earth also followed everything during their waking hours. The crew retired to their quarters for brief contacts with family back on Earth before going to bed for the best night's sleep of their lives. Everyone experienced vivid dreams of the events of the past day, combined with glimpses of imagery of yet-to-be-explored locales across that region of the Rim.

CHAPTER 20

A New Day

Early in the morning, the daylight was beginning to increase from above as the occultation barrier shrank away from the white dwarf star hovering above. The crew left Messenger in a group and headed in the direction of the nearest forest. They were simply following the children, as if they were on a stroll through a park.

David turned to Jennifer. "Is this the direction to Seth and Deborah's home?"

"We have no instructions, but it feels right," Jennifer replied. "It's as if we had come this way for years, even all of our lives."

She looked at him with a look of disbelief and shook her head with a smile at the wonder of it all.

The mood was light as everyone enjoyed the mild climate and gentle breeze. David noticed that even though the meadow was full of flowers in full bloom, there were no insects assaulting them. He wondered if parasitic insects, like mosquitoes, even existed here. Though no one perspired, the hike across the meadow to the forest took a while. It built up everyone's appetite, and their pace gradually quickened.

Near the edge of the forest, a low, modest stone structure could be seen. It had plenty of windows without screens or glass. The moss growing on the slate roof and stone walls suggested great age. Seth and Deborah could be seen near the entrance, awaiting their arrival.

About five hundred meters from their destination, everyone came to a halt, frozen at the sight of a huge African male lion crouching in attack posture. He was intensely focused on the astronauts—more specifically, Andy, Randy, Toma and Kushe who were in the lead a hundred paces ahead of everyone else. Before anyone could say a word, the lion broke into a furious charge straight for the children. Allison and Anastasia screamed. Petrus and Becky ran to intercept, but everyone could see that the lion would reach the children first. Helpless fear and panic filled everyone with the exception of the children, who had paused to chase a meerkat. They were oblivious to their peril until the lion was upon them. At the last instant, the lion halted in front of the children. Instead of the expected assault of vicious claws and jaws, the lion came to Toma and Andy and gently sniffed their faces. When Petrus and Becky arrived, they were unsure of what to do, so they simply stopped in wonder. Within a couple of seconds, the rest of the crew arrived. The oversized lion was unperturbed by the surrounding humans. He looked around and rolled lazily in the grass, remaining on his back as if waiting for someone to come up and scratch him. Seth and Deborah arrived shortly thereafter.

"I am sorry that the lion scared you," Seth said. "He loves to play and romp. It's been a while since he has seen children."

"The size, the gentleness!" David exclaimed. "Did you raise and feed him?"

"No, he is completely wild," Deborah answered. "None of the multitude of animals here hurt or kill, even these great lions."

"What do they do for food?" Toma asked as he rubbed and scratched away at the lion's belly.

"Like you, they simply imagine a favorite food, and it appears," said Seth. "None of them have ever had to kill to eat, nor have they ever had to fear humans."

"But they are so large," Maria remarked.

"Yes, you might be too if you could eat whenever you wanted and never get sick," Seth said. "Come on into our house for breakfast. There is much to discuss."

The crew was led through the sparsely decorated home to the patio area in the rear. It was a flagstone floor surrounded by verdant gardens and hedged by the trees of the mighty forest beyond. The air was permeated with the fragrance of life. Birdsong and other animal calls could be heard. In the center of the patio stood a large circular table with handmade wooden chairs all around its perimeter. Everyone sat down as if they were at home, and food began to appear before them, as it had at the banquet the night before. Deborah led everyone in a singing grace, and they began to eat and talk about the day.

They were joined by a tall, fair-skinned younger man who shared some facial features with Seth and Deborah.

"I would like to introduce our grandson, Eli," Deborah said.

Allison and Anastasia took immediate notice, as they stopped eating. Eli was even taller than Seth. He appeared to be about college age and easily would have qualified for any basketball team back home. His well-proportioned head was highlighted with curly blonde hair. It was his pale blue eyes that captivated Allison. Her pulse rose as she stared at him. When Eli suddenly returned her gaze, she blushed and looked away. To her horror, he came and sat down in a vacant chair right next to her. Eli immediately turned to face her with a slight smile, as if to begin conversation, but he remained silent, as if studying her face with the same intensity she had studied him. Allison felt a rush of serenity and acceptance, as if she had known Eli all her life. Her pulse was still racing, and her breath was halting. This was the most beautiful young man she had ever seen.

"I am not very good at words," Eli began in a resonant bass. "I use my voice for singing. My thoughts are conveyed in what you call 'telepathy.' Please forgive my clumsiness."

"Oh, I don't mind at all," Allison stammered. "I'm Allison, and this is Anastasia."

"It is wonderful to meet you both," he replied. "I sense that both of you have strong telepathic abilities. Would you mind if I were to help you awaken them?"

Allison felt fear rising.

"Please, I will not intrude into your private feelings," Eli said reassuringly. "You need only focus your thoughts, as if you were going to speak, and then listen for my reply."

Allison shot a glance at Anastasia, who looked as frightened as she did. Then, on impulse, Allison turned to Eli and thought, *Why not?*

Great! Eli responded. *You will master it in no time.*

Allison blushed again at the intimacy of hearing his voice inside her. She wondered if he could sense her intense attraction to him. If so, Eli never let on. He only continued to smile warmly at them both.

Can Anastasia hear me too? Allison wondered.

Yes, and I hear you both, Anastasia chimed in.

Allison turned to look at her with eyes full of wonder.

How is this possible? Allison wondered.

It is another one of the wonderful gifts that God has given you, Eli responded. *You were made for this. You just did not know it.*

How much do you know about me? Allison wondered, trying to look coy but scared that Eli could read everything inside her mind.

I know enough, he responded. *You and Anastasia are very talented young women with tremendous potential. Your minds are keen, and your hearts are pure.*

At the mention of hearts, Allison blushed so strongly that she felt like Eli knew everything about her. He must know that she was falling for him, but he gave no hint of that. She had no way of knowing how much he knew or could sense inside of her.

How did Anastasia feel about him? Would Eli prefer her? What if Anastasia could read all of this too?

Please relax, girls, Eli responded, taking Allison's hand into his own. *Both of you are becoming overwhelmed by this newly discovered ability. I assure you that I will keep a respectful distance from your innermost thoughts. I will look to see only what you want to 'say' to me.*

Allison nearly melted at his touch. She looked back to Anastasia, and both giggled slightly. Allison hated herself for being so immature. She was very unsure of this new telepathic ability. For her, it was the biggest discovery of the entire voyage.

Meanwhile, Jennifer and David were receiving surprises of their own as they conversed with Seth and Deborah over breakfast.

"There are so many questions," Jennifer began. "I hope you won't be offended if we keep asking."

"Not at all," replied Deborah with a reassuring smile. "It is wonderful that you are so eager to learn, and we are blessed to teach you."

"You have said that we will be here only forty days before Messenger returns us to Earth," Jennifer began. "Why such a short time and what can we learn to be of any help back home?"

"The One has determined the times of your stay and your mission to the people back home," Seth said. "Your world is in terrible trouble. Rescuing your solar system from the passing black hole was the easy part. The spiritual sickness on Earth has metastasized so quickly that it may not be possible to save your world from its coming self-destruction."

"We know of the politics and other social and international crises that have risen, but that is as old as our world," David replied. "Won't it all somehow work out in the end?"

"The intensity and speed are different," Seth said. "The spiritual ruler of your world has been at war with the One since the beginning of time. The coming of the Sphere terrifies him because his power and time are almost over. Desperation drives him to take as many of your people with him as possible."

"Do you mean the Devil, or Satan?" Jennifer asked.

"We do not use his name here," said Deborah with a hint of fear to her voice. "We have been blessed to have been free of his influence for nearly seventy thousand years."

"What is our role in this ancient conflict?" David asked.

"The One is preparing you three for the tasks of being messengers of the truth and light in the midst of the darkness being spread across Earth like a poisonous cloud," said Seth. "We do not know many details, but the One has made it clear that we are to share all of our knowledge and skills with you to prepare you for Earth's final conflict."

Jennifer and David looked at each other in shock at the gravity of these words.

"Our goal in coming out here was to learn and share so both of our worlds would benefit. So now the task becomes even more onerous," Jennifer said. "Let's get started."

"Our first task is to take all of you on a journey to see the outside of the Sphere," said Deborah. "Please gather your crew, and we will travel aboard Messenger."

Jennifer felt an inner thrill for the chance to see stars again. She wondered what changes might be seen in the patterns of the constellations.

As they left the house, Messenger drew near and hovered above, deploying a ramp for a short climb on board. Soon everyone was seated in the control room. The walls turned transparent as Messenger lifted high into the atmosphere, leveling off where the sky turned from blue to black.

CHAPTER 21

Class Begins

T he surface of the interior of the Rim appeared completely flat—so vast was the scale. It was natural to expect the distant horizon to fall away with a slight convex curvature. Instead, it rose ever so slightly in the misty distance that measured thousands of kilometers. Try as she might, Jennifer still could not discern any concavity. Their increasing velocity appeared in kph's on a digital monitor.

"It is truly wondrous," Seth remarked.

"I can't tell any curvature to the surface," Jennifer said. "Everything out here is so large that it all seems flat."

"How far will we go across the Rim?" Allison asked.

"About fifty thousand kilometers to the portal," replied Deborah. "It is only a small fraction of the way around the interior surface."

"What portal?" David asked.

"It is one of a dozen passageways through the two-million-kilometer Rim to the exterior of the Sphere," Eli said.

"You said that most of this interior surface is uninhabited," said Allison. "Will we pass over any of the thirty-six other civilizations that are out here?"

"Not this time," replied Deborah. "Contact with many of them will come later for the fifteen of you who will remain on the Rim to help prepare the way for the rest of your people back on Earth."

"Our people back on Earth?" Jennifer interjected. "Is everyone on Earth going to be relocated out here? If so, how and when?"

"The One has kept us appraised as to the deterioration of conditions back on Earth," Seth said. "The outlook is bad, and a mass evacuation will probably be necessary for the survivors."

"Survivors?" asked David. "We have kept up with the news even out here, and I had no idea that it could ever come to that."

"The prince of your world is desperate since his end is near. He has enflamed all of the old hatreds and fears of the people of your world, and the decline is accelerating toward a terrible catastrophe," Seth replied. "We have less than forty days to prepare you three to return with us to save as many as we can."

"Why us?" Allison asked.

"You were chosen for this," Deborah said. "Everyone is chosen for some unique part of God's plans. By now, you three are the best-known family in the history of Earth. Your influence is beyond measure. Millions have been watching and listening to everything you say and do since your voyage began."

Allison looked at her parents with a perplexed expression. "I'm not up to this," she said softly.

"None of us are," Jennifer responded. "Somehow, God has been and is preparing us. We must trust him. For now, let's enjoy what we will soon experience."

In the far distance, an enormous gray wall rose to block the horizon up to about one thousand kilometers above the surface. As they drew closer, the wall revealed a backside, where another section of the Rim's surface ran off into the expansive distance. The landscape appeared to be at a similar depth to the region they were about to leave. The ruddy hues on the land portions hinted at a widely variant plant life from what they had seen up close. Not far to the right, another massive section of wall met the first one at a perpendicular angle. In the middle of the junction on the top surface, a hole ringed with blue light surrounding a black center could be distinguished. Messenger was headed for it with a gradual descent. The gigantic scale of the Rim's interior had deceived them into perceiving everything with an earthen perspective. It took another five minutes to reach the opening, and the top of the wall was so wide that it nearly filled their frontal view. The monitor indicated a steady increase in velocity to above twenty thousand kph's. Seth, Deborah, and Eli remained relaxed as the eighteen astronauts all tensed up at the fast approach of the flat, dull, gray surface.

"What is that wall made of?" David asked, breaking the nervous silence.

"It's a steel, carbon, and silicon composite that has been knitted together on the molecular scale," Seth replied. "These walls divide the interior surface of the Rim into hundreds of separate regions that can be adapted to suit the needs of the biospheres of almost any planet. Presently, most of them are vacant. Our Earth region is a hundred times the size of the surface area of Earth. When the Sphere last came to Earth long ago, all life-forms were sampled and brought here, including a large sampling of the fossil record. Since then, several sections have been dedicated to restoring thousands of species of animals and plants now extinct on Earth."

Messenger continued to accelerate as the portal opening grew in size. The countdown to the entrance was ticking down ever slower as time dilated.

"Now I know what it would be like to be a bullet fired from a gun at a flat surface," remarked Becky Ishulutak as she held her twins closely in her lap to reassure them.

"I can't get over the massive scale of everything out here," Maria Quaupucura said. "Earth has always been our frame of reference. No wonder the cartographic atlas delivered by Messenger was so enormous."

A faint reddish glow could be seen as Messenger's energy field deflected the thin atmosphere. As the seconds to entrance ticked away to zero, everyone held their breath. In a blink, they were inside the portal. Messenger continued to accelerate into the inky blackness of the portal's passage. No light was discernible apart from the numbers on the readouts on the control panels inside of Messenger.

"How long will it take to get to the outside?" Anastasia asked.

"About two hours," Deborah said. "We will travel about two million kilometers."

"All of this matter should collapse into a huge star bigger than Betelgeuse," Jennifer remarked.

"Helium II is used to attenuate the gravity," Eli said. "The passageway in this portal is constructed of a tube of solid, transparent diamond that is five kilometers thick."

"How does the Helium II control gravity?" Alice Cly asked.

"When Helium II is chilled to a few fractions of a degree of absolute zero, approaching its ground state, it acts as a barrier or insulator against gravity," Eli answered. "By controlling its precise temperature and thickness, gravity can be regulated for each region of the Rim to suit the needs of the creatures residing there. It flows in subterranean channels and seas over a million kilometers deep about a thousand kilometers beneath the interior surface, which consists of granite and basalt rock, much like Earth and most other rocky planets."

After fifteen minutes of passage, a faint blue light could be seen all around, as if they were inside of a massive dark atmosphere filled with gossamer, blue clouds.

"What you are seeing now is the helium II, which emanates a faint blue light," Eli said.

"How do you maintain this vast structure and keep all of this matter from collapsing in on itself from the sheer force of gravity?" queried Vartan Bedevian. "By the laws of science and engineering as we know them, it is impossible to construct and sustain something of this magnitude, billions of times larger than a rocky planet like ours."

"The inner structure of the Sphere is a complex network of structural elements, energy generation, and gravitational attenuation, all controlled by advanced, hyperdimensional technologies on scales from complexes larger than Earth down to nanobots beyond count," said Deborah. "It is structured like a biological organism, with a nervous system for control, a circulatory system that regulates the flow of the helium II, a skeletal system of composites similar to the wall above, and a muscular system for effecting all of the functions of the Sphere. The structural elements even use the force of gravity to generate piezoelectricity. All components in the Sphere are constantly renewed down to the molecular level, similar to the cells and tissues of your body. Remember that it took almost a billion years and the matter from hundreds of uninhabited stellar systems to complete."

The astronauts all shared bewildered expressions in contemplation of what they were learning. Then Jennifer returned to the matter of contact with home.

"Houston, Odyssey here. So you still read us?" she said.

"Yes, loud and clear, Odyssey," came the reply on their headsets. "We are as full of awe as you are. When you arrive at the exterior, get a fix on our new position in the Galaxy if you can."

"Copy that, Houston," Jennifer said. "We will try to collect and record everything we see out there. Odyssey out."

Messenger displayed schematics of the interior structure and major systems of the insides of the Sphere's two-million-kilometer composition. The astronauts were like young children seeing and riding an airplane for the first time. The simplicity of the Sphere's organic design was deceptively complex, and all of it had been maintained for eons by artificial intelligence.

After half an hour, Jennifer turned to astronomical questions. "Will Earth and our solar system be returned to the original position?" she wondered. "When will that be?"

"We don't know," Seth responded. "The One has told us that the crisis on Earth is so severe that it could take years or even centuries. By then, most, if not all, of you would opt to stay out here on the Rim, even when the time comes to disgorge your system."

"Where will the Sphere go next?" Allison asked.

"Again, we don't know," Eli said. "None of the thirty-seven peoples on the Rim determine the timing or direction of the journeys."

"Who does?" asked Petrus. "Is it up to the artificial intelligence that maintains the Sphere?"

"I'll answer that one," interrupted Messenger. "No. The direction and mission are revealed to me, or us. We move the Sphere to the specified location and undertake the assigned tasks necessary to save each world we are sent to."

"Messenger, you said 'me' and 'us.' What does that mean?" asked Becky Ishulutak. "Are you the machine that runs everything?"

"Yes and no," Messenger responded. "There are millions of distinct units of what you would call artificial, or manufactured, intelligence. Yet we are all closely linked and access one another as the need arises."

"Who reveals your mission?" Becky asked.

"The One you know as God and Lord," Messenger said.

"Did he create you?" she asked.

"He created those who created us and inspired their work throughout the millennia," Messenger answered.

Turning to Deborah, Fatima al-Tarabin asked, "The people out here never seem to suffer and appear to live forever. Does anyone, your species or the others we have yet to meet, ever die?"

"No humans out here have yet died," Deborah answered. "Even when someone experiences an accident that would be fatal on Earth, they are resuscitated and healed. Several species that have resided on the Rim have left entirely during our stay. They simply vanished as the One had determined their time in corporeal bodies had ended."

"Where did they go?" Apiranoa Ngata asked.

"Above, beyond space and time," Eli said.

"When will our time come?" David asked.

"Only the One knows," Seth said. "It could be in an hour or another seventy thousand years."

"What do you do with all that time in your lives if you live for seventy thousand years?" Allison queried.

"We feel sorry for you with your all-too-brief spans of seventy or eighty years," Deborah replied. "Our years are full of learning, travels, longtime friendships, rich experiences, and best of all, a deep spiritual life. We have done so much. I have composed symphonies, written volumes of poetry and literature, and mastered every field of science and engineering; and there is so much more to do. Once you and your people have resettled here, you will adapt to the wonders of this longer lifespan."

The velocity readout indicated that they had passed one million kilometers per hour, topping out at 1.5 million kph. Then, like an elevator on a tall building, Messenger began a steady deceleration. A blue ring of light became discernible and grew as they approached. Everyone became silent as they slowed to less than ten kph. Suddenly, the blue ring passed by, and Messenger emerged above the Sphere. All around and beneath lay a dimly shimmering surface that stretched out to the remote horizon. Above them, the celestial sky of familiar stars, constellations, and the misty streak of the Milky Way shone forth in pinpoints of light that had dazzled humanity since the beginning. Jennifer began to cry for joy at the sight of the heavens that no one had seen for years. Gasps of awe could be heard among the crew.

Messenger slowly approached a substantial structure that rose a kilometer above the surface, then docked to a port on the underside of its oversized top level. Soon everyone had disembarked and risen by topless elevator to the flat open roof, which was about twenty meters in diameter and covered by a clear dome.

"Welcome to one of our observatories," Eli said. "Since the Sphere has moved only two billion kilometers from your original position prior to envelopment, the star patterns you call constellations are largely the same as before. Please have a seat and enjoy the show."

Twenty-one black, upholstered chairs in semireclined positions appeared before them. Having seen this sort of thing often aboard Messenger, the crew simply assumed the seats. Eli walked over to Jennifer with a helmet and a pair of gloves.

"Since you have studied these heavens and led your people here, please do the honors of directing our viewing," he said. "The rest of us will see on the dome above us what you see in your helmet. This helmet will interface with your brain and eyes, and the gloves will respond to your hand movements to rotate the view and adjust the magnification. You are familiar with optical interferometry. On Earth you might use a few dozen telescopes in an array to combine images with the help of computers to gain greater resolution. Here, the entire outside surface of the Sphere is covered with trillions of telescopic instruments in an array that combines through interferometry to cover the entire electromagnetic spectrum. The resolution here will enable you to see a grain of sand on a beach on a planet twenty thousand light years away."

Jennifer donned the helmet, which instantly changed the view of the dome. She then put on the gloves and began to get acclimated to their functions. Slowly, she rotated the field of view around the entire outside of the Sphere. As large as the Sphere was, it was quickly dwarfed by the vast immensity of the surrounding cosmos. The highlight for everyone was the luminous band of the Milky Way that ran in a rough belt all around. Jennifer asked for the larger two hundred stars to be labeled, and labels appeared next to each one. Then she added constellation asterisms and boundaries. All eighty-eight could be seen as the view rotated. Jennifer then dismissed all markings and began to zoom in on various nebulae. With combined enhancements from the infrared, ultraviolet, and x-ray frequencies, each of them glowed with greater clarity and detail than the Hubble Space Telescope had delivered. The incredible resolving power gave live views in the full range of colors. The Crab Nebula drew hums of awe as Jennifer explained its dramatic history. Everyone was enchanted by the Eagle Nebula and its Pillars of Creation. With the Ring Nebula, Jennifer was able to zoom in close to a protostar, giving detail much like solar images of the sun. She caught herself in midlecture as she had gone into detail about the types of nebulae. It was time to check out exoplanets.

"Let's look at an exoplanet with advanced multicellular life-forms," Jennifer said.

The system responded with the view of an earthlike planet, filling the dome above them. It was labeled Gliese 667 Cc, a mesoplanet (moderate temperature range in the habitable zone of its star), 23.6 light years distant. Fortunately, the planet was on the farther side of its star, revealing daylight across the surface. Jennifer then drew a deep breath as she zoomed in to reveal large continents separated by blue oceans of liquid water. Polar ice sheets covered the northern and southern regions to about fifteen degrees from the poles. As the image zoomed closer, the land showed evidence of vast tracks of crimson and green vegetation. Snow-capped peaks came into view. Larger lakes and rivers glistened in the light of their home star. The world was so earthlike that everyone tried to identify familiar landscapes of home. Jennifer made the zoom go even deeper, to where a large grassland resolved into view. Tens of thousands of large animals ranged across its surface, much like the Serengeti in Kenya. As the view came even closer, most of the creatures were four-legged herbivores, almost like wildebeests, but with variant colorations, horns, and heavy coats of hair. Predatory carnivores came into view, hunting in a pack. They walked upright in a bipedal manner until they dropped to all fours to run in pursuit of a prey animal. Their dark, hairy fur was reminiscent of mountain gorillas. Jennifer then backed the resolution out and looked toward the terminator. There was no hint of the artificial lighting of cities. She then turned to a major river channel and followed it at close range in search of any settlements or cities.

"Is there any civilized, intelligent life on this world?" she asked.

"No," said Eli. "About fifty thousand years ago, this world was also in crisis when the Sphere was sent and rescued them and this planet. These people are with us now on a far region of the Rim. Some of you will meet them soon."

"You say 'people,'" Jennifer said. "Are they humanoid?"

"Yes, in a general sense, but they are very different in appearance, social functions, psychology, language, perspective, and abilities," he replied.

"Can we meet some of them and the other peoples of the Rim?" Allison asked.

"You and your parents will not have time now," Eli answered seriously. "You must now be prepared for all that we will encounter on our return to Earth. Your mission is of utmost importance to humanity. If and when you return, I will be pleased to introduce you to each species and their world."

David suddenly noticed that their stargazing had taken six hours. He and the others were becoming hungry. Suddenly, an open-pit barbeque appeared before them, along with a table heaped with plentiful foods, both familiar and unknown. Jennifer removed her helmet and gloves, and the dome returned to the real view. After a prayer sung in gratitude for the food, everyone enjoyed a feast under the stars. After a couple of hours of feasting and small talk, Jennifer announced that it was time to return to the meadow near Seth and Deborah's home on the Rim inside the Sphere, so everyone returned to Messenger, and their return began. Some slept, while others were lost in silent reverie. What they had experienced for the past three weeks was but a dim shadow of the intense spiritual and intellectual training they were about to undergo.

CHAPTER 22

To a Whole New Level

The next morning, the astronauts all assembled with Seth, Deborah, and several dozen Edena, who were introduced and assigned to each adult crew member according to their specialty and tasks in preparing the Rim for receiving survivors from Earth. Seth announced that Jennifer, David, and Allison would now be separated from the rest for their training for the return to Earth alone in thirty-nine days. There were tearful hugs and reassurances shared among them all. Everyone hoped that there would be a joyful reunion in a couple of months. The kids were especially sorrowful, but none more than Allison and Anastasia, who had become fast friends. Soon the fifteen who were to remain on the Rim departed for various locations with their mentors. Jennifer was delighted to find that Seth and Deborah were to be their mentors. She and David had grown to trust these two ancient ones more than anyone they had ever known. Allison was terrified at the prospect of Eli being part of the mentor team, with her as his special pupil. All six of them made their way back to Seth and Deborah's home, returning to the garden-shrouded patio in the rear, where they took comfortable seats.

"We must quickly help each of you develop your full spiritual abilities," Seth said with seriousness. "First, we want to help you access the telepathic bond we share with others out here on the Rim. This will also help you mentally access the vast database from the cybernetic system you know as Messenger. You will retain these powers even when you return to Earth. For now, relax and remain seated."

Seth arose and approached David, Deborah approached Jennifer, and Eli approached Allison. Allison felt her pulse quicken and her palms sweat. She tried to suppress the blush she knew was betraying her. Each of the Edena faced their partners and, closing their eyes and placing their hands to the temples of their subjects, began to breathe deeply, chanting something indistinguishable. Allison opened her eyes briefly at the perception of a sudden breeze only to be astonished to see tongues of flame above Eli and his grandparents. She felt a surge of power within her mind and heart as well as a feeling of love and peace that made her want to sing for joy. For the second time in their voyage, Allison became acutely aware of Jesus near her and within her. In her mind's eye, she could see those around her and hear their thoughts. Allison looked to her mother and had an instant awareness of her thoughts. Almost like he was talking to her, she felt her dad and turned to connect to him. Out of awe, Allison opened her eyes to find Eli looking right into her eyes—herself. With tears in her eyes, she took a deep breath and released the love she felt for him. He smiled and nodded, conveying the response, *Yes, I know.* Before she could follow that further, Allison heard Seth in her mind saying, *It's as easy as breathing. From now on, we will all communicate with this telepathy. In a group, it is much like verbal conversation. You will be able to hear each 'voice' and must focus on the one you want to 'hear.' It can also wear you out until your abilities strengthen. You are much like blind people who have been given sight. Remember that you must not use this gift to invade or coerce the mind of another or your powers can be permanently lost. It is only with genuine love for another that you will be able to use this power. And now, I want to open you up for access to our knowledge base."*

Again the tongues of flame appeared above their heads as Seth, Deborah, and Eli chanted in a similar fashion, but this time, the tongues also appeared above David, Jennifer, and Allison. Allison closed her eyes and saw herself floating in a vast sea of widely varied shades and hues of flickering light. She tried to recognize what she was seeing when it resolved into a narrated diagram explaining the overall structure of the mental library. It finished within seconds, and she felt like she had used it all of her life. All it took to access a subject in verbal and visual forms was to think of it. She was even able to download vast amounts of knowledge into her brain. Allison experimented with Spanish, which had always challenged her back on Earth, to find that within seconds, she now had great fluency at the level of a native speaker. She was drawn back by a voice calling her name.

Allison, thought Eli. *You can lose yourself in this if you are not careful. Let's take a break for now. Would you like to go for a walk?*

With eager excitement, Allison looked to her dad for permission.

David knew immediately what she needed and nodded his ascent. *Just remember, Allison, he's a little older than you, and there's a world of difference between you. Also know that your mother and I can read your thoughts from a distance now.*

Allison and Eli walked off into the woods that halted at the gardens in the rear of Seth and Deborah's home. Sunlight streamed down through trees larger than the redwoods of Earth. Understory trees of exotic varieties were ablaze with fragrant blooms. The songs of birds filled the air. Allison was amazed that her allergies were dormant. They continued some distance in silence along the mossy banks of a flowing stream. A steep, rocky trail led down to a clear pool that was fed by a small waterfall from the stream. Allison felt thirst and tried a handful of water. It had a faint sweetness. She found a large rock on the bank and took off her shoes to cool her feet in the pool. Allison motioned for Eli to come and sit beside her. She had never felt so happy. If this wasn't paradise, she couldn't imagine what was lacking.

Eli, she thought, *Dad reminded me that you are almost seventy thousand years old, but, to me, you appear to be no more than twenty-five. You must have been married ages ago and have descendants by the millions. I can't imagine what that must be like.*

Allison, Eli responded with a look of mystery, *I am as old as you say, but I have never been married. Everyone else of my age was married long ago and generated many descendants.*

Why were you never married? Allison thought, with concern about this anomaly. *Weren't there any eligible women?*

I am unique in that I am one chosen for a special mission in ancient prophecy, he replied. *During all of these millennia, I have been learning extensively in many areas of study in preparation for that mission. My wife was prophesied as one who would come in a later age from Earth as a second wave of people. When the mission is complete, if I survive, she and I will be married.*

What prophecy and mission is that? Allison asked.

I am to depart with you, your parents, and my grandparents when you leave in under forty days, Eli thought. *Our mission is to bear the message of the One to your world in its last days during the final conflict.*

Allison began to mull over his words and built up the courage for the more personal question, as she thought, *Do you know who your wife is? Am I the gifted and chosen one you will marry?*

Eli looked into her eyes with a deep and loving look, as if he had known her forever. He gave no answer, and she was not able to discern his thoughts, but a deep happiness filled her with a joy that made her want to sing. Allison impulsively grabbed Eli, embraced him, and kissed him briefly on the lips. He raised an eyebrow as if to feign surprise.

All I will tell you now is that the mission is of ultimate importance to us, Eli thought. *Nothing must distract us from getting ready for what lies ahead. Let us return to continue our training. Now we must discover what your special gifts are and how they will be used.*

Allison grabbed his hand and led the way as they followed the trail back. She felt as if she could fly. Allison began to wonder how she would explain all of this to her parents. Her brother, Justin, had married at sixteen and so far, so good. But Allison was just fifteen. She knew better than anyone how much more she would need to grow before committing herself in marriage. A shiver of fear ran through her mind as she considered how strange it would be to marry such an old man, who wasn't much older than her physically but had lived much more life than anyone from her world ever had. Eli was even older than any living thing back home. He knew more than anyone on Earth could ever learn. What could they possibly have in common? But then there was this incredible bond through telepathy which opened her up like nothing ever had.

Allison wondered how Eli would relate with her family. What would Justin and Sarah make of him? How would Cerberus, their dog, take to him? She then realized how much she had missed that silly dog. He had been cared for by Sam and Ida Wilson out on their ranch. Allison wondered what kind of trouble Cerberus might have gotten into with all that open range to explore. She began to cry, and suddenly, with a bright flash of light, Cerberus materialized before her and Eli. Allison was as startled as Eli. She then grabbed the big dog and began to hug and pet him.

I believe we have discovered another one of your special gifts, Allison, thought Eli. *This must be Cerberus. He has missed you as much as you have missed him.*

How did this happen? Allison asked. *It's hundreds of millions of kilometers back to Earth. Am I just imagining his being here?*

No, this is really your beloved dog, Eli mused. *So you have a telekinetic ability. No one out here has ever had it so strong as to transport a living creature over such a great distance. I worry about the impact on anyone on Earth who may have seen his disappearance.*

As they approached everyone else on the patio, Cerberus barked and ran pell-mell to David and Jennifer, who were stunned in amazement.

Jennifer looked up at Allison with mixed emotions. "I think you have several major questions to answer for us," she said audibly and with gravity. "First, you, your father, and I will have some serious conversation with you about your new love interest." Allison blushed and gasped, realizing that her mom knew everything. "And second," continued Jennifer, "I want to know how you brought Cerberus here, across forty-nine AUs of space."

"I don't know, Mom," Allison said unconvincingly. "I thought about how much I missed him, began to cry, and then a bright flash appeared, and here he is. Eli tells me that I have an exceptional telekinetic power to transport living creatures. Should I send Cerberus home?"

"No, let's let him stay for now," said Jennifer. "But we will need to contact the Wilsons to let them know his whereabouts. Surely this is the farthest a dog has ever strayed. But that aside, I think it best that you stay with your dad and me for the remainder of our time here."

"Mom, nothing happened!" Allison exclaimed with embarrassed irritation. "You read my mind and know exactly what happened. Besides, Eli is a wonderful gentleman you can trust."

"It's not him I'm concerned about," replied Jennifer. "The intensity of your passion can easily overwhelm your judgment. You have little experience by which to manage your behavior, and with the openness of this telepathy, it all might prove to be too much for you to handle."

Allison had become exasperated to the point of tears when she sensed the loving feelings of everyone there focused on her. Laughter began to overtake her emotions as she chuckled through her tears. "I guess I made a fool of myself out there. I'm sorry, especially to you, Eli," she said.

Eli looked at her with that wondrously enchanting look that had captured her heart and verbally said, "No harm done. Your feelings are pure and true. Every one of us here loves you with all our hearts, and we will each do everything we can to help you grow through this to become the wonderful woman the One created you to be."

Then everyone joined together for a light lunch. David, Jennifer, and Allison then took a break to return to Messenger, a few hundred meters away, to check in with their family back on Earth.

At first, they checked in with Jennifer's mom and found her to be doing fine. She had spent most of her waking hours following them on the live feed from Messenger's transponder. She admitted that so much of it all had bewildered her, but she felt great joy over the wondrous experiences they had gone through.

Then Jennifer tried to initiate contact with Justin and Sarah, only to fail.

"Messenger, where are they?" Jennifer asked.

"I'm working on that, Jennifer," Messenger replied. "It is strange. Their cell phones and computers are active but nonresponsive. Their location applications indicate that these devices have been moved to a large building in Reston, Virginia. As for Justin or Sarah, I have no location information but will continue the search."

"I think I can expedite that," Jennifer said. "Messenger, connect me with General Morris."

Once again, the matter-of-fact poker face of the unshakable military friend appeared on the screen.

"Hello, General Morris," Jennifer said. "I hope I haven't caught you at a bad time."

"Hello, Jennifer," he replied. "With you, there is never a bad time. What can I do for you?"

"I'm worried because we tried to contact my son and daughter-in-law in Austin, where they're in college. Messenger indicates that their cell phones and computers are active, but nonresponsive, and located in Reston, Virginia. Is something wrong back there?"

"I'm sorry to tell you bad news, Jennifer," General Morris said gravely. "As for Justin and Sarah, my people are working on it. Nationally, President Barton has blown a gasket and has inflamed a great deal of trouble for our country. He's declared DEFCON 1 and ordered the arrest of all of the members of the opposing party and much of the military command personnel. He has held lengthy daily telecasts, where he launches into tirades against anyone who criticizes him in the media or elsewhere. He has stirred up fear and hatred of all of the various groups in society as well as incited riots and widespread civil unrest. He even tried to break off all communication from your mission, but his people couldn't find the hyperdimensional transmitter left behind by Messenger. It has been broadcasting in such a way that any wireless capable device can receive the signal. You are already aware that Barton had declared your mission to be a hoax. Now that has been altered as he stirs up fear that you and the people of the Rim are planning a massive invasion of Earth to make slaves out of us all. The joint chiefs of the military have quietly explored invoking the twenty-fifth amendment, but almost half of the country is still in support of this man. The vice president has gotten severely drunk and the speaker of the House of Representatives has been assassinated. The line of presidential succession is very uncertain at best. Other congressional leaders and the Supreme Court justices are scared into silence. I am currently in a secret location because of that little favor I did helping you and your crew into orbit. America is on the brink of a civil war. May God help us all."

Just then, an aide brought General Morris a note.

"Good news about your kids," he said with an uneasy smile. "While their apartment in Austin was raided by 'unidentifiable agents' yesterday evening, a neighbor reports that they had been gone for a couple of days. One of our inside sources in the CIA says that their computers and cell phones were seized and are being examined. I don't think these agents for the president have Justin or Sarah, but we don't yet know where they are. Give me a couple of hours; we will find them, and, if necessary, rescue them."

"Thanks for your help," Jennifer said, choking back tears. "You are a true friend. I hope we can repay you some day."

"I believe that you will," he said. "Please let me know if you hear anything before I do. Rest assured that we will find them, and soon. Good-bye for now."

The screen went blank, and Jennifer turned to David and Allison.

"David, what if Barton is holding Justin and Sarah as hostages?" she quivered.

"I don't think he'd have the guts to do something that stupid with our ability to go directly to almost everyone on Earth," David said. "Maybe we should do just that—turn on our communication gear and hold our own press conference."

"That might make everything worse," Jennifer replied.

"I think we have been so busy that we have forgotten the power we have been given as the most famous family on Earth," David said. "Most of the people back home have followed all of our daily events and are fascinated. Think of how much pressure eight billion people could bring to bear on a rogue politician."

Just then, their screen lit up with the image of Justin and Sarah in an unknown office.

"Mom and Dad," Justin said. "We're okay. It's great to see you. We're sorry if we gave you a scare."

"Where are you?" Jennifer demanded. "What has happened?"

"I had a premonition that something bad was about to happen to us with all the crazy things the president has been doing lately," Justin said. "Besides, it was getting hard to study at campus with all of the attention we have been getting. You probably don't realize that all three of you and us are now the hottest celebrities of all times. Students, friends, strangers, and even professors have been reacting in strange ways, treating us as if we had the power to make them happy, or rich, or whatever. Two days ago, we decided to get away, and left our electronics behind. We borrowed a friend's car and drove home. We're talking to you from Pastor Scott's office."

"I don't think you will be safe there for long," Jennifer said with concern. "General Morris told me that your apartment was raided by some kind of special agents yesterday, and your electronics are now with the CIA in Reston, Virginia. It's only a matter of time before they come looking for you in Fort Davis. I'll call General Morris back right away, and his people will get you out to a truly safe location. Lay low and don't be seen around town. God bless you and keep you."

"You too," Justin chimed in. "We love you all. And Allison, next time you decide to kiss a guy, no matter how old he is, make sure your com gear is off. Everyone on Earth saw you kiss Eli. It's been playing over and over on all of the news channels, besides going hyperviral on the Internet. You won't need to post that on Facebook. Remember that he still has to get my approval."

The screen went blank, and David and Jennifer turned to Allison, who had blushed scarlet all the way down her neck and arms.

"Young lady, remember who you are and whose you are," said Jennifer with a slight smirk on her face. "What is the old expression? 'Your sins will find you out.'"

"Jennifer," interrupted David. "That's not fair. Allison has suffered already for her impulsive gesture of affection. I'm sure she's already learning and growing from all of this."

"Thanks, Dad," Allison said sheepishly. "I believe I have made myself into the world's biggest fool. When I go home to Earth maybe I can land a job with Comedy Central."

Jennifer rose from her chair and hugged Allison. "Like Eli said, 'No harm done.' There are probably a couple hundred million women and girls back on Earth who would give anything to have been able to hug and kiss Eli. He's a wonderful man."

Jennifer turned to David with a perplexed look. "Let's go live on our com system," she said. "It's time for us to address the crisis back on Earth."

David nodded with a serious look. "What do you think we should say?" he asked.

"I believe we should address the fears that are rising and condemn those in leadership who are trying to exploit it," she replied. "Messenger, could you please set up a worldwide transmission for us through our com system."

"Certainly, Jennifer. Give me a few minutes," came the answer.

"Let's go outside and transmit from there," Jennifer said with rising confidence. "We're about to talk to more people than anyone ever has."

They put on their headsets and exited Messenger to stand out in the broad meadow, which blazed in glorious color in the midday light. A slight breeze ruffled their hair as they prayed together before commencing their talk.

"Jennifer, you are now live for almost all of Earth," Messenger said.

"Hello to all of you back on the good Earth," Jennifer started. "We haven't talked directly to you in some time, but we know that you have followed us closely through our communication systems. It's humbling to be seen and supported by so many. Perhaps someday, all of you will have a chance to see this beautiful world with your own eyes. Though we have been busy exploring this vast new world and are now training for our approaching return home, we have kept up with news of the events taking place even as we speak. Our hearts ache for the rising fear and social disruption. Much of the evil is the direct result of leaders who are seeking selfish gain and attempting to panic and divide you—the people of Earth. Weigh carefully what you hear, paying close attention to the facts. If a leader tells you things that make you fearful, consider it as a possible deception. Some of them allege that we and the Edena out here are planning an invasion and take-over when some of us return. As you can tell from our transmissions, nothing is further from the truth. If there's anyone to fear, it is anyone on Earth who tries to manipulate you with lies and fear mongering."

"We will return home to Earth in forty days," David said. "Please use this time to examine your own lives. Consider forgiving old wrongs, building bridges, and making amends in your relationships. If you have been abusing substances or people, stop and seek help right away. A new day is dawning for humanity, and you need to do your part to be ready."

"To the youth and children of Earth," Allison began. "I am amazed and humbled that I got to come here as one of you. Someday, you, too, can stand where I do now. You and I are blessed to be young when as all of this begins for humanity. Right now, it's hard to see all that lies ahead of us, but from what I have seen, I know it will be wonderful. We are soon coming to a day where none of us will be hungry, homeless, cold, hurting, or scared."

"In closing," Jennifer said, "God bless you back home, and God bless the good Earth. May the Lord bless you and keep you. May the Lord make his face to shine upon you and give you peace."

With that, Messenger ended the transmission, allowing Jennifer, David, and Allison to decompress.

"Mom, should I bring Justin, Sarah, and Grandmother here?" asked Allison.

"Let's wait until we learn more about your abilities," Jennifer replied. "There may be risks involved. We should ask Seth and the others about it."

Soon Jennifer contacted General Morris and hoped that his people would get to Justin and Sarah before the president's agents.

They then returned to Seth and Deborah's home for an afternoon of intense training in prayer and other spiritual disciplines. Allison's telekinetic abilities were new to the Edena and very little was to be found in the mental database, so the decision was made to wait until it became a matter of life or death. Their training was extremely engrossing but pleasant. The woes of Earth began to seem so removed from the paradise that they enjoyed; time passed easily, and anxiety faded.

When evening came, they took a break for supper, with a sumptuous Mexican banquet created by David and Jennifer from their memories of home. Seth, Deborah, and Eli dug in as if they had always known how to eat fajitas and tortillas. The guacamole was especially favored.

Allison's heart was so full of joy that she decided to share some special music. She closed her eyes and accessed the mental library to search for a special piece of solo music. Her mind began to fill and awaken with musical understanding she had never known. Suddenly, as if sent by the Spirit, a brief violin piece embedded itself in her mind as her fingers became aware of the skill to play. Allison's mind was reeling. She had to catch her breath. In a few moments, she looked at the table before her, and a violin materialized. She picked it up and immediately began to play it with deep love and great mastery. The tune revealed itself to be "Jesu, Joy of Man's Desiring." David and Jennifer were astonished at their daughter's newly found abilities. The others simply smiled and deeply enjoyed the music as it enveloped them.

As the evening wore on, they became aware that everyone was now communicating telepathically. David, Jennifer, and Allison had come to know one another better than ever. They had rapidly shared lifelong memories with their hosts and found themselves amazed at the depth and scope of their knowledge and experience. David and Jennifer even felt like novices in their own academic fields of biology and astronomy before these ancient ones. They had learned more in one evening than in years of advanced education. All of this mental exertion had left them exhausted. As the light faded with the occultation of the white dwarf star, David, Jennifer, and Allison were making their short passage to Messenger for a welcome night's sleep. Distant white dwarfs were visible across the sky in faded twilight, making a symmetrical nimbus of light above.

CHAPTER 23

Preparation and Return to Danger

The next day, Seth and Deborah joined Allison, Jennifer, and David on Messenger as they set out for a lengthy flight across the Rim to the interior of a vast desert more expansive than even the entire surface area of Jupiter. When they landed and disembarked, the searing heat lit up their nerves. Jennifer wondered if the star over this region ever got occulted into nighttime. Much to her shock, Messenger departed abruptly after they had walked a few hundred yards. They had not even brought any of their astronaut survival gear.

Seth and Deborah led them over to a forbidding rocky ridge that resembled an ancient shipwreck beached on a burning sea of sand. As they came closer, they could make out a trail that led up to several caves and up to the top. As they climbed up, Allison wished that Messenger had landed on the rocky, tablelike summit. Seth announced that it was here that their training would take place for forty days, out of touch with Earth.

It was here, in the most hostile place on the Rim, that they spent time in intensive prayer, fasting from food for extended periods, and enhancing their mental and spiritual powers. Time seemed to halt and race simultaneously. Visions and dreams blended with the stark reality of their extreme surroundings.

The Word of God came to them early in the process. Everything they had ever learned and more became amplified and expanded exponentially. David, Jennifer, and Allison found insight to both the smaller and greater details of life as well as clarity as to what God had done and was planning to do. They came to understand what their roles would be when they returned home. As quickly as it had begun, Messenger returned, and it was time to return to Seth and Deborah's home and to the farewells from the other crew members who would be staying.

A large banquet similar to their first welcome was held at the large pavilion on the hilltop. This time, the music and mood were somber, like a requiem, as if something dreadful was about to happen. News from Earth indicated that everything had rapidly deteriorated into war and social chaos. Across the planet, people had turned their fears into acts of terror and violence against anyone different in color, class, creed, or ethnicity. David and Jennifer worried how they would be received.

Soon the banquet was over, and the time had come to say good-bye to the rest of the crew, who had already begun to work in their new roles to prepare for the first wave of arrivals from Earth. Everyone tried to keep the mood upbeat, but the undertow of concern brought tears through the smiles, hugs, and well wishing.

Later, in the control room inside of Messenger, Seth, Deborah, and Eli joined Jennifer, David, and Allison in the comfortable chairs prior to lift-off.

Allison relished the thought of two weeks with Eli. She had missed him during their forty days of training.

We won't have two weeks, Eli's thought rang out in Allison's mind.

"Why not?" Allison said aloud in mild exasperation.

Messenger will take us there in three days, Eli replied.

"Mom, Eli says that we'll be back at Earth in three days," Allison said.

"Messenger, can you get us back that fast?" Jennifer asked.

"Certainly, though it will take much more energy," came the reply. "But the needs are great, and the time is short."

Seth, Deborah, and Eli indicated no surprise, as if they had known all along.

Much like their time in the desert, the three-day passage was all too brief, as the tiny speck of Earth drew ever closer. The chaos back home had silenced transmissions from NASA at Mission Control. The news-media outlets were ominously silent. Worst of all, there was no contact with Justin and Sarah or General Morris. These concerns kept conversations both verbal and telepathic to a minimum. A growing sense of discomfort increased with each passing hour. Allison began to wonder if they would lose all of their powers and knowledge once they returned. Her dreams were dark, and she often awoke with a sense of burning and suffocation.

As they entered Earth orbit, it seemed like they had been gone for a lifetime. It was somehow alien and hostile. There was no response from the International Space Station, but that presented no problem since Messenger could easily descend and land directly on Earth. There was no official contact or response to their calls, leaving Jennifer and the others uncertain as to how to proceed.

Messenger broke the silent impasse with the words that shot ice into their veins: "It appears that we are being welcomed with nuclear ICBMs headed our way from several sources."

(To be continued.)

Jennifer Bass; Icelandic–Scotch and Irish–American
  Astronomer-Physicist
  Child: Allison, age fourteen

David Lopez; Castilian, Basque, and Hispanic–American
  Exobiologist and Sociobiologist

(Petrus) N!amce Xamseb; Khoisan and San Bushman; older male
  Cultural Anthropologist
  Grandchildren: Toma, age ten, and Kushe, age eight

Aizam Mat Saman; Bejau; younger male
  Linguist

Fatima al-Tarabin; Bedouin, from Israeli Negev; younger female
  , from the Sinai and later, settlement township, Tirabin al-Sana
  Physician, Surgeon, and Internist

Vartan Bedevian; Armenian; older male
  Geophysicist

Timujin Ji; Mongol; younger male
  Mathematician

Apiranoa Ngata; Maori; younger male
  Ethnopsychologist

Theodora Melas; Greek; younger female
Historian, Poet, and Musician
Daughter: Anastasia, age fourteen

Alice Cly; Navajo; older female
Biochemist and Geneticist

Becky Ishulutak; Inuit; younger female
Electrical Engineer and Cyberneticist
Twin Sons: Randy and Andy Ishulutak, age four

Maria Quaupucura; Mapuche; older female
Geographer and Cartographer

GLOSSARY

abaya: A dark cloak that covers Bedouin women from head to foot

Aries rocket: The next generation of boosters for launching NASA's manned missions

astrolabe: A finely machined brass instrument used to determine latitude based on star and solar angles above the horizon

atabal: A small drum played by the Basque people in traditional music

AU: astronomical unit; The distance from the Earth to the sun, which is ninety-three million miles

bait ashshar: A black goat hair cloth tent for a Bedouin family

BAMC: Brooke Army Medical Center; An advanced hospital in San Antonio, Texas

Basarwa: The San Bushmen

Bertsolari: Basque men dressed in traditional costume who compete in folk songs

Black Project: The designation for ultra-top-secret military hardware and vessels, which is so called because their details are "blacked out" from congressional budget requests

CAPCOM: capsule communicator; An astronaut who handles all ground communication with the astronauts on the mission

carrack: A European sailing vessel of the sixteenth century with square-rigged sails

chamarra: A traditional Basque woolen cape

chronometer: A timepiece with great accuracy, often used in navigation

circumnavigate: To sail around the world

CNCI: Comprehensive National Cybersecurity Initiative; A classified, comprehensive program involving several federal agencies to collect and analyze large amounts of data to secure government computer systems from cyberattacks and detect foreign threats of other kinds as indicated by Internet and cell-phone traffic

cupola: A raised cluster of bay windows at the bottom of the International Space Station that form a ceiling for the control and command centers

cybernetic: Control and communication systems with some degree of intelligence

DARPA: The Defense Advanced Research Projects Agency, which handles all secret "black" projects

DEFCON: Defense Readiness Condition; There are five levels for degree of severity, with DEFCON 1 meaning nuclear war is imminent

DOD: Department of Defense, a branch of the American Federal Government which oversees the military

Dyson Sphere: An immense hollow sphere constructed by an advanced civilization; can be of a variety of sizes; named for famed astrophysicist, Freeman Dyson, who first postulated their existence in the 1960s

ecliptic: The plane on which smaller objects orbit a larger central body

edena: The inhabitants of the Rim who make first contact with the astronauts

el mus: A traditional Basque card game

EMU: Extravehicular Mobility Unit; The suit worn by an astronaut when outside of the International Space Station

envelop: To bring inside; what the Dyson Sphere did to the entire solar system

es-shigg: The portion of a Bedouin tent reserved for the males in the family

etcholak: A Basque shepherd's stone hut

Euskal Herria: The Basque homeland

Euskara: The Basque language

EVA: Extra Vehicular Activity; A space walk by astronauts

exoplanet: A planet in a solar system beyond ours, orbiting another star

FAA: Federal Aviation Administration

fatwa: A command ordering the death of someone who offended Islam

feteer: Handmade bread; a Bedouin staple

first contact: The event where humans make their first contact to intelligent extraterrestrial life-forms

fjord: A narrow bay of deep water connected to the sea

G: A unit of gravity, with 1 G equaling the level of gravity at sea level on Earth

gahwa: The traditional strong, bitter coffee served by Bedouins

Godspeed: A traditional blessing said as a farewell to astronauts upon departure

goum: A small cluster of tents in a temporary Bedouin settlement

goura: A five-stringed thumb piano made from the wood and played by San Bushmen

GPS: Global Positioning System

gravitic drive: Top-secret aeronautical propulsion system that channels gravity to assist in high-powered flight haka: A raucous Maori chant with ritualized posture and dance

Hawaiki: mythological ancestral homeland for the Maori

ICBM: Inter-Continental Ballistic Missile, used to deliver a nuclear bomb

IDF: Israeli Defense Force, or military

imam: Islamic clergyman

ISS: International Space Station

Juan Sebastián de Elcano: A sixteenth-century Basque sailor who commanded and finished the second half of Magellan's circumnavigation of the world

JPL: NASA's Jet Propulsion Laboratory in Pasadena, California, which specialized in robotic space probes

JSC: The Johnson Space Center, Houston, Texas, specializing in manned space flight

kaross: The traditional animal-skin garment or loin cloth worn by San Bushmen

kibr: A white cloak worn as an outer garment by Bedouin men

Launch Status Check: Go/no go poll of all systems controllers immediately prior to launch; Done by NTD (NASA Test Director) who then reports to launch director, who gives the final word to launch

LSS: Life Support Subsystem; A backpack with oxygen, water, and communication worn by an astronaut during an EVA mahram: The section reserved for women in a Bedouin tent

makhila: A Basque shepherd's staff

mansaf: A Bedouin feast with roast lamb, rice, pine nuts drenched in yogurt

meerkat: A small mongoose-like mammal that lives in colonies and forages during the day

Messenger: The name given by the astronauts to their vessel

moko: The traditional tattoos across a Maori man's chest and arms

NASA: The National Aeronautic and Space Administration; America's space agency

NSA: National Security Agency

occult: In astronomy, the darkening of a star by dust clouds or other large objects

Odyssey: The name given to the mission to the Rim by the astronauts

The One: The name for God used by the inhabitants on the Rim

optical interferometry: The coordinated use of a couple dozen telescopes in an array to combine images with the help of computers to gain greater resolution

Orion Capsule: The next generation of space vehicle for NASA astronauts

orlan: A Russian space suit

piezoelectricity: Electricity derived from pressure on a crystalline substance

PMA: Pressurized Mating Adapter; docking port on the International Space Station

polombière: A Basque tradition of setting nets to catch migrating pigeons

pottokak: A breed of small, sturdy horses indigenous to the Pyrenees

rebabe: A Bedouin flute

Rim: The vast interior surface of the Dyson Sphere

saha: A heavy cloth curtain that separates the male and female sections in a Bedouin tent

San Fermín: An annual Basque festival celebrated with singing contests and food

scramjet: Jet engine that works at hypersonic speeds up to Mach 12

scree: A deposit of loose rock, often left behind by glaciers or landslides

sentient: Self-awareness and capability of reasoning and memory, underpinned with language

skerm: A grass-and-stick shelter made by San Bushmen women, like a tent or a lean-to

skyr: A yogurt from sheep milk; an Icelandic delicacy

smagg: A red-and-white checkered Bedouin head covering held in place by a black agall

solar ecliptic: The plane of the solar system over which all the planets orbit around the Sun

SST Concorde: European Supersonic transport plane that flew over the Atlantic at speeds above Mach 1 between Europe and America for thirty-five years before being retired from service

SSTO: Single Stage to Orbit; A term applied to a vehicle capable of achieving Earth orbit without multistage booster assist

tarha: The black shawl worn by Bedouin women, covering their heads and shoulders

Tawhid wa Jihad: Means "Unity & Holy War"; a Bedouin terrorist group

tchirula: A Basque flute

telekinetic: The ability to affect objects by the will of the mind without physical contact

telemetry: Electronically transmitted information

telepathy: The ability to communicate thoughts without verbal or physical action

terminator: The moving line that separates night from day on a planet as it rotates

uruquin: Bedouin name for a sand dune

wadi: A dry streambed in desert areas of Africa and Asia, which can flood in rains

waka: A large ocean-going outrigger canoe used by the Maori

wayfinding: The ancient Polynesian method of using currents, birds, wave sequence and shapes, and star patterns to navigate the Pacific Ocean

werf: A temporary San Bushmen's cluster of grass lean-tos or skerms

white dwarf: A dense, hot star not much larger than Earth

Zamalzain: The oldest of all Basque dances, depicting the battle between good and evil

Printed in the United States
By Bookmasters